The Count's Daughter

By James Vincent

Author's Note

To my children: love is eternal and even transcends lifetimes. Though at times we may mess up life so badly that all seems lost, there's always hope.

TABLE OF CONTENTS

Chapter 1

What's That Taste?

The dull glow of the fluorescent light seemed a bit brighter than usual.

It's just my imagination. I thought they were the same lights I'd been under for the past ten years. Bright as they always had been.

Staring at the ceiling isn't my idea of a good time—but today, it's fine. I've never really been able to tell the difference between a good time and a bad one anyway. Come to think of it, that's probably why I'm strapped to this chair, looking up at the ceiling.

I've often wondered how things might have turned out if I could feel good or bad—or any emotion, for that matter. Most of my life, I just went along with the flow. But I did try to feel. I even tried embracing some of the more exciting elements of detachment, like joining the military and skydiving.

"Adam Drummer, you have been convicted of the crimes of kidnapping, assault, and murder," stated the guard to my right.

Oh, yeah. I tried all that as well. But the only thing I felt afterward was annoyance over the mess it left.

"You have been sentenced to death by the state of—"

"Just push the damn button already," I yelled at the guard. "I've waited long enough for this day, and I'd prefer to get it over with—without having to endure any more humiliation than I already have."

I heard a few more words come from the guard, but I wasn't listening anymore.

In a few more moments, I'll finally be free—from this emptiness inside me that is never full. I'll be free from never fitting in and from having to act like the people around me. Most importantly, I'll finally be free from all the annoying thoughts that never stop.

I will finally have the gift of being nothing.

1

James Vincent

I hear the click of the button being pressed.
I feel a cold liquid flow into my arm through the IV.
My eyes close, and I feel like I'm drifting off to sleep.

My last thought is a total surprise.
I've heard that some people have their life flash before their eyes.
All I had was a question:

What's that strange taste in my mouth?

Chapter 2

I Can Still Use This One

In a moment of pure cosmic perfection, I exist with no thoughts of my own.

I cannot sense anything.

All I know is that I exist.

I hear a voice from an unknown source. It sounds like a woman, but I cannot be certain. It has the softness I've come to recognize as feminine, but there's a roughness to it as well—something that leaves room for doubt.

"It seems like this one is missing something," the voice says.

"Don't worry, I can fix it. I can still use this one," replies a second voice—rough and sharp, clearly that of a man.

I open my eyes—and they hurt.

How do I have eyes?

My heart starts pounding as I look around. A strange, candlelit room surrounds me, full of people I've never seen before. I hear sounds coming from their mouths. I know they're speaking words, but I can't tell what language they're in.

And why do they all look so big?

This is bullshit. Where is the nothing I waited so long for?

Suddenly, one of the big people reaches toward me with a massive hand. It wraps around me and picks me up without effort. In that moment, terror shoots through my entire body, and I cry—loudly, uncontrollably.

Damn it. Why am I crying? Why am I afraid? Why do I feel this way?

I'm passed from person to person in the strange candlelit room. Some of them are smaller than others, but I'm too confused to make sense of it all.

I'm exhausted. More tired than I ever remember being—more than after a 20-kilometer ruck march back in my military days.

A large man says something in the strange language and sets me in the arms of a tired-looking woman. The next thing I know, something is pressed to my lips. I feel an overwhelming compulsion to open my mouth and start sucking.

When I do, I realize I have no teeth.

In that moment, it becomes clear.

I've been reborn.

The woman smiles down at me.

"Nisha," she says.

That sounds oddly feminine.

It's the last thought I have before drifting off into the best sleep I can ever remember.

"Have you ever been so tired that all you wanted to do was sleep, even after sleeping all day?"

That's all I felt for the first four months.

Instead of the sweet embrace of nothingness I'd expected, I'd been reborn. The "when" and "where" are still a mystery. From what I can tell, there's no indoor plumbing or electricity. The house looks ornate and large—fifteen rooms, from what I've seen while being carried around.

My father is a blonde man with European features, probably in his mid-thirties. My mother calls him Kelvis, but others, who seem like servants, call him Count Delwin.

My mother is striking—like an exotic princess with almond-brown eyes and shimmering silver-white hair that reflects like starlight. Her pointed ears are unusual. I try to feel my own ears to see if I have points, but for some reason, I can't get my hands to do what I want.

Her name is Vanisha.

There are two older children. Klovis, the eldest, has his father's blue eyes and his mother's silver hair. He looks to be about eight. Ranisha, my older sister, looks about six and shares the same silver hair and blue eyes.

Most of the servants blur together, constantly in and out, except for two: Milla and Armon.

Armon is tall and muscular, always with a sword, following my father everywhere. Milla is a maid—brown hair, rosy cheeks—whose job seems to be caring for me and assisting my mother. She's eager and gentle. I enjoy Milla. I enjoy Ranisha, too. She may not be much help to Milla, but she tries.

And speaking of enjoyment—that's the strangest thing of all.

Stranger than the voices, stranger than waking up here as a girl in a strange land:

I can feel.

Mostly it's been anger—hunger, tiredness, but there are moments, like when my mother smiles at me, when I feel something new.

I think it's called happiness.

Another mystery:

Why do I still remember my past life?

Does everyone here have memories of a past life?

I remember hearing a theory once—that all newborns remember their past lives but forget as they grow.

I wish I could forget.

With these new emotions, thinking back on the horrible things I did as Adam is... horrifying. It seems inconceivable that anyone could be so cruel. Yet every time I remember, I see *her*—her lifeless body, her blood on my hands.

Now, my desires are different. These people matter to me.

In my past life, I didn't care about anyone—not even family.

An old psychology lecture comes to mind: mirror neurons—those things that make a baby smile back at you. People with fewer show less empathy. Psychopaths have almost none.

Maybe my new body has more. Maybe that's the difference.

Or maybe it's more complicated than that.

Too much to think about now.

Mother just said something.

Milla just changed me.

And I'm tired again.

I think I'll take a nap.

Chapter 3

Baby Steps

We tend to take simple things for granted—like being able to walk.

For a six-month-old with no muscle development or coordination, it's nearly impossible.

Being carried is nice, but I want to explore.

So I start the way other babies do—grabbing onto things and pulling myself up.

It's harder than it sounds.

But after falling countless times, I manage to stand.

Now for the first step.

"Where do you think you're going?" Ranisha asks.

I can't form words yet, but I'm starting to understand the language.

I was about to go for a walk, I think to myself.

Ranisha walks over, takes my hand, and off we go.

As we round the corner into the hallway, we run into Milla carrying a stack of folded laundry. She stops in her tracks. The laundry hits the floor.

"My goodness!" she exclaims. "How is she doing that?"

"I don't know. She just does it," Ranisha replies.

"But she's too little to be walking!"

"She does it," Ranisha insists.

To make her point, she lets go of my hand.

"Go to Milla," she says.

Figuring there's no point pretending, I wobble toward Milla. She stretches her hand out. As soon as I reach her, she picks me up and heads for my mother's room, Ranisha following behind.

Mother is sitting at her desk, writing a letter.

"My lady, you need to see this," Milla says, clearly puzzled.

"See what?" Mother asks.

"This," Milla replies and sets me on my feet.

"She can stand already?" Mother says in surprise.

"That's not all. Go to your mother," Milla says.

Having already performed this trick, I walk to Mother. She picks me up and stares into my eyes.

She says nothing.

"What does this mean, my lady?" Milla asks.

"What does it mean?" *I think. It means I'm walking early. I knew kids who did that in my last life.*

"It means she's smart!" Ranisha says excitedly.

"I don't know," Mother replies. "I've never seen or heard of a child this young able to walk—let alone follow instructions."

Oops. I hadn't considered that.

"Perhaps it was just a coincidence," Mother says. "I'll give her a quick test."

She places me on the floor and lays out three objects from her desk: a key, a hairpin, and a ring.

"Nisha, can you hand me the hairpin?" she asks.

Every instinct tells me to play dumb. I sit there, unmoving.

See? I'm not special, my expression says.

But when our eyes meet, I know she knows that I know.

What's the worst that can happen? I think.

I hand her the hairpin.

A sudden scream of excitement bursts from me—loud and shocking.

It scares me.

And I soil my diaper.

Ranisha's laughter doesn't help. I begin to cry.

"At least that part of her is normal," Milla comments.

Weeks later, after I've explored every corner of the house, I lead Ranisha to the main entrance and point at the large wooden doors. She's become my unofficial translator—quick to figure out what I want.

"You want to go outside?" she asks.

I nod. We find Mother in the study.

"Mother, Nisha wants to go outside. Can I take her?" Ranisha asks.

Mother sets down her book and thinks for a moment.

"I guess it's alright—as long as you take Milla with you."

A few minutes later, I'm dressed warmly and standing at the main doors with Ranisha and Milla.

"Let me know if she gets too cold," Milla says.

"I will," Ranisha replies.

Milla opens the door, and we step outside.

Chapter 4

Doggies

Once outside, I immediately felt the cold air biting into my cheeks. That explained why I was wrapped up like a burrito. It must have been late fall or early winter, though there wasn't any snow on the ground. A tall brick wall surrounded the entire estate. I could see houses on the other side of the street through the iron bars of the main gate. There were several smaller buildings surrounding the mansion.

The first building we came to, we opened the door and all stepped inside. The interior reminded me of an indoor shooting range. I saw targets and mannequins. We were situated at the far end of the building, close to the entrance. Father Cuovis and Armon were already inside.

"What do I owe this surprise to?" Father asked. I could see that Klovis looked annoyed. He didn't spend as much time with me as Ranisha did. That's actually an understatement. From what I could tell, Klovis hardly noticed I existed.

"Nisha wanted to go outside, so I figured we'd stop by and see you, Daddy," came Ranisha's eager reply.

"Well, that was sweet of you. Is there anything I can do for you ladies?" Father asked.

"Can we watch you practice your magic, Papa?" Ranisha asked eagerly.

"Father, can't you just send them away? We're still in the middle of a lesson."

"It's not an issue, Klovis. They can stay and watch. Perhaps it will teach you to focus more," Father replied. "Do the last bell again and focus more on your mana consumption. And aim this time."

Magic, spells, mana? What are these weirdos going on about? I thought the entire setup felt ridiculous, like I was watching a silly stage production. Klovis held up his hand in the direction of the targets and started saying something strange.

"The fire inside me comes forth!" he spoke. A ball of fire about the size of a baseball appeared in front of him.

"Grow and devour!" he continued. The ball of fire grew to the size of a basketball.

"Go forth and destroy my enemies!"

The ball of flame shot out toward a round target at the back of the room. It missed and hit the back wall.

"I wouldn't have missed it if they had left," Klovis said, pointing at me and Ranisha.

"You missed because you were more focused on having an audience than hitting the target," came Father's reply.

"I thought you were amazing, Klovis," said Ranisha.

Magic. Real magic. If I could have spoken, I would have been at a loss for words. That also means that this isn't some distant land or pastime. This is a completely different world. This is a world with magic in it. And I'm going to learn everything I can about it.

As if she were having the same thought as I, Ranisha asked, "Daddy, can you teach me and Nisha to use magic too?"

"I can teach you when you get a bit older, but I'm afraid there won't be much use in trying to teach Nisha."

"Why can't you teach Nisha too?" she asked.

I'd like to know. Damn it, I thought.

"Mana flows along certain bloodlines and with certain traits," Father began to explain. "For my family, it's passed along with blue eyes. Your mother's family passed it along with their silver hair. You and Klovis both got it and, as a result, should make excellent mages someday. For whatever reason, Nisha didn't get either of those traits. It's strange, but blonde hair and blue eyes almost always come together. And Nisha got my blonde hair and your mother's brown eyes."

"Of course, that's not a complete explanation," Father continued, "but as a result, Nisha's mana capacity is probably really small."

Father pulled out a small stone from his pocket. He held it out in his hand, and it started to glow brighter and brighter until it started to feel unpleasant to look at.

"It isn't an exact measurement. But this Glowstone puts off more light with stronger magics." He came over and put the stone in my hand. The stone started to light up, and for a moment, I got my hopes up. Unfortunately, the stone stopped at a low glow that barely showed at all.

"It's just as I thought," he said.

That's so sad, I thought.

"No, it isn't," came Father's reply. "There are lots of people who have a low amount of capacity, and they live perfectly normal lives. And this one is incredibly smart. And beautiful," he continued. "She'll be just fine with that."

Father picked me up and kissed my cheek. "Don't worry about it, Nisha," he said. "She's perfect. Just the way she is."

What bullshit is this? What utter and complete bullshit.

As we left the trio to their magic training, I couldn't stop shouting inside my head. How could I really be born into a fantasy world with magic and not be able to use it? Was it a punishment for being such a horrible person in my past life? But I was executed for that! Surely the ledger was cleared!

We came to the next building. That wagon was in front of it. A big black dog came walking up to us.

"Hello, Asher," said Milla, reaching down to pet him. After Ranisha also pet Asher, he moved out of our way, and we kept walking toward the building with the wagon.

This looks like a horse stable, I thought as we walked inside. We were greeted by two men, a middle-aged man and a teenage boy who looked like his son.

"Hello, David," Milla said.

"Hello, Milla," the older man replied.

"Hello, Davis," Milla said to the teenager.

He blushed and replied, "Hello, Milla."

So it was a custom to give your child a similar first name, I thought. I had been wondering about that for a while, and now it was confirmed.

Whatever I was thinking at that point completely left my mind as I looked at the two giant 'not horses.' Without thinking, the word shot out of my mouth.

"Doggies?"

After a bit of a lengthy pause in which nobody answered my question, I pointed at the giant dogs and asked again, "Doggies?"

Milla finally stammered out, "That's right, Nisha, those are doggies."

I pointed at Asher, who was wagging his tail behind Ranisha. "Doggy?"

"Yes, Asher. He's also a doggie."

My mind was once again full of questions. Questions about how dogs the size of horses could exist. Dogs are carnivorous and pack hunters. Whatever they feed on would have to be absolutely massive, and they would have to be plentiful.

"I think she's asking why they are different," said Ranisha.

"Oh, that's a simple one to answer," said David, walking over to the two giant dogs. He patted one on the shoulder and said, "These are barrow dogs, or as some people call them, cart dogs."

After giving up on the logic of their existence—having realized that between magic and reincarnation, oversized dogs would be completely within reason—

"Would the young ladies like to pet them?" asked David.

I nodded my head excitedly, and Milla brought me over to the two giant dogs.

"Down," David commanded. Both dogs got down on their bellies.

As I brought my hand up to the closest one, the furthest away started pushing its head in closer to me.

"Don't get jealous, Hoba. Let Savo have his turn first," said Davis.

Hoba moved back and gave me what I think was a whine, but the pitch was so low that it didn't sound like any dog whine I had ever heard before.

I never could understand it in my past life. Dogs were messy. They had to be trained and fed, you had to take them out for walks, and you had to pick up their poop. Pets—and dogs in particular—were a complete waste of a person's time, energy, and money.

As I looked into Savo's big brown eyes and touched his cold, wet nose, I believed only a monster couldn't be in love.

Who cares about magic anyway? I'm going to ride on a giant dog.

Chapter 5

Joyride

At eighteen months old, I could definitely get around much better. I tried to keep my vocabulary limited. My words were few, so that nobody caught on to the fact that there was a killer's soul inside this toddler—for the most part.

I'd gotten proficient at blocking out the old, rotten memories. Only occasionally did they resurface—like when Melissa sliced her finger while cutting vegetables and started bleeding everywhere. Just the sight of that crimson trail triggered a flash of my old life. A quick glimpse. A reminder. A monster, that's what I had been.

All that aside, mobility had improved. But I had a new nemesis: doorknobs.

I could get around them if something was conveniently nearby to stand on. Otherwise, I enlisted Ranisha as my door-opener. Lately, though, she'd been busy with tutors, learning magic with her father and Klovis. That meant I was often stuck inside. Trapped. Like some kind of pampered, magical pet.

Occasionally, I'd walk through the kitchen and wait for one of the kitchen workers to go outside. Then I'd slip through behind them. But it had gotten harder since Mother caught me sneaking out to visit Hoba and Savo. Nobody found me until they checked the kennel and discovered me fast asleep between Hoba's front legs.

After that, the house staff had been told to keep an eye out for me trying to sneak off again. But as they used to say in my old world: *Where there's a will, there's a way.*

A hair ribbon or any other long piece of fabric could work, but it took several attempts before I figured out how to toss it just right over the door latch and pull it open. What worked best was a belt. I started making it a point to ask Milla for one when she helped me get dressed each morning.

On this particular morning, I was on a mission.

I headed to the back of the mansion, toward the servants' entrance. After waiting for the coast to be clear, I rushed to the door, slipped off my belt, looped it over the latch, and—with one last glance to make sure no one was watching—pulled it down and slipped outside.

I headed straight for the kennel.

Breakfast had already been served, so the kennel master, David, and his son, Davis, were likely off for the moment. Today was going to be different. I wasn't just going to see Hoba and Savo.

Today, I was going to *ride* one.

Once at the kennel, I waited until I was sure David and Davis were gone, then slipped inside. Hoba and Savo sensed something immediately. They were more excited than usual, their tails wagging like heavy ropes.

I chose Savo—he was the calmer of the two. There were saddles and tack meant for riding burrow dogs, but it was far too heavy for me to manage alone. Besides, I had been building a relationship with these two. They'd listen to me.

I climbed up to the latch of their pen and pulled it open. Back on the ground, I looked at Savo and Hoba, both doing a sort of excited doggy dance, bouncing from one front paw to the other.

"Down," I commanded.

They instantly dropped to their stomachs.

Climbing onto a burrow dog reminded me of scaling a cargo net in boot camp—if the net was made of soft, warm fur. If it hurt Savo, he didn't show it. I grabbed onto a tuft of fur, dug my feet in, and worked my way to his shoulders. Wrapping my small hands into his thick coat, I called out, "Up."

Savo stood.

"Get the door."

I had seen them do this neat little trick before. Savo trotted over to the kennel's double doors. They were held closed by a wooden beam. He wedged his snout beneath it and lifted it free of the iron hooks.

16

As for my plan?

There wasn't really one.

A tall brick wall surrounded the entire estate. I figured we'd just run around the property a bit. If anything went wrong, adults were nearby. The worst that could happen was a scolding from Mother or Father. A fair price to pay to ride a giant dog.

But my simple plan was instantly met with disaster.

Just as Savo pushed open the kennel doors, the main gate to the estate— open briefly to let in a carriage—stood wide open.

Savo and Hoba saw their opportunity.

They made a mad dash for the gate.

The exhilaration was instant. In seconds, we were out.

I clung to Savo for dear life, sure I'd fall at any moment. As we passed the open gate, I saw a team of burrow dogs pulling a carriage. That explained the timing.

Savo and Hoba ignored them. They just kept running.

When I finally found my voice, I shouted for Savo to stop, but he was deaf to reason. We tore through the town. People screamed and scattered as we passed—two huge dogs and a toddler clinging for life.

As the houses thinned and buildings faded into farmland, I finally sat upright. The town lay far behind. Crops stretched out on either side. Ahead, an open road curved toward distant hills.

I had wanted to ride a giant dog. And here I was, doing it.

The wind roared past. The scents, the sights, the movement—all of it swept over me. And for a moment, I just let myself enjoy it.

Eventually, even the crops disappeared, giving way to endless grassland.

Savo turned off the road, dashing through tall grass. At last, he stopped at the edge of a sparkling lake. He and Hoba dropped their heads and lapped up water in loud, rhythmic gulps.

Time to regain control.

"Savo, sit—"

But before I could finish the command, something lifted me by the back of my dress. I twisted around.

Armon.

He was riding another burrow dog—sleek, lean, and built for speed. He didn't speak as he pulled me into the saddle in front of him. Silently, he tossed ropes around Hoba and Savo's necks and turned us back toward the road.

My mind raced. I had to come up with an excuse. Riding around the estate was one thing—but this? I'd frightened half the town and nearly lost the dogs. Panic crept in. Wild thoughts: a dungeon, a beating—though neither parent had ever done such things.

Calm down, I told myself. Just the imagination of a child-like mind.

Then Armon spoke.

"Did you enjoy your ride?"

It was the first thing he had ever said to me.

I knew, from the way he asked, that I would be all right.

For some unknown reason, I started to cry. Not sadness. Not fear. *I felt* safe. Emotions are strange.

At some point on the ride back, I fell asleep.

The next thing I remembered was hearing Mother and Father calling my name as we passed through the main gate. Armon rode up to them and handed me off to Father, then turned over Hoba and Savo to David and Davis—both of whom apologized profusely.

"Sorry, Papa. Sorry, Mama. Please don't be mad at Mr. David and Mr. Davis. I let the doggies out," I said.

"Her speech is remarkable," remarked a thin woman I hadn't noticed before. She had long, silky black hair and pale blue eyes.

"Never mind all that," Father said, turning stern. "You, young lady, are in big trouble. Mrs. AnnaLisa—" he nodded to the woman "—and the

18

other guests have arrived from the central palace to see you."

"That will have to wait until tomorrow," said Mother. "Any punishment you have for her can wait too," she told Father. "You'll have to excuse me, Lord Delwin. I must attend to Her Royal Highness."

Her *Royal Highness*? That got my attention. *Who exactly is visiting us?*

"You, young lady, are filthy," Mother declared. She called for Milla to take me upstairs to be cleaned, fed, and put to bed.

Before Father handed me over, he leaned close and whispered, "Don't ever scare us like that again," and kissed my cheek.

It was then I knew: whatever punishment awaited me, it would be light, and worth it.

Chapter 6

Krisstina XVIII

The next morning, I was brought down to the dining hall where the rest of the family was already gathered. The next to arrive was Lady AnnaLisa.

"May I present to you, Your Royal Highness, Princess Krisstina the Eighteenth."

Just then, another servant entered, holding a young girl in her arms. I say "young," but she looked a bit older than me. I watched as Mother and Father bowed, and I tried my best to copy their movement.

There was no mistaking Krisstina for anything but Royalty. Her golden eyes were so bright they nearly glowed, and her hair—blue like the deep ocean—looked nearly black until light caught it. Nothing in my past life even came close to it.

The princess didn't stay long. As soon as the introductions were over, the maid carrying her left, and we all bowed again.

"Lady Nisha," AnnaLisa said before departing, "please come up to the princess's guest room after breakfast."

After a quick meal, Milla and I met AnnaLisa outside the princess's room.

"How can Lady Nisha be of service to you, Lady AnnaLisa?" Milla asked.

"Please, just call me Anna. I've heard that Lady Nisha is quite clever for her age. After seeing yesterday's... display with the dogs, I'm inclined to believe the rumors."

"It wasn't their fault. Hoba and Savo are normally good boys. It was all my fault they got out," I replied quickly.

"It isn't the incident with the dogs I'm interested in," said Anna. "What intrigues me is that I'm having a conversation with a child who isn't even two years old yet. How is it that you can speak so well? Who taught you?"

"I did," I answered.

"You taught yourself?" she asked again.

"Well, Milla would talk, and Ranisha would talk, and I would listen," I said, doing my best to sound reasonable.

"Be that as it may," she said, still sounding somewhat skeptical, "I'd like to ask you for help with the princess."

"I'll try," I said. "What can I do?"

"Princess Krisstina is almost two years old. She doesn't walk, doesn't talk... and we can't explain it. When the Queen heard about you, she hoped sending the princess to visit might inspire her."

"I see... But people are more complex than that," I thought silently. "This isn't going to work."

"All of us learn at our own speed," I replied diplomatically.

"I agree. But the Queen... she is not one to be denied. Would you please just spend time with the princess? At the very least, I can report that we tried."

"I'll do my best," I promised.

This is ridiculous, I thought as I entered the room and introduced myself to the toddler Royal. *What am I even supposed to say to a normal toddler?*

"It is a pleasure to meet you, Your Highness. My name is Nisha Delwin."

Krisstina just stared at me with her golden eyes.

"Would you like to play with me?" I asked. I dragged over a box I knew usually had some stuffed animals and began pulling them out.

"Are you going to come over and play with me?" I asked again.

The maid who had carried Krisstina down earlier came over, picked her up, and brought her to the play area. *Why walk when you've got someone to carry you everywhere? I thought.*

"Can you excuse me for a moment?" I asked the maid, then pulled Anna aside.

"She's never going to learn to walk if she has no reason to. The maid carries her everywhere."

"I know what you're saying," Anna replied, "but if we don't move her, she just sits there. She won't move at all."

"Can you leave us alone for a bit?" I asked.

"Ordinarily, I would never leave the princess alone with a stranger... but under the circumstances—and the fact that you're smaller than her—I'll allow it."

Anna waved the maid to follow her, and the two adults left the room.

I walked over to Krisstina. She was still watching me silently. I picked up two stuffed animals.

"Do you want the dog or the lizard?" I asked. At least, I *thought* it was a lizard.

I held both toward her, but she made no move to take either. I kept pulling animals from the box, one by one, offering each. Nothing.

Sigh.

"Okay, maybe stuffed animals aren't your thing."

I got up and walked over to the closet. I pulled off my belt, looped it over the latch, and opened the door. After a quick look inside, I turned around—and nearly jumped out of my skin.

Krisstina was standing right behind me.

"So you can walk. You just choose not to?" I said.

She didn't respond. Instead, she grabbed my hand and pointed to the door latch leading to the hallway. *All that poking and prodding didn't get a response, but my door trick did?*

I walked over and opened the door. As we stepped into the hallway, Anna turned to see us—me holding Krisstina's hand.

"Can we go for a walk?" I asked.

22

Anna leaned down and whispered, "How did you get her to do that?"

"She already knew how," I replied. "She just didn't feel like she had a good reason—until now."

"Just don't leave the mansion," Anna warned.

"We won't. I promise."

As soon as we rounded the corner and were out of sight, I looked at Krisstina and whispered, "Wanna meet my friends Hoba and Savo?"

For the next few days, Krisstina was glued to my side. Everywhere I went, she followed. I didn't mind. In fact, it felt nice—important. In my old life, I never really cared if anyone looked up to me. Maybe things would've turned out differently if I had.

No use dwelling on it. The past can't be changed.

Eventually, I introduced Krisstina to Hoba and Savo, but only after convincing Anna to take us to the kennel. That woman was like a ninja. Every time I thought I'd gotten away from her, she appeared around the next corner. I suspected she had some kind of magic that kept her informed of everyone's whereabouts.

Each morning, Krisstina would bring her maid—Tamara—and Anna to the dining room before I even got there. She wanted to see me as soon as possible. After breakfast, we'd visit the dogs.

I tried my best to get Father or Armon to let us ride, but Anna was firm. "The princess will not be permitted."

Eventually, the day came for Krisstina to return home. Honestly, I felt a little sad. Anna thanked me for helping and told me I was welcome to visit when I came to the capital.

As they prepared to climb into the carriage, Krisstina turned and wrapped her arms around me.

"Bye, Nisha. See you again," she said softly.

"Yes," I replied, hugging her back. "See you again."

Chapter 7

Lila

After Krisstina's visit, we both made it a point to see each other as much as possible. Fortunately, the capital, Sirikk, wasn't far from the city. Father had to travel to Sirikk about once a month on business. He couldn't always take me with him, but he liked to when he could. Likewise, though far less often, Krisstina would come to visit me. Anna said it was doing her good to spend time with me.

Since we started spending time together, Krisstina had become much more independent. Something in me started to change too. Even though I felt much older due to my lifetime of past memories, I began to see Krisstina—or Kriss, as I called her when we were alone—as my best friend. Granted, apart from Ranisha, who was becoming increasingly busy with her studies, I didn't have anyone else to socialize with. But I liked having someone to call my best friend.

By Krisstina's fourth birthday, she had learned to read and do basic math. I think she was motivated by a desire to catch up to me. Krisstina was often hailed as a genius by her parents and the other nobles, even though I was the one who taught her how to read and do math. I didn't mind, though. It took the spotlight off me.

When Kriss and I were together, we spent a lot of time sneaking around the castle or the mansion—depending on whose home we were at—and pretending to be on grand adventures. Anna called it "being up to something," but it was never anything too wild. From terrorizing the Royal staff to stealing sweets from the kitchen, Kriss and I had become inseparable.

All of that changed the day we met up shortly after her fourth birthday.

"Nisha!" she shouted, running over to hug me.

"Let's go to the garden. I want to show you something," she said.

When we got to the garden, Kriss held up her hand and pointed at a stone wall.

"The fire inside me came forth," she said, and immediately, a blue ball of flame appeared before her. It was much brighter and bigger than the ones I'd seen Klovis start with.

"Grow and devour," she continued.

"Absolutely not in the garden!" Anna shouted.

Kriss froze, and the fireball vanished. "I'm sorry, Anna. I was just excited to show Nisha what I'd learned."

"I can understand your enthusiasm, but the Royal princess should not be blasting holes in palace walls," Anna said firmly.

"I'm sorry," Kriss muttered.

"Kriss, that's so amazing that you can do magic," I said.

Even as the words left my mouth, I realized something was off—not with Kriss, but with me.

Kriss and I spent the rest of the afternoon playing and talking. She started to speak excitedly about her magic lessons, but I interrupted her mid-sentence.

"I have to find my father."

Sensing something was wrong, Kriss asked, "What's wrong?"

"I'm not feeling well," I lied. I hugged her and promised I'd come to see her soon. The moment I was out of sight, I ran as fast as my legs could carry me.

When I found Father, I asked him to take me home.

"This is unusual," he said. "Usually, I have to hunt you down before we leave. Is everything all right?"

"Yes," I lied again.

"All right," he said gently. "You don't have to tell me now, but give me a few moments to finish wrapping things up, and then we'll head home."

Normally, riding in my father's lap on a borough dog would make me happy. But not today. I felt angry. I felt sad. I felt... other emotions I couldn't even name.

"Will you tell me what happened?" Father asked.

It took a while before I could swallow the knot in my throat.

"Kriss showed me her magic today," I finally said.

"Oh, I see. And how did that make you feel?" he asked.

"I'm happy for her," I said.

Father sat in silence for a while.

"It isn't fair," I finally blurted. "You can do magic. Mama can do it. Klovis and Ranisha can do it too. Now, Kriss can do it. Why can't I? Why do I have to be the useless one?"

"Is Milla useless?" Father asked.

"No," I said.

"Why not?"

"She can't use magic, but she takes care of me when I'm sick and helps me all the time."

"Right. And what about Hoba and Savo? They can't use magic either."

"But they're big and strong and can do things I can't."

"That's exactly my point," Father said. "Everyone has things that make them special. As I've said before, there are many people in this world who can't use magic—and they aren't useless."

"Then what am I good for?" I asked.

"You're good for making me smile when you say, 'Come with me.' You're good for getting my heart racing when you do something dangerous. You're still so young, my beautiful daughter. What you will do is still not known. But the most important thing you're doing is this..."

"What's that?" I asked.

"Being my daughter."

I didn't say anything for a while. After riding in silence, I finally said, "I'm glad I'm your daughter."

He held me tighter and said, "Me too."

Being jealous was painful, I decided. But magic or no magic, as far as second lives go, I got pretty lucky.

"Papa, can I ask you for a favor?"

"If it's reasonable," he replied.

"Can you ask Armon to teach me how to fight?"

Father thought for a moment. "I'll see if I can find you an instructor."

"I need Armon to teach me to spar with him."

Father looked back at Armon, who was following behind us. "Do you think she's available?"

"She's available, my lord. I can find out. But I don't think you should use her to instruct anyone—let alone a child."

"Send her a message anyway. If she's available, we'll test it. She might not be the right person, but I have a good feeling about it."

"As you wish, my lord," Armon said. "But don't say I didn't warn you."

"Who is she?" I asked.

"My sister," Armon replied.

Every chance I got, I hunted down Father and Armon to ask if there was any news.

"I'll let you know when I know something," they would say.

"What's she like?" I would ask Armon.

"I wouldn't want to spoil your surprise, my lady," he replied.

Finally, just when I was starting to think she would never come, Father told me she had just finished a long job and would be arriving in several weeks.

One morning, I rushed through breakfast because Armon was going to give me a riding lesson on the dogs.

"Finish your breakfast," Mother said. "Honestly, sometimes the way you behave, it's like I have two sons."

"Sorry, Mama," I said, stuffing another huge bite in my mouth.

When I had enough food to qualify as "eaten," I ran out to the kennel. As I got closer, I heard the sound of metal clashing. Around the corner, I saw Armon and a woman I had never seen before dueling with swords.

Their movements were a blur—precise, practiced, and graceful like a dance.

"I can't believe they let someone as fragile as you protect the Count," the woman said.

Armon may have been many things, but fragile was not one of them.

"And I can't believe they let something as wild as you out of a zoo," he shot back.

Every time it looked like one of them was about to win, the other would pull off a move so fast and fluid I couldn't follow it. The duel ended with both of them lunging forward and stopping their blades just short of each other's necks.

"You've gotten better, little brother," the woman said.

"I couldn't let you keep winning forever," Armon replied.

"That was amazing," I breathed.

"Who's the runt?" she asked.

"That's Lady Nisha Delwin," Armon said. "Lady Nisha, meet my sister Lila."

Lila looked nothing like Armon. While he was always polished and sharp in his attire, she had auburn hair, blue eyes, and wore a cropped leather jacket with black leather pants. She had a sword on one hip, a large knife on her thigh, and bits of armor strapped to her limbs. She looked like she belonged in a biker bar from my old world.

In short, she was the very essence of cool.

"You've got to be joking. This is the child you want me to instruct?" Lila scoffed. "This one doesn't even look housebroken. How old is she?"

Feeling insulted, I stood up straight. "I assure you, I've already broken quite a few things in the house. And I'm almost four," I said with as much attitude as I could.

"It isn't me who's asking. It's Count Delwin," Armon cut in.

"And what exactly does he expect me to do with a grumpy little three-year-old? Any training I give her is going to be too difficult."

"She'll pick it up. Starting this early gives you a chance to mold her before any bad habits form," Armon reasoned.

"Does she even realize what she's asking to get into?" Lila asked.

"Probably not. But most of us didn't before we started. Her father is well aware of what's involved. So long as you don't completely break her, you should be fine," Armon replied.

"Kid, why do you even want combat training?" Lila asked me.

"I don't want to be useless or rely on others to protect me."

"You're rich. You'll probably never even be in a situation where you need to fight."

"Maybe not. But things change, and life offers no guarantees."

"This will be harder than anything you've ever done. The second you quit, I'm gone. No second chances."

"I won't quit."

"Famous last words. Armon, give me the contract."

As Lila signed it, she looked down at me and smirked.

"I'll be done with you in less than a day."

"Do you really think you can teach me everything you know about fighting in less than a day?" I jabbed back.

"That smart mouth of yours will be the first thing to go," she muttered.

Chapter 8

That Isn't Training

"You're late," Lila said.

"I got here as fast as I could," I replied. "I also had to figure out how to put this on." I gestured to the dull gray outfit I was wearing—it felt like a cross between a sweatsuit and a burlap sack.

"Your father made it clear that any of your regular clothes damaged during training would come out of your pay. So get faster at putting them on. Training starts after breakfast."

She added, "From this point on, you will call me 'Master.' That will only change if you can defeat me or I tell you otherwise. Is that clear?"

"Yes, Master. I'm ready to learn," I responded.

"I don't need the extra words. Just 'Yes, Master' or 'No, Master.' Understood?" Lila barked.

"Yes, Master."

"Good. Now that we have all that sorted out, come with me."

She led me over to the wall and handed me a bucket just small enough that it didn't drag on the ground when I carried it.

"I want you to fill up that barrel over there," she said, pointing to a large barrel placed about a hundred yards away from the well.

"How full do I have to fill it?" I asked.

"All the way. To the top."

"Yes, Master."

I get it, I thought. It's like the military—they tear you down first. Well, she has no idea who she's dealing with.

Lila found a spot in the shade and sat down.

Drawing water from a well would be a simple enough task for almost anyone—except a small girl. I quickly learned I couldn't draw a full bucket. Not even half. The first time I got a partially filled bucket halfway up, my arm slipped, and I had to start over.

Eventually, I managed to get some water into my carry bucket and began the long walk to the barrel. It looked a lot closer from the well. I had to stand on tiptoe, lifting the bucket over my head to dump the water in.

It slipped out of my hands and spilled all over me.

From her spot in the shade, Lila laughed. "Had enough yet?" she shouted.

I pulled myself up and walked over to her.

"Master, the barrel just needs to be filled to the top, correct?"

She thought for a moment, then said, "Nobody can help you."

I brought the transfer bucket back to the well and flipped it upside down. Then I went over to the barrel and started pushing. It didn't budge at first, but I got it to rock back and forth until it finally toppled. I rolled it to the well and stood it upright. Using the upside-down bucket as a stool, I began filling the barrel directly from the well bucket.

Little by little, the barrel began to fill. By the time water spilled over the top, it was nearly noon, and my hands were covered in blisters.

Lila walked over. "That was a pretty clever solution you came up with. It would've been even more clever if you'd found something to protect your hands from the rope. That's enough for today. I'll see you in the morning. Don't be late."

"Yes, Master."

It had been hard, but I was victorious.

When I returned inside, Milla had a change of clean clothes ready.

She looked at my hands. "I'll get some ointment for you."

"Please don't tell Mother about this," I begged.

"I won't," said Milla. "But promise me you'll let me know if it gets worse."

"I will. I promise."

The next morning was all running.

Lila was like a beast. I tried everything I had to keep up. After what felt like a dozen miles—though it probably wasn't even one—I tripped and fell face-first.

"Quitting on me already?" Lila called out.

"No, I just needed to take a quick nap," I muttered.

The day after was more running, plus push-ups and squats.

And so, my new life began. Every morning except one day a week was filled with exercise of some kind.

Once, after returning from my morning routine, I overheard my parents talking.

"What about her other studies?" Mother asked. "Don't you feel like she's being neglected?"

"What is there to teach her?" Father replied. "She can already read and write better than I can. This makes her feel like she has a purpose."

"It still doesn't sit right with me," Mother protested.

"I'm okay, Mama. I don't mind it," I said, stepping into the room.

"I know, sweetheart. Just promise to let me know if it becomes too much."

"I promise."

Two weeks after starting training, Father asked if I wanted to go to the capital with him. I was exhausted, but there was no way I was missing a chance to see Krisstina.

At the palace, I hunted down Kriss and Anna.

Kriss ran over and hugged me. I winced.

"Are you all right?" she asked.

"I'm okay," I said, and told her about my training.

"That isn't training!" Kriss exclaimed. "She's just being mean to you."

"It's called 'condition training,' Your Highness," Anna explained. "It's much different than training to use magic."

"It's true," I added when Kriss didn't look convinced.

"Fine, but I don't like Miss Lila. Here, let me help you."

"Let the life within me restore," Kriss chanted, then touched my chest. I felt warmth flood through me. I was awake—fully, vibrantly awake.

Birthdays in this world were similar to those in my old life, with a few differences. No cake. The focus was more on food than gifts. Though presents were still a thing, you were more welcome with a pie than a present.

When I came downstairs, Milla stopped me after the first flight.

"Everything looks in order," she said. "For the daughter of the Count."

Birthdays were also political events—opportunities for marriage proposals. Thankfully, I was still too young. You didn't get those until you were ten.

Even then, Ranisha—with her silver hair and blue eyes—was the prime candidate. Not me, with my blonde hair, brown eyes, and lack of magic.

After greeting a slew of nobles clearly there to curry favor with Father, I saw AnnaLisa and Krisstina.

"I didn't know you were coming," I said.

"I wouldn't miss your birthday! I also have something for you," Kriss said, handing me a small box.

Inside was a silver pendant with a green stone set between two metal rings.

"It's beautiful, but what is it?"

"A healing rune," Kriss said. "Channel magic into it to heal wounds."

"Thank you, but... I can't use magic."

"Yes, you can," she insisted. "Everyone has some mana. Anyone can use magic."

Anna added, "It won't let you cast spells, but you can heal minor injuries."

"How do I use it?" I asked.

"Hold it between your thumbs. Clear your mind. Then imagine energy flowing from you into the rune."

It took a few tries, but it glowed. I held it to my chest and felt warmth radiate.

"This is amazing. Why doesn't everyone use these?"

"Several reasons," Anna said. "First, any decent mage can cast better spells. Second, runes are expensive."

"How expensive?"

"It's not polite to ask how expensive a gift is," Anna scolded gently. "Just be careful who you show that to."

"I will. Thank you so much, Kriss. I love it."

"I knew you would," she said, hugging me.

"Anna, where could I find a fire rune?"

"If you had the money, you could buy one from an artisan. Or you could find a firestone in a dungeon and bring it to an artificer to craft into a rune."

"They're mainly used to start fires and light paths," she added.

"Thanks, Anna. If I get one, I'm sure I'll put it to good use."

Chapter 9

Dungeon Crawl

The day after my fourth birthday, training with Lila began in earnest.

Every morning started with a brutal workout like the one she'd introduced me to before, followed by a sparring match. Well—as much of a match as you could call getting the crap beaten out of you by a seasoned warrior. On one hand, I knew it was all my choice. I wanted to get stronger, and if I wanted the pain to stop, all I had to do was quit.

On the other hand, Janos probably belonged in prison for standing by while Lila beat the living hell out of a child. But different worlds, different standards.

After Lila had her fun thrashing me, she would have me practice the basic swordsmanship forms she'd taught. I couldn't see any change or progress. But any day I could still walk at the end of sparring, I considered it a win.

Still, what I really wanted was to land a hit on her. Just one. That thought became my ultimate goal. If I could just get in one good shot, I could die happy. Better yet—I was working on a plan to make it happen.

One morning, shortly after my fifth birthday, I decided to seek out Klovis. It was my day off from training with Lila, and I had a plan to make the most of it.

"Milla, have you seen Klovis?" I asked.

"Not yet. He might still be asleep," she replied.

I found him fast asleep in his bed.

"Klovis, I need your help," I said.

No response.

Time for more direct measures. Klovis and I got along fine as siblings, but with eight years between us, he mostly ignored me. I climbed up on his bed and started rolling him off the edge.

Thunk.

Judging by the sound, his head must have hit something wooden—a noise I was all too familiar with from Lila's training sword.

"What are you doing, Nisha?" he groaned, rubbing his head.

"I have the day off, and I need your help doing some research."

"It's always something strange with you. It isn't more research into microscopic organisms again, is it?"

"It's microscopic organisms—and yes, they do exist. And they make people sick," I replied firmly.

In my past life, I'd hoped that pointing someone in the right direction might jumpstart some important discoveries. But the real issue turned out to be the quality of glass and mirrors in this world. They simply weren't good enough to make an effective microscope. Some things just had to be rediscovered the hard way.

"This is something completely different," I said. "Are there any kinds of powders that explode? Probably black, maybe used for mining or blowing up rocks?"

"Not that I've ever heard of," Klovis replied.

"Then how is mining done? How do they remove large stones?"

"Mages who specialize in explosive magic, I'd guess."

Figures. With magic available as a solution to so many problems, technological development was slower. Why invent explosives when you already have fireballs?

"What about a yellow powder that smells like rotten eggs? Or a white powder that helps plants grow?"

"I don't know," he admitted. "But I might know someone who does."

"Can we go see them?" I asked.

"Any chance you'll leave my room and let it go if I say no?"

"Not on your life," I said cheerfully.

"Let me get dressed. Meet you at the front gate after breakfast."

"Thanks, big brother. You're the best."

A little positive reinforcement never hurt.

"Out," he said, pointing at the door.

About 45 minutes later, we stood by the front gate.

"Who are we going to see?" I asked.

"An alchemist. When we get there, promise me you won't touch anything. He has a lot of strange stuff in his shop. Keep your hands in your pockets."

"I'll be careful. I promise."

Fifteen minutes later, we arrived at the market center. We turned into a row of shops marked with symbols rather than words—probably a sign that literacy rates weren't great here. We entered one marked by a flask with a snake wrapped around it. The air was a strange blend of dried herbs and animal musk.

An old man with gray hair sat behind the counter.

"Good morning, Mr. Prinsky," said Klovis.

"Good morning, young lord. What can I do for you and your adorable young friend?" he asked.

"This is my sister, Nisha. We were wondering if you might know anything about certain powders. If they exist," Klovis said.

"They do exist," I cut in. "Mr. Prinsky, have you ever seen a black powder that burns quickly or explodes when confined?"

"Such a well-spoken young lady," he said. "I suppose that's the benefit of being raised in the Lord's mansion. But no, I haven't heard of anything like that."

"What about a yellow powder that smells like rotten eggs and burns blue when lit?"

"Ah, that I know. You're talking about Devil's Breath." He pulled out a sealed jar of yellow powder. "Don't open it unless you're ready to use it. It'll stink up everything."

"Anything else?" he asked.

"Yes. Do you have any white fertilizer that might come from birds—or creatures that live in caves?"

"I think I know what you mean. Diatherfly dung is white and used to grow special plants."

"Do you know where I could get some?"

"You could try a flower shop—or go straight to the source."

"Where's the source?"

"The Tantum Dungeon, north of town."

"Thank you so much!" I said.

We paid for the Devil's Breath and a bag of charcoal, then headed out to find a flower shop.

"That wasn't so bad," I said. "Why'd you make me keep my hands in my pockets?"

"The first time I went in there, I broke something. Smelled so bad, they had to burn my clothes."

"Do you remember what it was called?"

"Forget I said anything. The last thing I need is for you to get strange ideas."

"Sounds like I'd make a good distraction if you ever need to make a quick escape," I said.

The flower shop didn't have any dung in stock, but confirmed it was easy to collect from the dungeon.

"When are you going to collect more?" I asked.

"In about two months," the owner said. "Won't have anything growing that needs it until then."

"Klovis?"

"No," he said immediately. "I'm not taking you into a dungeon."

"Why not? We know exactly where we're going and what we need."

"If anything happens to you, Father will kill me."

"If a flower shop owner can go in and out, surely a trained noble mage like you can handle it."

"I see what you're doing. It's not going to work."

"Please? This is really important to me."

"You still haven't told me what it's for."

"I can't land a hit on Lila. This might help level the field."

"And how do you know how to make it?"

"It's just in my head. Like how I knew mathematics."

I didn't enjoy lying, but the truth was worse—I had the memories of a killer from my past life. I wasn't Adam Drummer anymore. I am Nisha now. I had a family. A life. And despite the weight of my past, I wanted to do something good.

"You really are something," Klovis said, breaking my thoughts.

I looked up at him and felt a sudden rush of gratitude.

"Klovis, bend down."

He sighed and leaned over. I wrapped my arms around his neck.

"Thank you for being my brother. I love you."

He awkwardly returned the hug. "Fine. I'll take you to the dungeon."

"I love you too," he added.

We walked in silence for a bit before he muttered, "That was a dirty trick."

"I really do appreciate having you in my life," I said.

"You don't have to feel sorry for my future husband. I find the idea of marriage disturbing."

"Well, you're only five. You might feel different later."

"Oh? Has someone made you feel different?"

Klovis's cheeks turned red. "We're done with this conversation."

"Can we go to the dungeon on your next day off?"

"That should work. Gives us time to plan."

Over the next few days, we gathered supplies: lanterns, food, a couple of knives. Klovis stashed everything behind some bushes near the main gate.

"Are you ready?" I asked the night before.

"Ready for what?"

I spun around. Ranisha stood behind me, wearing a traveler's cloak.

My mind raced. "I asked Klovis to help me with mana control training."

"That sounds interesting. Can I join?"

"No!" I blurted. "I have almost no mana. I'm nervous about people watching."

"It would only be me," she said gently. "You know I'd never make fun of you."

"I know. But I'd still rather not have an audience."

"Okay, I get it. I'm not invited," Ranisha said, turning to walk away.

"It isn't like that," I tried to explain. But it was too late.

"She'll be fine," Klovis said. "Now get some sleep."

The next morning, I acted like everything was normal. Nobody suspected anything.

After breakfast, I slipped out to meet Klovis at the gate. He handed me a pack, and I hooked a dagger onto my belt.

"I know you've been training with Lila, but you're still small," he said. "If we run into trouble, stay behind me. I can't cast if you're in the way."

Just as we were about to leave, the gate opened again.

Ranisha walked out in a traveler's cloak, looked us over, and asked, "So, where are we going?"

"Training," I said, trying to keep up the lie.

"Don't give me that nonsense," she said, grabbing a pack from behind another bush. "You two aren't as good at making secret plans as you think you are."

"It's dangerous," I protested.

She just looked at me and said, "Do we really need to have this conversation? Besides, if I'm not going, I'll tell Father that you're heading off to Tantum Dungeon. Two mages are better than one."

I finally relented. "Is anyone going to be wondering where you are?" I asked.

"No more than you two," said Ranisha. "I said I'd be out at the market."

"So what's inside the dungeon that we're after?"

"Ditherfly dung," I said.

"What could you possibly want with that stuff?" she asked.

"Nisha has this wild idea that she can use it to create explosive powder," said Klovis.

"It isn't just a wild idea," I said.

"Couldn't you just get a mage who knows explosive magic?" asked Ranisha.

"I want to be able to do things for myself."

It took us about two hours to reach the entrance of the dungeon. The entrance was about as high as a barn door and had a pillar on each side. A sign was posted that read:

"Parties larger than four recommended below Floor Five."

"That shouldn't be an issue," said Klovis. "Ditherflies are on the second floor. I've been here several times with Father and Armon, so this shouldn't take long."

"Those sound like famous last words," said Ranisha.

41

"We'll be fine. Whatever's inside there can't be worse than Leela," I said.

Once inside, darkness enveloped us. Klovis lit a small lantern and handed it to me.

"Stay close," he said as we turned left and headed into the dungeon.

"What does a ditherfly look like?" I asked.

"You'll see soon enough," Klovis replied. "There isn't much that comes up to the first floor, but some of the bugs and insects that feed on the surface hide on the second floor, where it's cooler. Most are harmless unless provoked."

After walking for about ten minutes, we came to a fork in the road. The path on the right had a sign that read:

"Second Floor."

Following the sign, we moved down a sloping path. It dropped about a hundred feet before leveling out again. Somewhere in the darkness, we heard a steady *tap, tap, tap.*

I held the lantern as high as I could. The light bounced off the carapace of a beetle the size of a cat.

The fire inside me stirred—*Grow and devour*—

"No! Don't yell," said Klovis. "It's harmless. And it smells awful if you kill it."

Ranisha lowered her hands. "It looks so creepy."

"He probably thinks the same thing about you," said Klovis.

"What should we be looking out for?" I asked.

"On this floor, not much. Ditherflies will swarm if agitated, but they can't do much besides bite. Occasionally, there are slimes, but they're easy to take out with fire."

"Sounds simple enough," I said. "How much farther until we find the ditherflies?"

"They should be just up ahead. The path opens into a giant room," said Klovis. "We'll hear the buzzing before we see them."

We kept moving, and it wasn't long before the buzzing sound of thousands of flying insects filled the air. Just as Klovis said, the tunnel opened into a large cavern. I turned the lantern to full brightness. Along the walls were thousands of gray, moving shapes.

Ditherflies.

They were about three to four inches long and looked like a cross between a housefly and a dragonfly.

"As long as we aren't too loud and stick to places they avoid, we should be fine," said Klovis.

"Can we make this quick? This place gives me the creeps," said Ranisha.

"Over there," I pointed. There was a pile of white substance clear of flies. Dig Marx in the pile showed others had collected from it before.

I pulled out some jars and hand shovels. "Let's get to it."

After several minutes, the jars were full and packed away.

"Now we can leave, right?" asked Ranisha.

"Yes, we can go now," said Klovis.

"That was really easy. We could have done this last week," I said.

"Never underestimate a dungeon," Klovis replied. "Father always says bad things happen when you aren't prepared."

"Let's just get back to the first floor and go home," said Ranisha.

We were about halfway back when we started hearing voices.

"Nisha, turn the light off," whispered Klovis.

"It's just other people," I said.

"Humans aren't the only things capable of speech," he replied.

We stopped and waited in the dark, the voices getting louder.

"I can't tell what they're saying," I whispered.

"Could be bandits—or goblins," said Klovis. "Nisha, get behind me."

The voices were not human. Klovis's voice was barely audible:

43

"Kobalds. They must've wandered up from the lower levels."

"Ranisha, when they get close, we'll try to burn a path through. Wait for my signal."

I pulled my dagger out. I wasn't sure how well my small body would hold up in a real fight, but Leela had been beating the crap out of it for a year now.

Klovis and Ranisha started chanting fire spells. The kobalds were surprised and stopped—but only for a moment. They rushed in.

The first two caught fire and burst into flames. The flash lit the tunnel, revealing at least a dozen more.

"This isn't good," Klovis muttered. "Hit them again!" he shouted.

Two more ignited. "Ranisha, take Nisha and run!"

They were too close. One kobold swung a club at Klovis. He tried to dodge but couldn't clear in time. The club caught him in the chin, and he fell.

Ranisha pulled at my arm to flee. For a moment, I considered it.

But the thought of giving up... *I'll bet they don't hit as hard as Leela.*

I tore my arm from Ranisha's grasp. "Don't quit!" I shouted, running toward the kobold that hit Klovis.

It swung. Too slow. Time seemed to move on its own.

I rolled beneath the swing and slashed its Achilles tendon. As it came down, I jumped and drove my blade into its eye.

It took more effort to remove the blade than to strike.

Another one charged.

I remembered a range instructor's advice: *A shot to the groin is almost as fatal as one to the head.*

Let's see if that's true.

I sidestepped and stabbed the next kobold in the groin. The blood spray was massive, drenching half my body.

A fire spell shot over my head and hit another—*Ranisha*, I thought.

The remaining kobalds turned to flee.

I put everything I had into my arm and threw my dagger at the back of the closest fleeing kobold. The dagger buried itself into its back, and the kobold fell to the ground.

I ran over to Klovis and held my ear to his mouth. He was still breathing.

"Ranisha, I need light," I said.

"Here, I got one."

The voice was not Ranisha's.

My heart filled with terror.

"Master. What brings you down here?"

Crack.

The next thing I remember was waking up next to Klovis. We were outside the dungeon. Armon and Leela were standing next to a cart hitched up to Hoba and Sabo.

"You have to admit that the bladework on those last three was pretty clean," said Armon.

"True. But I don't need her developing an oversized ego just yet. Too much confidence early on kills a lot of students," replied Leela.

I slowly got up. Ranisha and Klovis were already on their feet.

"Are you okay?" I asked Klovis. "I saw you get hit, and it had me worried."

"I'm all right," he said. "Mr. Janos is pretty good at healing magic. It's a good thing your instructor showed up when she did. That could've ended a lot worse."

"Master, how did you find us?" I asked.

"Three well-dressed children heading out of town with Pax tend to draw attention. Maybe next time you try to sneak off on an adventure, you'll try not to stand out like a sore thumb," replied Leela.

"How did you even know to come looking for us?" I asked.

"Astronicia. All three of you said you were headed off to the market. You could've just shouted that you were up to something and been less suspicious," said Armon.

"What were the three of you doing in the dungeon, anyway?"

Not wanting the full truth to come out, I spoke up. "It's my fault. I kept begging Klovis to show me what a dungeon was like. He told me no, but I kept asking until he agreed. I wanted to see if my training was working. I can't tell when I'm always losing to you, Master."

"You could've just talked to me about it," said Leela. "I was planning on taking you to a dungeon soon anyway. I've been training you for over a year now. Of course, you've gotten better. Do you think I keep wasting time on you if you weren't?"

In all the time I had known her, that was the closest to praise I had ever gotten from her.

"No, you're a good instructor," I replied.

I couldn't help but smile. There was an overwhelming sense of satisfaction burning inside me. I had been... praised. Sort of. By my master.

"What's with the creepy grin?" Leela asked.

"I'm just happy to see you coming to save us," I replied.

"We'll see if you still feel that way after training tomorrow," said Leela. "It's getting late. Get in the cart so we can get you kids back home."

I climbed into the cart and sat next to Klovis.

"Thanks for going along with my story," I whispered to him.

"It was mostly true anyway," he replied, checking to make sure no one else was listening. "Do we still have it?"

"Yes, we still have your precious bug poop," he said.

That was still a silver lining.

There was a sliver of daylight left when we got home to the estate. Mother was waiting just inside the gate. She immediately started going in on Klovis and Ranisha.

"Just what were you thinking? Wait until your father hears about this!"

As she walked around to the side of the cart, I stood up and started explaining that it was my fault. Mother's eyes locked onto me, and I watched as all the color drained from her face. The shock was too much for her, and she hit the ground.

I must have made quite the sight, all covered in blood and dirt from the dungeon.

"We should have cleaned her up before bringing her home," said Armon.

"You don't say," replied Leela.

Chapter 10

Artificer

"Grounded?" I asked.

"Forever," came Mother's reply.

But Papa only gave Klovis and Ranisha two weeks.

I protested.

"That's because we all agree the dungeon idea was yours," said Mother.

I tried to play the age card. "I'm only five. And Klovis is the one who took me."

Mother saw right through it.

"Nice try, young lady. You already claimed responsibility. And seeing as fate decided to give you a second life disguised as a little girl, I'm inclined to agree with you."

That one hurt. I thought maybe it was because it hit close to home, knowing the monster inside of me. Still, I couldn't help but cheer up. I knew she was right.

"I'm sorry, Mama."

"You know why I'm so upset, don't you?" she asked.

"I do. And I didn't mean to disappoint you, Mama."

"You didn't disappoint me. You scared me," she said.

"I didn't mean to. I forgot to clean off the blood before coming home."

"It wasn't the blood—or not only the blood—that scared me. Wild animal or not, I can't replace you," she said.

"I'll be more careful," I promised.

"You better. Now come give me a hug, and then go to bed."

My lifetime sentence ended up being reduced to two weeks, which I made use of by drawing out the ditherfly dung, pulverizing it, and mixing it with potash. Remembering the ingredients for gunpowder is only the first step. It takes some experimenting to get the right ratio.

Klovis and Ranisha were eager to see the fruits of our trip to the dungeon. Through trial and error, I finally got the ratio where it burned bright.

Klovis and Ranisha seemed disappointed by the simple flash.

"An open pile made all that work just for that?" said Klovis.

"Hang on."

I dumped some into a small cloth bag, twisted it tight, and tied it closed. I placed it on the basement floor and made a trail of powder leading up to the bag.

"Get behind something," I said.

Klovis pushed over an old table.

"Ranisha, can you use a spell to light the end of this trail closest to us?" I asked.

"I think I can hit it," she said.

She cast her spell, and the line of powder ignited.

"Get down!" I yelled.

When the line hit the bag, the explosion shook the entire mansion and shattered a basement window.

I could tell how this was going to play out, and I instantly took off running. As soon as I did, Ranisha and Klovis were right behind me. You can't be blamed if you can't be found.

All three of us headed for different hiding places. I made it into the garden tool shed and hid behind some bags of sod. At some point, I must have fallen asleep.

When I woke up, it was late in the afternoon, and I was still hidden. I figured one of the others must have been found and punished already. I got up and snuck back inside the mansion. If I could get to my room, I could say I had been there taking a nap.

As I checked the dining room, I saw Ranisha and Klovis sitting at the table. I pulled my head back and started sneaking the other way when I ran into Milla.

"You'd better go back to the dining room," she said.

I walked all the way inside this time, trying my best to act as innocent as possible. Mother was standing there, looking between me and the two already seated.

"It's a month this time," she said.

I had been waiting over a year to get back at Leela. I could get through another month.

During that month, I used my sparring time with Leela to practice putting distance between us.

"You can't kill anything by running away!" she yelled as I backed off.

"I can survive a bit longer," I replied.

Leela caught me with a leg sweep and kicked my training sword out of my hand.

"And you'll still be just as dead in the end," she said.

"Maybe I'd have a better chance if I actually had a fair fight," I said.

"It will never be a fair fight. You are small. Even when you're fully grown, you'll still be at a disadvantage."

"Really? Explain."

"You will have to work twice as hard as a man just to keep up. Even then, most who are trained to fight will be bigger and stronger than you. And the beasts out there will eat you whole and crap you out while you're still whining about fairness."

"If you want things to be fair, put down your sword right now and go learn something else," she concluded.

"I get the point," I said. "I'm always going to be at a disadvantage."

"I don't think you do," said Leela. "I said it won't be fair. If you're at a disadvantage, that's on you. Now, quit complaining and find a way to not be at a disadvantage. Now try to attack me."

A month passed by, and I still hadn't found a way to level the playing field against Leela. But I had a plan to change all that. I needed an artificer to help me realize that plan, but Klovis said the closest one was in Circa.

The next time I went to see Kriss, I asked Anna if she knew where to find an artificer.

"Is there something wrong with the rune necklace the princess gave you?" she asked.

"No, there isn't anything wrong with it," I replied. "I would like to have something made, but it's far beyond my skills."

"His Majesty keeps a very skilled artificer employed here at the castle," said Anna. "I could introduce you to him, if you'd like. Just be warned—he's not the easiest person to get along with."

"That's okay. I'm getting better at making friends," I replied.

As Kriss and I followed Anna, the castle seemed to get dustier the further we went.

"This part of the castle doesn't get any visitors," Anna said, sounding slightly embarrassed.

We finally stopped at a large wooden door. Anna knocked firmly.

"Samuel, are you there? Are you in at the moment?" she shouted.

"That depends on who's asking," a man's voice shouted back through the door.

"It is I, your one true love, Lady AnnaLisa," she said with a playful voice full of jest.

"He has a bit of a thing for me," she whispered to us.

"What do you want?" he asked.

"I have a potential customer for you," said Anna.

A series of locks could be heard unlatching. When the door opened, a young man in his early twenties with brown hair and blue eyes looked out at us.

"Where is this customer?" Samrail asked.

"She's right here." Anna pushed me forward.

"I don't make toys anymore," said Samrail.

"I'm not here for a toy. I need help building a weapon," I said.

"Aren't you a little too young to be using weapons?" he asked.

"Aren't you a little young to be a Royal artificer?" I shot back.

"Fair point," he said. "Come on in. Just be careful what you touch."

We followed him into his workshop, where he had various projects laid out all over.

"So, what lies has Anna told you about me?" he asked.

"She did say that you fancy her," said Kriss.

"In her dreams," Samrail shot back defensively.

"Oh, don't try to hide it," said Anna. "I've seen the way you look at me when you think nobody's watching."

"You are delusional," said Samrail.

"What about you, Anna? Do you like Samrail?" I asked.

"I'm not sure," she replied. "I could probably find out if he ever asked me out," she added.

"Do you want my help or not?" Samrail asked, redirecting the conversation.

"It's not much, but I have some preliminary drawings," I said, cutting into their banter.

I pulled the drawings out of my bag and handed them to him. He took a few minutes looking them over.

"These are really good. Did you make these?" he asked.

"The concept is mine, but my brother Klovis helped with the drawings," I said.

"He's very talented," said Samrail. "I'd like to meet him sometime."

"I'll let him know when I see him."

"I can see that the general purpose of the device is to expel projectiles at extreme velocity," said Samrail.

"Not just that. It gives even non-magic users the ability to cast defensive spells," I said.

"Most people would call this an offensive weapon," he replied.

"I guess it depends on how it's used," I said.

"I can see that it uses mana to activate a fire rune, but I've never heard of this explosion powder before," Samrail said.

"It's something I've developed," I replied.

"Can you give me a demonstration?"

"Do you have a safe place where I can set off an explosive?" I asked.

He pointed to an empty corner of his workshop. "Over there should be fine, if it's small."

I set up the powder the same way I had in the basement at home, but with a smaller amount. "Kriss, will you light it for me?"

She shot a fire spell at the trail. "Cover your ears," I warned.

After the explosion, Samrail looked at me, wide-eyed. "Do you have any idea what you're asking me to make? A way for anyone—mage or not—to cast a lethal spell instantly, without any incantations."

"Exactly," I stated.

"It still has limitations," I said. "Each shot takes time to load, and you have to carry all the supplies with you."

"If someone could get their hands on enough fire rune stones, they could build an army overnight," Samrail said.

"Wouldn't it be impossible to get that many?" Anna asked.

"Difficult, maybe. But not impossible," he replied.

"So can you make it?" I asked.

"I can. But a better question is—should I?"

"Yes, you should. Mages can already cast lethal spells. This just makes things a bit more even for everyone else," I replied.

"It's a lot to consider, but if it is just the one, I think I can make it. But the price may be out of my reach, even for the daughter of a noble," Samrail warned.

"How about this? You cover all the expenses. In exchange, I'll share the formula for the powder if you agree to a contract: that formula isn't shared or sold without both our consent," I offered.

"That's very generous of you—leaving me covering everything," he complained.

"You know that the value of this formula is far more than what I'm asking."

Samrail looked over the drawings. "Give me about two months. The next time you come by, I'll have the contract ready for the formula."

"Now that business is out of the way," I teased, "are you going to ask Anna out on a date?"

"Get out of my workshop before I change my mind," he grumbled.

A month later, I was back at the castle visiting Kriss.

"Samrail said he needs to see you when you come by," said Anna.

We made our way down to the workshop.

"Who is it?" Samrail called out when Anna knocked.

"It's me, darling. I brought Nisha down to see you," Anna said.

Samrail opened the door. "You know, someday someone who doesn't know any better will hear you and think you're serious. Maybe someone like His Majesty the King."

He rolled his eyes. "I have the contract ready," he said, handing it to me.

I read through it. "It looks good, but how is it enforced?"

"I have two copies. You and I sign both on the mana circuit line. Focus mana into the circuit, which prevents tampering and pairs the copies."

We signed both with a pen. The contracts lit up as the mana circuits activated.

"That was my first contract," I said.

"I hope it was fun. But now come over here," Samrail said. "I need to measure your hands."

Over on a bench, there were several wooden stocks set out for pistols.

"Hold this one," he said, handing me the smallest.

"That's what I thought," he muttered. He made some Marx and then handed me one closer to a rifle stock. He marked around my shoulder and hands.

"Which one are you making?" I asked.

"Both. I'm not sure which will suit your needs best, but I thought it best to get data back on both versions. Be sure to give me feedback—that's my price for making two."

"Do you have a piece of paper I can use?" I asked.

He handed me one, and I wrote down the formula for the powder.

"It's so simple," he said.

"It is—but without a need, nobody developed it."

"What do you call it?"

"I was thinking of calling it boom powder."

"I'm not calling it that."

"Fine. Take all the fun out of it and just call it black powder."

"Now that's a name I can agree with."

My sparring matches with Leela were not going as well as I'd hoped. Every time I tried to gain some distance, she closed in instantly, undoing any progress I made. I couldn't just shoot her at random—it had to be during a match. Otherwise, it wouldn't be a win. And Leela definitely wouldn't accept it.

Lying on my bed after training, I screamed into my pillow. Then, suddenly, inspiration struck. It would be risky, and I'd only get one chance.

Two months were finally up. Mother was coming, and the carriage was hitched. I was practically pushing everyone to get going.

"You seem eager to get going," Father said.

"I'm always eager to see Kriss," I replied.

"Being eager is fine," said Mother. "But harassing everyone is not."

At the castle, when I met Kriss, she saw the look on my face.

"You used to come to the castle to see me."

"I still do. But just like you were excited about learning magic, I'm excited about this."

"Okay, we'll go see if Samrail is finished. But if he's not, you have to promise to play with me instead."

"I promise," I said.

"I've already tested them myself, and they're ready," Samrail said after we entered his workshop.

"Why didn't you wait for me to test them?"

"I wasn't going to put something in the hands of a child that might explode."

He had a target set up in the corner with some paper cartridges already made. Both the pistol and the rifle had two barrels and used paper cartridges. They had no primers, just open backs like a break-action shotgun. You loaded the cartridge, closed it, and focused mana into the rune stone.

"The lever in the center selects which barrel to fire first by closing off the mana circuit to the other. Center fires both," Samrail explained.

"Got it," I replied.

"They've got a bit of a punch, so be careful."

I picked up the pistol, loaded two cartridges, set the lever, and fired. The first shot was a little left, so I adjusted and fired again—dead center.

"You're a little too good at this," said Samrail. "Is this really your first time?"

"Nisha's always been a fast learner," said Anna.

"If I hit the center of the target, you have to take Anna out on a date," I said.

"Fine."

I picked up the rifle, tilted it, aimed, and fired. Direct hit.

"Why do I feel like I was set up?" Samrail asked.

"So am I actually taking you out, or just buying dinner?"

"Let me be clear: you're picking the activity, we're doing it together, and then you're taking me to dinner," Anna replied.

"So it really is just about getting a free meal," he muttered.

"I think Anna and Sam are going to get married—and Samrail won't even realize it," said Kriss.

"I think I'd have to agree," I said.

"There's just one last thing I need to test," I told Samrail. I modified a cartridge by replacing the bullet with a half-dried slime ball.

"What is that?" he asked.

"Half-dried slime. It should splatter on impact. I need you to shoot me."

"Absolutely not!"

"I'll be fine. Kriss can heal me. Just don't miss."

"All right. Just remember—you asked for this."

Bang.

The impact knocked the wind out of me. I doubled over, and they all rushed to me.

"I'm okay," I gasped, checking the red lump forming on my stomach. I healed it with a rune from my neck.

"That worked perfectly."

"That scared the crap out of me," said Samrail.

"I can't believe you would injure a child!" Anna exclaimed.

Samrail turned to her and said, "You really don't want dessert, do you?"

Chapter 11

Nisha Vs. Lila

All the preparation that could be done had been done. It wouldn't be a fair fight, but I had a way to overcome my disadvantage.

I met Lila for physical training. This particular morning's task was dragging weights across the ground. I had to dig my heels in just to get enough traction to move them. Sweat was rolling off my forehead when Lila finally said, "That's enough."

"Can we wait a minute before we get started, Master?"

"Your enemies won't give you a minute," she replied flatly.

"I understand, Master. But Princess Krisstina has been asking to watch one of my sparring matches with Master Swordswoman Lila." I made sure to use her title, hoping the formality might sway her.

"You have five minutes. If she isn't here by then, we will start anyway."

I dashed to the corner of the mansion where I saw Anna, Samrail, and Kriss standing around looking lost.

"Over here!" I shouted.

They followed me back to the sparring area, where I rejoined Lila.

"I don't know what Her Highness hopes to learn from this other than how pitiful my student is," Lila said dryly.

"Her Highness the Princess hopes that having an audience might motivate her friend to reach greater heights," Anna answered smartly.

"And who's he?" Lila asked, pointing at Samrail.

"That's my boyfriend and Royal artificer, Samrail," Anna replied with a mischievous grin.

"One date does not make us a couple," Samrail protested.

"It's fine by me if she wants an audience to her humiliation," Lila said, returning her gaze to me. "Today I won't be an easy target, Master."

"Sure you won't," came her biting reply.

But I meant it. If I didn't give this fight everything I had, Lila would sense something was off. My timing would have to be flawless.

Training swords drawn, we faced each other.

I pressed in first, coming high and fast. Lila blocked easily and sidestepped me.

"That was sloppy, and you know it," she said.

I adjusted, bringing my arms in closer for better control. I came at her faster this time, and she had to jump back, but she still countered. I kept pressing, pouring everything I'd learned into my attacks.

To an outside observer, it must have been clear Lila was holding back—passing on offensive openings. But I was doing everything I could to bait her into attacking.

I had to get creative.

After my next strike was blocked, I stomped on her foot. My size and weight made it a minor hit, but it had the desired effect. She lifted her knee to drive me back—and that's when I ducked, slamming my forehead into her knee.

The impact threw me backward, and I landed flat on my face and stomach.

"Get up!" Lila barked.

But my hand was already gripping the pistol. Powered by mana, it made no sound—no springs or metal mechanisms to give it away.

"Don't tell me a little hit like that knocked you out," she said, stepping closer.

I stayed perfectly still.

She nudged me with her foot. I didn't move.

She crouched to roll me over—and as soon as my hand was free, I pointed the pistol up and fired both barrels directly at her.

The twin explosions, smoke, and sudden sting to her chest shocked her completely.

Curses and screams poured out in an incoherent mix.

I jumped to my feet, triumphant. "I win, Master!"

Lila glared at me with murder in her eyes. I knew in that instant that I had to run.

I managed two steps before something hard collided with the back of my skull, and the world went black.

I woke up to Kriss leaning over me.

"Sorry, I lost it on you, kid," Lila said. "Your friends explained what you hit me with. That was your win."

"Thanks, Master," I muttered. "Didn't think you'd be more gracious about it—what with you always going on about finding ways to not be at a disadvantage."

"That's true," she admitted. "But I never had a student go and invent a whole new kind of weapon as a solution. One that's loud, smelly, and stings like hell."

"It would only work once, you know," I said.

"I do, Master. But it was worth every bit of planning it took just to see your reaction and finally get one over on you."

"I hope you thoroughly enjoyed the show," Lila said darkly, "because now that you've shown me what you're capable of, training is going to get much more dangerous. We're going to start taking trips down into dungeons."

"That sounds exciting!" I said. "But I've only ever landed the one hit on you, Master."

"You've shown me that you can make up for your disadvantages. It only makes sense that we test you in a more serious environment."

"Can I come with you on these trips to the dungeon?" Kriss asked eagerly.

"I have no issue with you tagging along," Lila said, "provided you don't hinder my student's training. But—" she turned, pointing to Anna, "—I'm not paid enough to guarantee the safety of a princess. So the decision is up to your minder."

Chapter 12

Politics and Proposals

In order to take on dungeon bounties and get paid for them, you have to be registered as a hunter. Hunters can then accept bounties based on the overall capability of their party. Party ranking is determined by the average rank of its members.

Hunter ranks start at Rank F—the lowest—and go up to Rank A. Technically, there are two higher ranks: Double-A and Triple-A. Most hunters, even lifelong professionals, never make it higher than Rank A or B.

Leela's rank is Triple-A, which allows us to accept just about any bounty from the Hunter's Guild. The downside is that most of the credit from our bounties goes to her. After almost three years, I'm still only ranked D. Kriss, on the other hand, has managed to reach Rank C—not because of her Royal status, but because mages are generally in high demand, especially those proficient in support and offensive magic. Kriss is an exceptional mage. Someone of her talent usually ends up working for the military, so there aren't many like her in the Hunter's Guild.

Today's bounty had us down on the seventh floor of the Tantum Dungeon, hunting saber bears. The best description for them? A koala bear from hell. They run on two legs, and the claws on their front paws are four inches long and shaped like sabers. They're wicked fast but not too intelligent.

"Remember," Leela said, "the bounty calls for twelve mostly intact hides. That means no fire spells or slashing kills."

"How do you want us to do this?" she asked me.

"I'll have Kriss build the kill zone with Earth Wall. I'll go antagonize a group and lead them back to the rest of the party," I explained. "You'll have to be fast. They're aggressive, but the shots might scare them off. Other than that, it's a good plan."

"I picked out a spot with some boulders to hide behind for the ambush," I added. "Can you keep an eye on these for me, Kriss?" I asked, setting down my pack and rifle.

"I can do that for you," she replied. "But be careful. I'd hate to think what would happen to you if they caught you."

"Well then, don't think about it. I'll be quick," I said with a smile. "Besides, death isn't all that bad."

"That's not funny. And how would you know anyway?"

"Just a hunch," I said. I couldn't exactly tell her I'd already done it once before.

"Nisha," Kriss said seriously, "you've had a pretty carefree attitude lately and have been taking risks with your life that you don't need to."

"It's not extra risk. My confidence and skills have just been improving," I explained. "Maybe I've been a bit heady with my capabilities at times, but Leela makes it a point to humble me often."

"Just be careful," she said.

I stepped away from the party and headed toward an area where I had seen saber bears before. The pistol was off-limits until I got them back to the kill zone, so I had my short sword at the ready. This part of the dungeon was a massive cavern lit by a giant glowstone hanging from the ceiling. The light level was about the same as dusk on the surface.

After about twenty minutes, I found what I was looking for: a group of saber bears outside a cave. Perfect. Speed was the name of the game.

Three bears lounged near the cave. One was asleep, and the other two were fighting over a bone. Sword in hand, I crept up on the pair. With a quick thrust, I stabbed one in the back of the head. My sword pushed the bone out of its mouth, and the other—now in full possession of the bone—rolled onto its back in surprise. I pulled my sword from the first bear and lunged at the second, stabbing it through the bottom of the jaw into its brain. Both died without much fuss.

I walked over to the sleeping bear and kicked it. It blinked up at me, dazed. I kicked it again, and it screeched. Once it had made enough noise, I stabbed it through the eye socket.

Noises echoed from the cave. I didn't wait to count how many were coming—I ran.

As soon as I was certain the first bear had seen me, I bolted. Judging from the pounding footsteps behind me, there were a lot of them. I could shoot some to slow them down, but that risked scaring them off, just as Leela had warned. That was a last resort.

I weaved through the cavern, creating as many obstacles as I could, but it didn't make much difference. They were just as good at climbing and dodging as I was. Their footsteps drew closer. The kill zone was in sight, but I wasn't sure if I could make it. I reached for my pistol and was about to turn and fire when I heard Leela shout:

"Keep running!"

If she believed I could make it, then I could. I gave everything I had and dove behind one of the earth walls Kriss had erected.

Before I could turn to help, one of the bears swiped and caught my face with its claws. Blood streamed down my cheek. I punched the bear in the face, and as it staggered, I shot it. It dropped instantly.

Over the wall, Kriss was casting spells while Anna and Leela dispatched the rest of the bears with swift, efficient strikes. I vaulted back over the wall, sword in hand, and took out two more before the last one fell.

Leela looked at me. "You got careless. If you'd just thrown a rock to get their attention, you would've made it back without a scratch."

"Of course you were watching me," I said, wincing.

Kriss walked over and cast a healing spell on my face. "This is exactly what I've been talking about," she said sternly.

"I know," I said. "I guess I've become a little arrogant. I'll try to think things through better going forward."

"I hope so," said Kriss. "I can heal a lot, but I can't replace an eye. If that bear had gotten any closer, you might've lost one."

As for my life... the second one wasn't so bad. But I didn't know if I'd get a third chance. I figured I'd better start taking care of the one I had.

All together, there were nineteen dead saber bears. The bounty only called for twelve hides, but we could always sell the rest to the guild. While the rest of the party cleaned and processed the hides, I headed back to the cave to retrieve the three I had killed earlier.

Processing hides wasn't pleasant, but it was every party member's responsibility. I'd heard of groups that hired people specifically to handle the mess. Must be nice, I thought as I worked on the second bear.

Once I had all three hides, I took a look into the cave. A foul stench drifted out. If this were a video game, I figured there'd either be a boss fight or some treasure inside.

Nisha's curiosity got the better of her.

I crouched to enter and pulled out a lightstone, feeding it mana. The foul stench intensified. Deeper in, I found the source: the mostly eaten corpse of a hunter, swarmed with dither flies.

I vomited.

When I finally stopped, I stumbled back out and went to get Leela. She'd know what to do. The image of that corpse kept flashing in my mind.

Why was it getting to me so much?

It wasn't my first encounter with death. I certainly hadn't cared when I was the one causing it. Whoever that was... those voices I heard before waking up in this world... They did something to me.

They must've given me a conscience. A soul.

Because I never cared about the death of others in my past life.

"Master, I found something you need to see. There's a dead hunter in a cave where I found the saber bears," I announced as I returned to the party.

The party made its way to the cave, with Leela, Janos, and me heading inside while Kriss and Anna waited outside.

"You shouldn't explore areas like this on your own," said Leela.

"I'll remember that, Master."

"I think it was a woman," said Janos. "Can't be too sure, but the long hair and small boots suggest it."

"It's an unfortunate consequence of being a hunter," Leela said solemnly.

I was still struggling to stay composed around the corpse.

"Nisha, I want you to gather up her remains and take them outside the cave. Once she's outside, start removing all clothing and personal items. We'll bury the corpse but take her effects back to the guild for identification."

There wasn't much to take outside besides boots, bones, and a few scraps of clothing.

"Over here," Janos called, holding up the end of a broken staff. "Must have been a mage," he added.

Once I'd taken the hunter's remains outside, I summoned what willpower I had and started sorting the remains from her gear. Kriss saw what I was doing and came over to help.

"You don't have to touch anything. I can take care of it," I said.

"I'm a hunter too. I'm not going to stand around while you do all the dirty work," she replied adamantly.

"Thanks, Kriss."

I wrapped the clothing and personal items in a blanket, and we buried the remains. Leela marked it with a large boulder.

"Are any of you religious?" she asked. Nobody said anything. After a moment, Leela bowed her head.

"To the elements of the heavens and earth, please watch over this lost soul. That's about all I can do for her."

We turned in the bounty, sold the extras, and handed over the personal items to the guild.

"It may take some time to identify her," said the guild clerk. "Hunters go missing all the time, unfortunately."

"Well, that took a dark turn," I said.

"You'd better get used to it if you want to keep hunting," Leela replied. "As your rank increases, the danger only gets worse, and the odds of a party member dying only go up."

"Then I'll just have to train even harder so I can keep myself and everyone I care about alive," I replied.

"Did I hear you right? Did you just hear my student ask for harder training?" Leela said with a smirk.

"Hey, Kriss, are you and Anna going to come to Renisha's birthday celebration?" I asked, trying to change the subject.

"We wouldn't miss it," Kriss replied.

"This has been an eventful day," said Anna. "But I need to get this one back home," she added, looking at Kriss. "Morning comes early, and my student has asked for harder training. I would be a poor instructor if I didn't ensure she's properly challenged."

"Sometimes I wish I had just been born of age. Then I could just practice casting spells all day," I said sarcastically.

"You should have quit while you had the chance," said Leela. "I have too much time invested in you to let you walk away now."

Renisha's fourteenth birthday was coming up. Though not of official significance, it was similar to a sweet sixteen celebration in my old world: more food, more preparations, and more people. As the oldest daughter of a count, Renisha's hand in marriage was highly desirable. Add to that her beauty and talent with magic, and nobles and Royalty from other countries were interested in her as well.

Renisha knew she was popular among the noble class, but she never acted like she cared for it. Her good nature always seemed to shine through. She even still found time to dote on me every once in a while. In essence, she was amazing. I was very fond of Renisha, and it would be a cold day in hell before I let some snot-nosed noble or Royal who didn't deserve her have her.

The day finally came, and everything was in motion.

"Milla, have you seen Nisha?" asked Mother.

"I believe she's still training, my lady. Would you like me to go retrieve her?" asked Milla.

"No, I'll do it. I want to speak with Leela anyway," Mother replied.

"So the left hand charges the lightning rune, and that flows into the slime round. Then the right charges the fire rune like normal?" Leela asked.

"The hand you use doesn't matter. You could be a left-handed or right-handed shooter," I said. "But you've got the concept down."

"And you're sure this won't kill him?" she asked.

I was showing Leela the newest version of the firearms from Samrail's workshop. The lightning rune turned the slime around into a tasing round. She currently had the gun pointed at Janos.

"He'll be fine," I said.

Mother walked out just as Leela pulled the trigger and dropped Janos like a sack of potatoes.

"There you are," Mother said to me. "I need you to go get ready. And for the love of all that is dear, can you please not cause any problems tonight?"

While watching Janos finally start to move again, I replied, "I can do that. But why are you singling me out?"

"Because it's always you, Nisha. This night is important for your sister, and for once, I'd like people to see that you are domesticated," Mother replied.

"I put my socks on before my shoes just like everyone else does, I'll have you know," I said. "Just promise you'll behave tonight, please."

"I promise I'll behave," I said.

"Leela, you'll be in attendance as well?" Mother asked.

"I wouldn't miss it, my lady," she replied.

"Good. Can you meet me in my dressing room once you're done here, then?" asked Mother.

"I'll see you there, my lady," said Leela.

"What was that about?" I asked after Mother left.

"Your mother likes to dress me up like a doll," replied Leela.

"Oh, Master, you would look amazing in some of my mother's dresses."

"Shut it, otherwise I'll shoot you too," said Leela.

After getting dressed, changing because I looked like I was looking for a fight, getting dressed again, changing again because I didn't put any thought into my dress, then getting dressed again—this time with Milla's help—I was ready for the evening. To be fair, it was challenging to find something that I could hide a knife in, had mobility, and mother's approval.

The result was a blue dress and some sharpened hairpins. There wasn't much for me to do after that. Some of the guests had started showing up, but I typically had no interest in socializing with other children—besides Kriss, and she hadn't shown up yet.

I wandered around until I found myself in the courtyard. There was a group of boys sparring with training swords. As I got close, I picked up on their conversation.

"Take it back!" shouted one boy.

"I will not," said a boy with jet black hair and yellow eyes. "Of this entire pitiful kingdom, you are the worst excuse for a noble."

Both boys looked to be about ten or eleven years old.

"What makes you think you're so much better?" asked the other boy.

"Everything," replied yellow eyes. "I'm simply from superior stock. My mind is superior, my training is better, and my blood is far superior. Come on, I'll prove it to you."

"I don't think I've ever seen anyone that arrogant before," I thought.

The other boy charged. Their swords crossed three times before yellow eyes smacked the other boy's hand and made him drop his training sword.

"Pick it up," he said to his defeated opponent.

The boy grabbed the training sword and charged again. This time, yellow eyes beat him in two moves.

"Pathetic," he said.

"My turn," I said, picking up the dropped training sword.

"I'm not going to beat up a girl," said yellow eyes.

"That's what a coward would say," I replied.

"Who do you think you are, talking to someone like me—like her—that way?" he asked.

"Someone better," I said.

"You're going to regret this," he said.

I sprinted at him, knocked the sword clean out of his hand, and pointed mine at his chest. Yellow eyes were seething.

"Again," he said, picking up his sword.

"When you're ready," I said.

"I'm ready," he replied.

I came at him even faster this time and knocked him all the way to the ground.

"Had enough, or do I need to keep proving that I'm better?" I asked.

He didn't say a word, but I could see he was livid. I turned and started walking away. Then I heard chanting behind me. He was trying to cast. He was still mid-incantation when I struck his sternum with the hilt of the training sword as hard as I could. The force knocked the air out of his lungs, and he collapsed to the ground.

"Like I said... a coward," I spat.

"There you are," said Leela.

She was wearing a black dress that hugged her fit form beautifully.

"Master, you look amazing," I said.

"I always look amazing," she replied.

"What's this about?" she asked.

"Just a friendly sparring match," I said.

"Come inside. It's time to start." She gave me a sideways look. "You know, boys won't like you if you beat them up."

"Is that why you're always alone?" I shot back.

"You don't know as much about me as you think you do," she replied with a smirk.

We entered just as the announcement of Kriss's arrival rang through the hall. Kriss walked in through the entrance, with Anna right behind her, escorted by Samrail. Anna looked quite pleased with herself; Samrail, on the other hand, looked stiff as a board, his glance shifting from side to side like he was searching for an escape route.

"Nisha!" Kriss shouted and ran over to me.

"You look amazing," I told her.

Kriss was wearing a green dress, coincidentally styled similarly to my blue one. The dresses complimented each other nicely. Her beautiful blue hair was done up in dozens of small braids that came together in the shape of a flower. The work must have taken hours.

I pointed it out.

"It did take a long time," she confirmed.

"I don't think I could sit still long enough for something like that," I said. "But it looks amazing."

"I think you're a bit early, but wait until you see Leela. Mother made her look gorgeous."

"What are you two little birds gossiping about?" asked Leela as she walked up.

"Nothing," I replied—probably a bit too quickly.

"Oh my, I almost didn't recognize you, Leela," said Anna.

"Everyone keeps acting like they've never seen a woman in a dress before," Leela replied.

"There aren't any other women here with a figure like yours," said Samrail.

Kriss threw her hand over her mouth in shock, sending a death glare to Samrail, who was completely oblivious to the statement he'd just made.

"What's my figure like, Samrail?" Anna asked, eyes narrowing.

"You have a normal figure, Samrail," he replied—still unaware of his blunder.

Before Samrail could dig himself into a deeper hole, another guest announcement was made:

"Presenting His Royal Highness, Prince Marx of House Berosa."

Standing at the entrance with two bodyguards was the boy with jet-black hair and yellow eyes.

"Why is a member of the Royal family of Berosa here?" I asked.

"Count Dylan is an important man, and Trassa is a major trading city between several kingdoms," Leela explained.

"Do you suppose he's here to propose to Lady Renisha?" Anna asked.

"That's a high possibility," said Leela. "The girl is popular enough in her own right, not to mention the political influence."

"Father won't allow it," I said. "Renisha is too good for him. That boy has a rotten disposition. Besides, he's younger than she is."

"Rotten disposition or not, that boy is a prince. And age doesn't matter in political marriages," Leela replied. "Ties with other kingdoms can't be simply ignored—not even by your father. He'll have to consult with King Hallid before he can officially deny or accept a marriage proposal."

"I won't let him take her," I growled.

"This is not your decision to make. If it happens, don't try anything foolish—otherwise, I'll stop you," said Leela firmly.

"Don't worry. I'll talk to Father. He won't make Renisha marry that boy," said Kriss.

"You are all getting ahead of yourselves," said Anna. "There are any number of reasons why he's here, and you don't know that a marriage proposal is one of them."

"She's right," Leela agreed. "There's no point in worrying about something that hasn't even happened."

I gave it some thought. I had only heard part of the conversation anyway, and I had been the aggressor. Maybe I had misjudged Prince Marx.

"Anyway," I said, "if his reputation is accurate, then—"

"Then I'm afraid not," Anna interrupted. "The Berosa family has a long-standing reputation for arrogance and superiority, even among nobles."

As Marx and his guards made their way to the ballroom, I brought up a strange point.

"Why was he out in the courtyard if his arrival was only just announced?"

"It takes time to get through all the arrival announcements," Anna explained. "Some parties at the castle take over an hour before your arrival is read."

Our group followed Marx into the ballroom.

"Those guards have some serious training, so whatever plan you're thinking of to attack him—just stop," said Leela.

"I wasn't thinking about attacking him," I replied.

Leela looked at me.

"Not enough to do serious harm, anyway," I added in protest.

After we arrived at the ballroom, it was about fifteen minutes before Renisha made her grand entrance. She wore a beautifully made white and blue gown that accented her silver starlight hair and vibrant blue eyes. Her hair was styled in many small, elegant braids.

Every eye turned to her as she walked in. She moved to the center of the room and gave a low, exaggerated bow. Music began to play, and the dancing started.

The first to dance with her was a boy with red hair, around sixteen. I looked at the line of men and boys waiting their turn to dance with her— and to my surprise, Marx wasn't in it. I found him off to the side of the room, skulking and excluding himself from the dance.

Well, at least he hasn't asked for her hand in marriage, I thought.

The dancing continued for another forty-five minutes before there was an intermission. A number of boys had danced with Renisha, and I was positive she had already received multiple marriage proposals.

Then I saw Prince Marx approaching Father.

I made my way over and found a spot behind a large nobleman, just close enough to overhear.

"Count Kelvis, this is a wonderful party you've hosted this evening," said Marx.

"Why, thank you, Your Highness. It's my pleasure to host such a highly regarded guest as yourself," said Father.

"I appreciate your generosity, Count. And if you would indulge me, I'd like to intrude on it further," said Marx.

"I am at your service, Your Highness. Just tell me what you request," Father replied.

"Your daughter is exceptional. I came to this event to request her hand in marriage," said Marx.

"I would be honored to grant your request," Father said carefully. "But as an international matter, I would need to consult with King Hallid and seek his permission first."

"But of course, my dear Count. I'm sure the King will see no issue, as it will serve to strengthen the bond between our two great nations," said Marx.

"Well said, Your Highness. Have you spoken with Renisha yet about your intentions?" asked Father.

"My apologies, dear Count. I failed to clarify," said Marx. "I mean to take **Nisha's** hand, not Renisha's."

Chapter 13

Problems and Solutions

"Do forgive me, Your Highness, but Nisha hasn't even eaten yet. But throwing those before ten is quite uncommon," Father explained.

I was completely lost. Why would this little monster want me? I can't even cast spells, I thought to myself.

"It's the same in my country as well," explained Marx. "Naturally, the wedding ceremony wouldn't take place until we both come of age. But, as is custom in my country, she would come to live in my household once she turns twelve."

"Why would she come to live with you then?" asked Father.

"It is so that she may be trained in the ways and customs of my home," replied Marx.

"As I said before, I'll have to consult with the king before agreeing. It is also a bit odd that you would bring this request on my eldest daughter's name day and not on Nisha's," said Father.

"I confess that I was sent here tonight to seek a betrothal with your eldest daughter. I was captivated by Nisha. I meant no disrespect towards your eldest daughter," replied Marx.

His tone was so precise and arrogant. The more he spoke, the more I was filled with rage. I stepped out from behind the fat nobleman I had been hiding behind. I was going to let this good-for-nothing prince know that it would be a cold day in hell before I agreed to a betrothal with him.

A hand shot out from behind me and covered my mouth. I was spun around, and I heard the voice of my master.

"You need to calm down and think. I'm going to release you now, and when I do, you're going to be as polite as possible," Leela whispered into my ear.

When Leela turned me around, she said, "Sorry about that interruption, gentlemen. Lady Nisha had some food on her face and I couldn't let her present herself that way."

"Prince Marx, it is so nice to formally meet you," I said while forcing a bow.

"Nisha, have you met the prince before?" asked Father.

"We had a small run-in at the courtyard before my formal announcement," said Marx.

Just then the music started playing again, signaling the end of the intermission. Marx held out his hand.

"Lady Nisha, might I ask you to join me for a dance?"

"Of course," I said, taking his hand.

To the onlookers, it must have been adorable—two kids dancing. But most were completely unaware of the true battle taking place.

"I heard your conversation with Father," I said.

"Good," replied Marx. "Then we can skip over that part. What is it you really want?" I asked.

"Is it revenge for defeating you?"

"That has nothing to do with it," replied Marx. "That was simply a misjudgment on my part. If I had known you had been trained by the legendary A-Rank Hunter Leela, I would have thought better of it."

"You know who my master is?"

"Everyone has heard of Leela the Hunter," replied Marx.

"I can't cast spells. By every measure, Renisha is a better marriage candidate, especially for a family that is concerned about superiority," I said. "So what are you really after?"

"You're right about your sister. Most would think she's the better catch," said Marx.

"And you don't?"

"Nisha, you're so clever. You were walking at six months old, talking soon after. Then you taught the princess to walk, to talk too. I'll bet you think you have everyone around you fooled."

"Someone has good spies," I said. "But me being a quick learner doesn't explain anything."

"I know it was you who came up with those new weapons that guard King Kravis," said Marx.

"The Royal artificer developed those," I explained.

"He's clever, but he doesn't have memories and knowledge from a past life like you do."

A deep panic set in, and I became unsure how to handle the situation.

"I don't know what you're talking about," I replied.

I stopped dancing and tried to walk away, but he held on to my hand.

"You aren't the first it's happened to. Four hundred years ago, someone else was born with memories of a past life, and he created the Berosa Kingdom from nothing."

"I don't know how to create kingdoms," I replied.

"Maybe not, but your knowledge is the true gift, and I intend to use it."

"And if I refuse?"

"Then I'll take sweet Renisha as my bride instead. I'll ask Kriss to talk to her father, and you won't have anyone in the Kingdom of Elris as a bride."

"That might work, but relations between Elris and Berosa aren't what they used to be. And they might become even worse."

"You would start a war over me?"

"The knowledge you possess would be worth it," said Marx.

"You're despicable," I said.

"I'll come by tomorrow morning for your answer," he responded as he let go of my hand. "Now, if you'll excuse me," he said and walked away.

Kriss came up to me after Marx left.

"You seem upset," she said. "What did he say to you?"

"Nothing important," I lied, holding back tears of frustration.

I couldn't sleep that night. I kept weighing my options over and over. I could try staying in denial, but even without hard evidence, Marx was convinced I had memories of a past life. There might be a way to convince him he was wrong, but I couldn't see how.

I could come clean to everyone—tell them about my past life. No. Adam was a vile person, and I wouldn't tell them about him. Maybe just don't tell the whole truth. But then, how would that make everyone see me—Mother, Father, or Kriss—if they found out I had the memories of an adult and kept it secret?

Round and round, problems and solutions swarmed around my head, but none of them felt like the answer. I watched the sun come up and finally settled on a way forward. It wasn't the best solution, but it was something.

It was a few hours after breakfast when Marx arrived. As he came up to the house, I walked over to him.

"I accept your offer and would love to become your bride."

I wrapped my arms around Marx and whispered into his ear, "If it takes me the rest of my life, I will make you regret having ever been born."

"We'll still need the king's approval to make it official," said Father.

I had four years to find a way to break a betrothal and prevent a war. It wouldn't be a simple task, but the second chance was worth fighting to protect.

"Father, would it be all right if Marx and I went for a walk by ourselves to get to know each other better?" I asked.

"I don't see why not," he whispered.

I held my hand out to Marx, and he took it. Once we were far enough away from the others that nobody could hear us, Marx started to talk.

"There's no reason for you to be hostile about this betrothal," he stated.

"Sure, there is. You threatened my sister and the entire kingdom if I refused," I replied. "What is it that you think I could do for the Kingdom of Berosa anyway?"

"To be honest, I'm not exactly sure. The founder of our kingdom, King William, often stated in his personal diary that he could have conquered the rest of the continent if he hadn't spent so much time bringing a single kingdom together," replied Marx.

"And what does any of that have to do with me?" I asked, still playing dumb.

"I see," said Marx. "Those weapons you have and the artificer made— they're called firearms, aren't they?"

"Call them whatever you like," I said.

"You aren't very good at subterfuge. Your expressions give you away," replied Marx.

"We've only just met. How would you know how to read my expressions?"

"I'm the third prince. I have no birthright, so I've learned to read people. When it comes to politics, everyone is a liar," explained Marx.

"King William stated that if he had known how to make firearms, he could have significantly reduced the time it took to seize power."

"It's not like knowing how to make them will change anything," I said. "We already have one in our possession. We know that they require fire runes in order to make them, and therefore, mass production will be difficult."

"If you already know all that, then you don't need me," I said.

"I doubt that very much," replied Marx. "In fact, I'll bet you've already thought of a way to get around the issue of mass production."

"Has anyone ever told you that you make too many assumptions?" I asked.

Marx laughed. "When I come to collect you in four years, we'll see if I'm wrong."

"Why tell me this now? Why give me a warning four years in advance? I could do a lot of damage to whatever plans you might have in that time," I added.

"I came early because I already had to convince Father that the firearms you have now aren't a significant threat to the Berosa Kingdom. Who knows what he might think if Elris had another technological development."

"So you came to tell me to stop making things?"

"I think we've come to an understanding between each other quite well," said Marx.

"Not too well. If I'm forced to be your wife, I might accidentally slit your throat at night. I am prone to night terrors, you see."

Marx laughed again. "Once you come to live in Berosa, I'm going to have fun breaking you of your defiance," he said.

I stopped walking, looked Marx in the eyes, and said, "I've been broken before. So do your worst."

"I think we've spoken enough for now," said Marx.

We walked back to the mansion in silence. Once we got there, Marx spoke to Father.

"I'm departing, but I'll return to sign the betrothal agreement once King Hallid has given his blessing," said Marx.

"Very well. I'll send word once he's made his decision," said Father.

"Goodbye, my darling. I'll see you again soon," Marx said.

I stood in silence as he climbed into his carriage and left.

I wasn't the only one to receive a betrothal offer. It turned out that the boy with the red hair—the one who first danced with Renisha—had also made a request. His name was Darius, the son of a baron.

"Do you at least like him?" I asked.

"He seems very genuine," said Renisha.

"But you didn't give him an answer?"

"Not yet. But I did say he could call on me again."

"And how about Prince Marx?" she asked.

"He's nicer than his family's reputation would have some believe," I said, doing my best to sound convincing.

"Nisha, you don't have to keep up pretenses with me," she said softly.

"It's important—to the kingdom—to maintain favorable relations. I have four years to either learn to like him or convince him that he'd be better off with someone else."

Renisha wrapped her arms around me. "You don't have to do anything you don't want to do. Just say the word, and I can get Father to call it off."

I hugged her back. "I'll let you know if it comes to that," I replied.

The next morning, I was sparring with Leela when she knocked me to the ground.

"You seem like you still need to wake up," she said with a grin.

"Master, can I ask you a question?" I said, brushing dirt off my arms.

"Technically, you just did. But sure."

"Have you ever gone up against an enemy you didn't know if you could defeat?"

"Many times," she replied without hesitation.

"What's the trick?"

"Visualize yourself defeating your enemy. You have to believe it's real. Then the rest falls into place."

"Is it really that simple?"

"Simple, yes. But not always easy. It can be pretty difficult to visualize defeating a monster when it just crushed the head of one of your allies."

She paused, looking more serious. "It can be very difficult to visualize victory against a powerful adversary."

"Is this about the prince?" she asked.

"Partly," I admitted. "I just don't like the whole idea of being betrothed."

"Then visualize yourself finding a way out of it."

"I could be out of it tomorrow if I wanted—but there would be consequences," I said.

"Add them in. Visualize a way to deal with the consequences, too. It's simple... but probably not easy."

"Thanks, Master. Can I ask one more question?"

"Sure."

"Who were those two men you kept dancing with at the party?"

Leela smirked. "Looks like you're feeling better now."

"Shut up and come at me again," I said, raising my sword.

Chapter 14

A Way Forward

Shortly after Renisha's 14th birthday, King Hallid granted permission for Prince Marx and me to be betrothed. Several weeks later, he returned to the estate, and we signed the contract. As we stood close to each other to place the seal, Marx leaned over and whispered into my ear, "Remember to stay out of trouble until I come to collect you."

Somehow, I managed to stay composed, but it took every ounce of self-control not to drop him to his knees. Fortunately, after the betrothal, I didn't see Marx for the next two years.

During that time, Renisha accepted Darius's proposal and was set to marry him after her 17th birthday. I had almost managed to land several hits on Leela using her visualization technique. It was like magic the first time it worked. Our blades crossed faster and faster, movement seemingly without thought. I visualized a deflection and a palm strike, and it happened just as I had imagined. Leela congratulated me—then proceeded to unleash the most aggressive attacks yet. Apparently, she had still been holding back.

Another change had come to the weapons I had developed with Samrail. They now utilized preloaded cylinders. With Samrail's help, we solved the indexing issues, allowing the entire six-shot cylinder to be changed quickly. I'd gotten the idea from an old Clint Eastwood movie whose name I could no longer recall.

"We need to keep this change between us," I explained to Samrail. I told him Berosa had already worked out the older versions. Marx had warned me about advancing technology too far, and I needed a way to shift military might, which currently favored Berosa over Elris.

One solution I shared with Samrail was the potential of solid, self-contained cartridges—stacked bullets, automatic weapons. But making even a small number would be difficult in a world where most metalwork came from blacksmiths. The precision to build thousands of identical cartridges simply didn't exist.

To get that kind of precision would take time—time I was quickly running out of. So, I returned to a simpler idea: build guns that used paper cartridges and make a lot of them, fast.

But that returned me to the root of the problem: rare and expensive fire runes. Thankfully, with Klovis's help, I found a potential solution. Theoretically, runes could be made through molten glass. A strong enough mana user—like Klovis, Renisha, or Kriss—could focus mana through an existing rune stone, transferring the circuits to molten glass.

Unfortunately, all attempts had failed. The rune stones exploded from the mana overload.

"We need a bigger rune," Klovis said. "One larger than any in the kingdom. About the size of a man's fist."

"Why do you need this so badly anyway?" he asked.

"You do realize the significance of being able to produce rune stones?" I responded.

I gave the same answer to Samrail and Anna when they asked. It seemed to satisfy them.

I began researching where fire runes were found. Most were found in dungeons after killing powerful monsters, or near volcanoes and surrounding mines. The largest fire runes, at least according to legend, were gastraliths—or gizzard stones—found in dragons.

I talked to Leela.

"I've never seen one myself," she said. "But there are old stories of them far to the South—and far to the North."

"How far North?" I asked.

"Definitely outside the kingdom. Further north than Alza."

My 10th birthday was coming up, and I had a plan. It might not be a good one, but it held hope. I had to go north. Far north. Find a dragon. Kill it. Bring back its rune stone and hope it was big enough.

I was still small, but I had strong muscles from my training with Leela. In spite of my size, I had become a B-rank Hunter. The plan was simple: gather supplies and money, then, after my birthday, borrow one of the borrow dogs and ride north.

A side note during my research: I found a brief mention of one Professor Lehman Borrow, who used magic and selective breeding to create the first borrow dog—named after him, not the mystery I'd been trying to solve.

I had nearly two years to find a dragon and kill it. I would leave a note. If I didn't make it back, Marx would assume I had died.

I didn't want to leave, but this world—this kingdom, my family, and Kriss—mattered to me. After living a life not caring about anyone, it felt good to want to protect someone.

I couldn't ask anyone to come with me. Leela and Klovis would stop me. Renisha and Kriss—I couldn't put them in danger.

On the morning of my 10th birthday, I woke up as usual and got dressed for training. As I passed through the back of the mansion and rounded the last corner to meet Leela, the entire family was waiting.

They must have all gotten up extra early—usually, I was the first one awake.

"Happy Birthday!" they all shouted.

I walked over, and they hugged me one by one.

"This is a bit of a surprise," I said.

"That's the whole point," said Renisha.

"Well, half the point," Father corrected.

He whistled, and Kennel Master David came out, leading a massive black borrow dog. He had rust-colored markings like a Rottweiler or Doberman. His build was somewhere in between—strength and speed combined.

"He's so beautiful," I said. "What's his name?"

"It's whatever you want it to be. He's yours," said Father.

My heart felt like it would jump out of my chest.

"He looks like a king... I think I'll call him Elvis."

"Elvis, down!" I commanded.

Elvis instantly got down on his stomach.

"It's such a strange name," said Mother.

"I think he likes it," I replied.

"Thank you all... This is the best birthday ever," I said.

"Master, can I—"

I wasn't able to finish my question.

"Yes, obviously you have today off," she said.

Elvis was already saddled. I hopped up on him, and he stood tall beneath me.

"Let's see how fast you are," I whispered with a grin. I turned him toward the back of the estate and slapped the reins. Elvis took off like a bullet. He was fast—faster than any dog I'd ever ridden. The back of the estate wasn't nearly big enough. Elvis had to drop his haunches low and slide nearly to the ground just to stop short of the back wall.

I turned him around and raced back to where everyone was watching me.

"It's not big enough in here to let him go all out," I explained, exhilarated. "Can I take him outside the estate?"

"That should be fine," Father said. "Just give Armon a minute to get another dog ready. In case he needs to catch you... or chase you down again."

A few minutes later, Armon and Leela rode up on their dogs. The main gate was open. Once outside, I let Elvis run as fast as he wanted.

I had no way of knowing exactly how fast he was going, but it must have been close to freeway speeds—if not more. The sensation of riding him made me feel like I was flying. The road I picked was empty, and within minutes, I was certain we were out of sight of the estate.

I pulled Elvis to a stop, turned him around, and sped back.

When I returned to the gate, Leela smiled and said, "Why don't we go for a ride?"

"Okay. Where to?" I asked.

"Just follow me," she replied.

She started off slow, heading in the opposite direction. The farther we got from the estate, the faster she rode. It wasn't long before we were outside the city. We passed hills and woods, and about an hour later, we stopped on top of a large hill overlooking Trash.

Armon had kept pace right behind me. I rode up beside Leela, who stared down at the city.

"How long have I been training you?" she asked.

"A little over six years," I replied.

"The time is coming very soon when I'll have nothing more to teach you—from a technical standpoint," she said.

"What are you talking about, Master? I'm still nowhere close to being able to best you. There's loads you can still teach me," I protested.

"Oh, you still have a lot to learn," she said, "but you'll have to learn the rest from others—and from your own experiences."

I knew what she was saying. But I needed to hear her say it.

"So... does this mean you'll be leaving, Master?"

"Not right away," she replied. "But it would seem so."

"When?" I asked.

"Soon," was all she said.

"Hop down for a minute," she said.

We both dismounted. Armon rode over and handed her something long, wrapped in cloth. She took it in her arms and turned to me.

"When I first met you, all I saw was a mouthy little runt," said Leela. "You're still a runt, but you've proven that you have a lot of heart—and a

87

desire to keep pushing even when you don't stand a chance. I consider it a privilege to be your master."

She held out the object wrapped in cloth toward me. I took it with reverence.

"Thank you, Master. I'm proud to be your student."

I unwrapped the object and found a very exquisite sword. It wasn't as thin as a rapier but resembled an extra-long dagger. Its length made it a short sword, with a leather and silver-wire-wrapped handle. Despite its size, it was much lighter than it looked.

"Thank you, Master. It's beautiful."

"The blade is made of a rare composite," she explained. "It'll eventually lose its edge and need to be reworked, but it'll last much longer than any steel blade."

"I'll be sure to always treasure it, Master."

"That's another thing we need to discuss," she said. "From this point on, call me Leela."

"I can't do that—it would feel wrong," I said.

"I don't care how you feel about it," she replied. "From now on, call me by my name."

"...Okay, Leela. Can I give you a hug?"

"Only if you want me to hit you," she said with a smirk.

We stood in silence for a moment before she added, "I guess I can make an exception—this once."

The words had hardly left her lips before I wrapped my arms around her. The dam I'd been holding back finally broke, and I sobbed as she hugged me back.

"Seems like it's starting to rain. We should probably head back soon," Armon said.

"It would seem so," Leela agreed.

Chapter 15

Runaway

The day was fast approaching when I knew I would have to leave. I also knew that the longer I put it off, the harder it would be. Kriss would take my absence hard—*especially* hard. So I took every opportunity I could to spend time with her.

We were on what I suspected might be our last dungeon run together. We were collecting scorpion stingers from black scorpions the size of small ponies. Kriss had just sent out an ice wall, freezing half a dozen of them, when a much larger one—nearly three times the size of the others—crawled out from the hole they'd been spilling from.

"I got the boss!" I shouted, charging it.

I took out some of its eyes with my revolver, which got its attention. It reared, and I dove to the side as it slammed its stinger into the ground—just the opening I'd been waiting for. I rushed between its pincers; with its tail in the way, it couldn't grab me. I pulled the shotgun from my back and unloaded both barrels directly into its face. Its head exploded in a burst of green ooze. The legs twitched for a moment before going still.

I drew my sword and cut off the stinger.

"Not bad," said Leela, observing. "If you'd kept taking out its eyes from a distance, it would've been less of a mess."

"That's true, but it would've taken longer," I replied. "And a little bit of bug guts never hurt anyone."

"Some of the bug guts on the lower levels will melt holes right through you," added Anna.

"That's fair. But I knew these guys didn't have that issue."

We harvested the stingers and started our way back to the surface.

"Your Highness," said Anna, "I'll be taking a leave of absence soon. This may be the last dungeon run I'm part of for a while."

"Does that mean he accepted your proposal?" Kriss asked.

"He did, yeah. I don't think he'll fully understand until the wedding ceremony," Anna replied.

"Isn't the man supposed to ask the woman to marry him?" I asked.

"You know how Samrail is. If I'd waited for that, I might've died of old age," she replied.

"When's the wedding?" Kriss asked.

"Next month," said Anna.

Great. Another thing I'm going to miss, I thought. There would be a lot I'd miss over the next two years, but it was unavoidable.

"Of course, all of you are invited," Anna said.

"I wouldn't miss it," I said.

I wanted to tell Kriss goodbye, but I couldn't think of a way to do it without tipping her off. Without thinking, I asked, "Kriss, will we still be close friends in two years?"

"Obviously," she replied. "Are you asking because of your betrothal to Prince Marx?"

"I think so."

"It doesn't matter where you go, or how long it is—we'll be friends forever," said Kriss. "And if I find out Marx isn't making you happy, I'll come take you from him."

"Thanks, Kriss. I'd do the same for you."

We returned our bounty at the Hunter's Guild and went our separate ways. I wondered if I'd ever see Kriss and Anna again.

The night finally came.

I made it a point to hug everyone and tell them that I loved them.

"What's this about?" asked Father.

"Nothing. I just wanted you to know I love you."

"Well, I love you too, sweetheart."

I stayed awake all night. Around two in the morning, I left a note on my bed. It read:

> *I can't say why I have to leave, but it's for a good reason. I love you all so much. If I'm not back before two years, then I'm probably not alive. Take care of each other, and I'll work hard to come back home. P.S. Don't fire Floyd.*

I packed light and brought some valuables to barter in another town for more supplies. I slipped out the back of the mansion and made my way to the kennel. I saddled Elvis and loaded my gear into his saddlebags.

As we approached the main gate, a guard called out, "Who's out there?"

I pulled my hood back. As I drew closer, he saw my face.

"Lady Nisha? What are you doing out at this hour?" he asked.

I pulled out my revolver and shot him with an electric slime round. He dropped to the ground.

"Sorry about that, Floyd. I left a note asking Father not to fire you," I said as I opened the gate and climbed onto Elvis.

I had about ten minutes before Floyd got back on his feet—and maybe thirty more before anyone realized I was gone. The nearest town to the north was Lazista, about two hours away. If someone followed me north, I might be able to lose them there.

I pushed Elvis as hard as I dared without wearing him out. By the time we reached Lazista, the sky was still dark. I couldn't hear anyone following. Rather than ride through the town, I went around it. A ten-year-old girl on a burro-dog would leave a strong impression.

We headed northwest. According to my map, there was a last trading town about 160 miles away called Berrin, just south of the border between Elris and Alza.

The sun began to rise. Elvis was getting tired—and so was I. About three hours past Lazista, I pulled off the road into a forest clearing, scouted the area, and found no high points where we could be spotted.

"I know you're probably hungry, but this'll have to do until I can hunt something," I told Elvis, handing him half a roast from my pack.

Burro-dogs were faster than horses, but they were gas hogs. Where horses could graze, burro-dogs needed meat—and lots of it. Fortunately, this world had plenty of large beasts. Like other dogs, a well-trained burro-dog would stick close to its master, and whoever trained Elvis had done a fantastic job.

I removed his saddle and brushed his coat, scratching the spot where the saddle rubbed. He let out a contented low howl.

"Careful, buddy. We don't want to give ourselves away."

It was probably around 8:30 when I flopped down beside him and leaned against his side.

"I'm going to take a quick nap. Keep me safe, buddy."

I closed my eyes and drifted off.

Tap. Tap. Tap.

I woke to the sound and feel of something tapping my head. My eyes adjusted, and I saw Leela and Armon standing over me.

"Have a nice nap?" she asked.

"Elvis! Why didn't you wake me?" I shouted.

Elvis looked away, clearly guilty.

"Don't blame him. He knew it was us coming from a long way off. Now explain what the hell is going on," she demanded.

"I can't. If I could, I would've said so in the note."

"That's dog shit. I just spent all night chasing you down, so give me a better answer."

It's all or nothing now, I thought.

"I know things," I said.

"What does that mean?" Leela asked.

92

"I know things I shouldn't. I've known them since I was born. I don't know why."

That wasn't a lie. I really didn't know why I had kept my memories—I was born with knowledge from another world.

They were silent for a moment.

"That... actually explains a lot of things," Leela finally said. "But it doesn't explain why we're out in the middle of the woods."

"I wasn't the only one born like this. King William of Berosa was too. He left a diary explaining it to his descendants. When Samrail and I made guns for the Royal Guard, Prince Marx figured out I had otherworld knowledge."

I paused, making sure they were following.

"He blackmailed me into agreeing to the betrothal. First, he threatened to have Renisha take my place. Then he threatened war with Elris."

"If I want to shift the balance of power to Elris quickly, I need something."

"What?" asked Armon.

"You have to swear this doesn't leave this spot. If Marx finds out, he might start the war anyway."

"I swear," said Armon.

"I swear too," said Leela. "Now out with it."

"I need a giant fire runestone. One from a dragon. I can use it to make more."

"Making runestones is impossible," said Armon.

"No, it isn't," I said.

"I wish you'd told me sooner," said Leela.

"I didn't think you'd believe me."

"That's because you're the smartest idiot I know," Leela muttered.

"Armon, let the Count know I'm with Nisha and I'll keep her safe."

"And what do I tell him about your quest?" he asked.

"Tell him… Nisha wanted a real adventure before being confined to the Berosa Palace," she said.

Chapter 16

Varlyn

As we rode towards Varlyn, the wind blowing through the trees made it clear we were heading further north. Winter was still a few months away, but the morning air already had a nip to it.

"Tell me more about this other-world knowledge," said Leela.

"The easiest way to explain it is that most of it is useless," I said.

"What do you mean?" she asked.

"Well, you know what a sword is—but do you know how it's made?"

"Of course I do. I've seen it many times."

"But do you *really*? Do you know where to find the ore? How to smelt it into steel? How to forge the blade? What temperature—"

"I get your point," she said, cutting me off. "Maybe I don't know how to make a sword."

"Exactly. I know a lot about things, but not always how to make them. Some stuff I know more about than others, and I can usually figure out the parts I don't."

"Like the guns we built."

"Exactly. Even then, I doubt I could have done it without Samrail's help."

"What was this other world like?"

"More advanced. But no magic."

"No magic? I'll bet that made things more equal."

"No. People are still people. They always find a way to treat others like trash."

"That sounds more like memories than knowledge," Leela said.

95

"I'd rather not remember that life. I was a horrible person."

We rode in silence for a while before she finally said, "I don't know that person from the other world. I only know you. And I know you're a good person."

"You might not say that if you knew what I had done."

"It doesn't matter. Those are other-world problems, and you haven't been that person for some time now. Seems to me that you need to let go of whatever happened, because here and now, the only person it's affecting is you."

"I know you're right, but it's not that simple. I've been trying to let go for years."

"It is that simple. It just might not be easy."

"When did you become so wise, Master?"

"I told you to call me Leela. Don't make me beat it into you."

"Elvis needs to eat."

"Baslim's probably ready to eat, too. We won't reach Varlyn until this evening, so let's stop to feed them. There should be a meadow up ahead."

About ten minutes later, the trees fell away, opening up into a wide meadow. The far side forest was visible ahead, but the ends were hidden by hills.

"Let's split up. I'll take the left, you take the right. We'll meet at the far side where the forest starts again in an hour," Leela said.

"You mean where the meadow ends?"

"Yes, that's what I said."

"No, you said where the forest starts again."

"Same damn place," she muttered.

"You all right?"

"Yeah, I think my brain is still mush from lack of sleep."

"If you get lost, turn back to the road. I'll find you."

We split up. I took my rifle and climbed the nearest hill. I spotted a herd of pullards near the forest. Pullards are like deer, but with one large, spiraled horn growing from the back of their head.

I looped around to get downwind and crept closer. Ten minutes later, I was in position. I aimed at a large male and shot—a clean kill. As I began dressing it, something grabbed me by my pack and tossed me. I hit the ground hard and got pinned. I reached for my revolver just as Elvis charged in, jaws clamped onto the creature attacking me—a cat the size of a mountain lion.

He shook it violently, bones crunching under the force. Once it was dead, I shouted, "Drop it!"

He did, and I finally got a good look. "Good boy, Elvis. You saved my life."

Once I dressed the cat as well, I strapped both kills to Elvis and returned to the road.

Leela was already there with two large birds tied to Baslim.

"What took you so long?"

"Cat problems," I replied.

"Must not have seen him. Cats are cautious."

"It attacked while I was dressing the pullard. Elvis got it."

"How are they for eating?"

"Too gamey for me, but the dogs will love it."

We cooked the meat for the dogs and rested before continuing to Verland. We arrived late, and I nearly fell off Elvis from exhaustion.

Leela got us a room at an inn with a kennel. After putting the dogs away and hanging the kills, I sat by Elvis. Leela walked in.

"Get up. I paid good money for that room."

"I'm good. I'll just sleep here."

"Not a chance."

I grabbed my pack and followed her.

Once inside, I dropped my pack and took off my boots. The next thing I remembered was waking up the next morning to sunlight streaming through the window. Leela was gone, but her pack remained. I washed up, got dressed, and headed downstairs.

The innkeeper greeted me. "The other lass said you'd be hungry when you woke."

"She was right. I'm starving."

He served me stew, bread, cheese, and a steaming mug.

"What is it?"

"Nothing special—apple cider tea with a dash of mead."

It was delicious.

"Did she say where she was going?"

"She went out for supplies. Said she'd be gone most of the day."

After finishing my meal, I grabbed a hairpin from my pack—something ornate I planned to trade—and headed out. Verland wasn't huge, but it was big enough to get lost in.

Eventually, I found the pawnbroker. A middle-aged man with a crooked nose greeted me.

"What can I do for you, young miss?"

"I have something to sell."

I showed him the hairpin. "One gold piece."

He examined it. "Beautiful. How'd you come by it?"

"It was a gift."

"Two gold. It's stolen, isn't it?"

"It's not stolen. And if you won't offer a fair price, give it back."

"How about we talk to the town watch?"

I was about to lose my temper when a man with flowing golden hair stepped in.

"Why don't you stop shaking down a child and offer a fair deal—before your nose gets broken again."

The pawnbroker glanced at the man standing beside me, his eyes lingering on the weapons and armor that marked him as a hunter. Not wanting to make things worse for himself, the pawnbroker relented.

"Five gold pieces," he said.

It was what I'd expected all along. I collected the coins into a small pouch and turned to the golden-haired hunter.

"Thank you," I said.

"Don't mention it," he replied with a shrug. "There's a lot of unsavory people who'll try to take advantage of you just because you're a kid."

"I'll keep that in mind," I said. "But for all you know, he could've been right. It could've been stolen. You might have just helped a thief."

He raised an eyebrow. "Just the way you carry yourself—and that sword? I'd bet you're not a thief. More like a child of nobility."

"I won't confirm or deny that," I said, giving a small smile. "But thanks again."

I turned to walk off, but he followed me.

"What brings a child of a noble all the way up to Verland?" he asked.

"Look, mister—"

"It's Warrik," he interjected. "Just Warrik."

"Look, Warrik, I don't mean to repay kindness with rudeness, but it really isn't any of your business," I said, trying to be diplomatic. "Suffice to say, my master and I are gathering supplies for a journey."

"And where will this journey take you?"

"North," I said bluntly.

We passed a few more shops as we walked.

"So, who is this master of yours?"

Just then, I spotted Leela at a wagon lot, her back turned as she inspected a cart.

"That's her right there," I said, pointing.

We walked up to her as she bent over to inspect the wheels.

"Do you have a list of what we need?" I asked.

"Not yet," she replied. "But I was thinking we could probably use a wagon for all the extra dog food we'll need."

"I didn't expect your master to be such a stunning woman," Warrik remarked.

Leela froze at the sound of his voice. She turned slowly.

"Warrik," she said, her tone neutral. "I didn't think I'd see you again so soon."

"It's been a while since our last encounter. Seven years, if I recall correctly," Warrik said.

"I was thinking that was still too soon," Leela replied with a sweet smile. She reached up and patted his cheek lightly. "I was thinking seeing you at all in this lifetime was too soon."

Then she drew her hand back and, still smiling, slapped him hard across the same cheek.

"I probably deserved that," Warrik admitted.

"Oh no," Leela said. "You deserve much worse. Fortunately for you, I'm an even-tempered woman."

The irony of that statement wasn't lost on me. I could feel the rage she was holding back. My instincts screamed at me to stay silent, but I had to ask.

"So... were you two lovers in the past?"

"You know, that is a damn good question," Leela said, sarcasm dripping from every word. "To be lovers, you'd have to love someone, wouldn't you?"

"I considered us very dear and special friends," Warrik offered.

"Eat shit and die," Leela snapped.

She turned away from him and walked over to the cart dealer. She handed over a few gold coins.

"I'll take this wagon and harness for two dogs," she said coolly. "We'll be back later today to pick it up."

Warrik didn't say another word. Seemingly defeated, he walked off, his final insult lingering in the air unspoken.

I wanted to ask more, but I decided it was best to wait until Leela was in a better mood.

"What still needs to be done?" I asked.

"I traded our wet meat for dried food for the dogs. Go to the clothing shop and get some warmer clothes. It's going to get colder the further north we go," she instructed. "I'll get the dogs and the wagon, and take them to the general goods store to pick up our order. Meet me there when you're done."

An hour later, I had a new coat, overcoat, gloves, and thick wool socks. I found Elvis and Beslim hitched to the wagon Leela had chosen earlier. One section of the wagon was already loaded with dried meat for the dogs, but there was still plenty of room for our packs, saddles, and other supplies.

Leela came out of the general store just as the last items were being loaded.

"Do we really need this much stuff?" I asked.

"It's better to have more than you need than less," she said. "We're heading into rough country."

"I get that, but all this must've been expensive."

"It's not an issue. You didn't think your father was paying me in praises all those years I was training you, did you?"

"No, but I still have money to help out."

"Save it for now. I'll let you know if I start running low."

"Okay," I said, "but you better let me pay you back someday."

"Don't worry," she said with a grin. "I'm keeping receipts. I'll turn them into your father when I get back."

I let the issue drop at that.

"It's late in the day," I said as we packed up. "We still have one more night already paid for at the inn."

"We'll leave in the morning," she confirmed.

We returned to the inn and stabled the dogs and wagon. I gave Elvis an extra-long back scratch.

"You spoil that dog too much," Leela said. "He's a working dog, not a house pet."

"He can be both. Plus, he saved my life from that cat the other day."

"All right. But don't say I didn't warn you when he starts demanding more attention."

Dinner was a delicious baked meat pie that Bon had prepared.

"Go ahead and head up to bed," Leela said. "I've got my room key. I'll be up later."

"Going to yell at Warrik some more?" I asked.

"No," she replied a little too quickly. "I'm going to drink and try to forget about him."

"Okay. I'll see you when you come up."

I went upstairs and must've fallen asleep waiting. When I woke in the morning, Leela was flopped across her bed, boots still on, a wine bottle in her hand.

As I got up, I heard her mumble something.

"What was that?" I asked.

"Just say it, you bastard..." she muttered.

Chapter 17

Bandits and Skirmishes

"Do you have a travel pass to get us past the border?" asked Warrik.

"Of course I do," replied Leela. "Just wake me up when we get to the border," she added.

"Have you been to Duvors before?" I asked Warrik.

"A couple of times. It's about the same size as Varlyn, except for the military garrison there."

"Why do they have a garrison there?" I asked.

"Elris and Moltura are constantly at odds and have regular border skirmishes," Warrik explained.

"Is there any particular reason why?"

"It's always about some perceived slight that one country claims against the other. If you want specifics, you'll have to ask someone from Alza," said Warrik.

The road out of Varlyn to Duvors was filled with twists and turns as it wound through a mountain range that formed the natural border between Elris and Alza. Several hours after leaving Varlyn, we finally arrived at the border crossing into Alza.

"We're here," I said, waking Leela.

Two guards stood in front of a large wooden gate that spanned the road. As we approached, one of the guards held up his hand to indicate for us to stop. Warrik pulled the wagon to a halt beside him.

"What business brings you to Alza?" asked the guard.

"Our own," said Leela, holding out a silver plate stamped with writing.

"This is a diplomatic pass," said the guard.

"I know," replied Leela.

The guard handed the pass back to Leela and waved us through the gate.

"Why do you have a diplomatic pass?" I asked.

"It's a long story," Leela said. "But the short version is that some Alza Royal owed me a favor, and this is what I asked for. Now keep it down while I try to get some sleep," she added.

"So why do you need to go north?" I asked Warrik.

"I'm not sure yet," he replied.

"What do you mean by that?"

"It means he has no direction in life and does whatever he wants," said Leela. "Now shush, I'm trying to sleep."

We rode on through the mountains. By late afternoon, dark clouds began to gather in the sky. The wagon had a canvas cover to keep our supplies dry, but we still had to close and tie up the ends. When we stopped to secure the wagon, Leela woke up.

"What's going on?" she inquired.

"There's a storm coming," said Warrik. "Do you want to stop for the night or keep going?"

"There's still plenty of daylight left. Let's keep going for now. If it gets too bad, we'll stop for the night."

I put on my overcoat and was getting ready for the rain when Leela told me to trade places with her. I hopped into the back of the wagon, and Leela moved to the front with Warrik. As the rain began to fall, I felt a little guilty watching Warrik and Leela getting soaked while I stayed warm and dry in the back.

The rain wasn't light, but it wasn't heavy either. I was about to drift off to sleep when Leela called out, "Something isn't right."

"What's wrong?" I asked.

"Stay hidden in the wagon and have your rifle ready," she instructed.

"Viva, tell Warrik to stop the wagon."

"I count ten," said Warrik.

"Me too," replied Leela. "But I bet they have a mage or two hidden with them."

The dogs started growling.

"Calm down, boys," Leela said, calling out to them. "Come on out, we know you're there already. We can smell you a mile back!"

One by one, heads began to appear from behind trees. One of them called out, "We have you surrounded. Drop the wagon and your weapons, and we'll let you leave with your lives."

"You better have more men with you than this lot, otherwise you won't stand a chance against me," said Leela.

Two more men emerged, their hands raised, ready to cast spells.

"You don't have a chance," shouted the bandit who had spoken earlier.

"Can you get both?" Leela asked in a whisper.

"I got it," I whispered back.

"Do it."

I fired at the farthest mage, and he dropped. The crack of the rifle stunned not only the bandits but Warrik as well. I took advantage of the confusion, lined up my sights, and dropped the second mage while he was still trying to figure out what had happened to his companion. Leela pulled out her pistol and shot two more bandits.

"Don't just sit there like an idiot—fight back!" Leela shouted at Warrik.

He jumped off the wagon and cut down one of the bandits with his sword. Leela cut down two more with her blade before the rest of them finally decided they had had enough and fled.

After the last of them ran off, Leela called out, "Is everyone all right?"

"I'm good. But what in the world is that?" asked Warrik.

"They're called guns, and they do just what you saw them do," replied Leela. "Nisha, are you all right?"

I stood there in dumb silence for a moment. "It's... different," I finally said.

"It is, and it isn't," Leela replied.

"What's different?" asked Warrik.

"Nisha has only killed monsters up to this point," Leela explained.

"Oh, I see," he replied.

"Are you going to be all right?" she asked me.

"I'll be fine," I said. "I just need to sort it all out in my head."

"You know, they would have likely killed us after they robbed us," said Warrik.

"I know. I just need to process it," I replied.

I had killed before—but that was as Adam. Back then, I killed simply to try and feel something. I had ended the life of another person for the most inconsequential of reasons and felt nothing. Yet here I was, having every justification for killing two men who would have likely killed me without hesitation—and I felt as if I had robbed the world of something precious.

"Why should I feel remorse for those men?" I asked. "Why do I feel bad for doing what I knew I had to?"

"It's because you know how precious life is," Leela replied. "These men either never learned that—or more likely, they forgot."

Suddenly, I felt incredibly tired. "Would either of you mind if I took a nap right now?"

"That's fine," said Leela. "Warrik, let's check the corpses and then put as much distance between us and here as we can before nightfall."

A few minutes later, the wagon started rumbling down the road again. Although I was troubled by my thoughts, the fatigue, the sound of rain hitting the canvas, and the rocking of the wagon lulled me to sleep.

That night, my dreams were plagued by visions of the woman I had killed as Adam. I kept seeing her face on the two bandits I had shot—over and over again.

"I'm so sorry," I called out. "I wish with all my heart I could take it back. I wish I could go back and change the past. If I could be reborn in another world, then why not go back and change the past?"

As I slept, filled with regret, that thought finally stuck in my mind. Wishing to change the past wouldn't make it any more real—so why hold on to that fantasy? All I could do was try to make the best of the present.

With that thought, I drifted off into an even deeper sleep, where memory does not follow.

Something smelled delicious.

There was no sun, just lots of clouds. The normal cold was amplified by humidity. I got up from my sleeping spot in the wagon.

"Are you feeling better?" asked Warrik.

"I think so... but the dreams I had last night were really confusing."

"I think there are very few of us who can easily make sense of our dreams," he replied.

He handed me a plate of food: biscuits, eggs, and seasoned meat. I took several bites and savored the taste.

"This is really good. Thank you," I said.

"A chef is always pleased to know his food is enjoyed," Warrik replied with a grin.

"How much further is it to Duvort?" I asked.

"We're still about a day and a half away," said Leela. "There will likely be more situations ahead like last night. Are you going to be able to handle it?"

"You mean... more killing?" I stated. "I'll be fine. I didn't enjoy it, but I'm grateful to be here, eating delicious food."

"That's good to hear. Eat, wash, do what you need to do quickly—we have another long ride ahead of us," said Leela.

Thirty minutes later, I was hitching Elvis back up to the wagon. He looked at me and whined.

"I'm sorry, buddy. I promise I'll take you for a ride tomorrow."

He seemed to perk up at that, though I was pretty sure the only word he understood was "ride."

The sky was still gray as we rode on our way, but no rain fell.

"Do you think we'll run into any more bandits?" I asked.

"Hopefully not," said Warrik, "but being this close to the contested border, it's likely. Those bandits last night looked like deserters—but from Alza or Multra, I couldn't say."

"Just remember to stay alert and we'll be fine," said Leela.

Save for a passing wagon headed in the opposite direction and a few solo riders, the rest of the day was uneventful.

As evening approached, we came upon an old, abandoned stone watchtower. It sat atop a hill, offering a good view of the surrounding area. A section of wall midway to the top was missing, and the lower stones were covered in moss.

"It's an old Imperial watchtower," said Warrik.

"I'm confused. Alza is a kingdom," I replied.

"About six hundred years ago, Alza and Berosa were part of the same country—it was called the Luminous Empire."

"What happened to it?"

"The same thing that happens to all kingdoms and empires. Time," he replied simply.

"We'll camp here for the night," said Leela.

"Won't that leave us pretty exposed?" I asked.

"Maybe, but we'll be able to see anyone coming up to us from a long way off," she replied.

Since Warrik had joined us, he had taken over the role of cook for our group. I didn't mind—it was clear he was more skilled at it than Leela or I were.

Darkness settled as we ate. After dinner, we put out the fire and split the watch shifts. But before anyone went to sleep, I spotted hundreds of lights off in the distance.

"They look like torchlights," said Leela, squinting. "Probably about a mile out."

There were two groups of torchlight, separated by several hundred feet.

"It looks like a battle is about to happen," said Warrik.

"Should we get moving?" I asked.

"We should be fine from here, and we're of no interest to whoever they are," he replied.

One side had far more torches than the other.

"This will be one-sided," I muttered.

"Not necessarily," said Leela.

Nothing happened for about thirty minutes. Suddenly, the army with fewer torches began moving toward the larger one. Just before making contact, the larger army charged forward. We couldn't see much in the dark, but the shouting and yelling reached us clearly.

Before the clash, the smaller force turned and began to retreat.

"I guess they weren't as brave as they seemed," I said.

Just as the larger army was about to catch up, the rumbling of cavalry came from the woods. Torches from the larger army began to go out one by one.

The retreating army—which had now become the larger force—turned and attacked.

"That was a bold feint," said Leela. "But it looks like it worked out well. Whoever is in control of that winning army is either clever... or lucky."

The yelling and sound of swords clashing began to die down quickly, and in a matter of fifteen minutes, it was all over.

"Get some sleep," said Leela. "I'll wake you up when it's your turn to watch."

The rest of the night was uneventful. Warrik took the last watch so he could start making breakfast early. I got up and threw my saddle on Elvis.

"Where are you going?" asked Warrik.

"I promised I'd take him for a ride yesterday," I replied. "You know Leela won't be happy if you're gone when she's ready to go."

"I'll be quick," I said as I climbed into the saddle.

Elvis was ready to run after pulling the wagon for the past few days. I ran him up and down the road a few times. Out of curiosity, I went to look over the aftermath of last night's battle. I could see where the ground was stained red, bodies scattered across the field. I decided I'd seen more than enough.

Just as I was about to ride off, a man wearing plate armor and sitting atop a white burrow dog came riding up to the battlefield. He was flanked by two other men on horses. The three of them spotted me and began riding in my direction.

I thought about running, but figured they would probably give chase if I did. Besides, I had nothing to hide.

As they approached, the man on the burrow dog spoke. "What is a child doing all the way out here?"

"The road from Varlyn to Devour is just behind that hill," I said, pointing behind me.

"She could be an enemy spy, sir," said one of the horsemen.

"Then why didn't I run?" I asked. "I'm not a spy. Just a hunter on my way to Devour."

"And what brings a hunter from Elvas up to Devour?" the man on the burrow dog asked.

"I'm looking for dragons," I replied.

I figured it would sound ridiculous, but maybe I could get some information by throwing out such a wild claim.

"There haven't been any dragons in these lands for hundreds of years," said the dog rider.

Just then, Leela came riding up.

"There you are! Beezlem won't like pulling the wagon by himself, so get your butt back to camp," she said.

"I'm Captain LeRoy of the Alsan Royal Forces," the dog rider said. "Is this child your daughter?"

I let out a gut-busting laugh. "Do I look old enough to be her mother?"

The captain, not quite sure how to reply, chose to move past the question.

"What business brings you this way?" he asked.

"We're hunters on our way to Devour," Leela replied.

"And what business do you have up in Devour?" he asked again.

"Our own," Leela said, tossing him the silver plate she'd shown the border guards.

"This is a diplomatic pass," said the captain, tossing it back. "Enjoy your stay in Alza."

"We saw the battle last night from the old watchtower. How did you know they'd fall for your feint?" Leela asked.

"It was simple," said the captain. "The first group I sent to attack turned out to be less brave than I thought. So when they started running, I sent the men on horses to attack instead of leaving them out there."

Leela stared in disbelief. "Is your captain joking, or is he an idiot?"

One of the men on horse just shrugged his shoulders.

"Have a good day, madam," said Captain LeRoy before riding off.

"What a strange man," I said.

"Let's get back to the wagon and be on our way," said Leela.

We returned the dogs to camp and hooked them up to the wagon.

"Where did the two of you run off to?" asked Warrik.

"We got held up by an Alsan captain—the one commanding the army we saw last night," I replied. "They thought we might be spies."

"We need to get going if we want to make it to Devour before nightfall," said Leela. "We've wasted enough time already."

We'd only been on the road for another hour when we heard shouting and the sound of metal on metal. As we rounded a bend, we came upon a scene of mayhem. Captain LeRoy and his army were engaged in another battle.

Unfortunately, this fight wasn't going as well for him as the last one. The numbers were close to even, and it wasn't clear who would win. The captain and his guard were surrounded by troops wielding spears and had been separated from his main force.

"I hope I don't regret this," said Leela. "Nisha, use your rifle and start clearing a path for the captain."

I braced my weapon against the back of the wagon. From several hundred yards out, I began shooting, trying to open a hole in the wall of men surrounding the captain. They didn't notice at first why their comrades were falling. It was difficult with only two shots before needing to reload, but eventually they realized the distant wagon was responsible.

With their attention split, the captain managed to rally his remaining guards and push back to his main force. Taking advantage of the distraction, Captain LeRoy reorganized his troops and began driving the enemy back.

I took two more shots at the retreating Molturan forces when Leela called out, "That's enough. Save your ammo. This fight is over."

With the last Molturan soldiers surrendering, we rode forward through the carnage. Captain LeRoy came riding up to our wagon.

"I have no idea how you did it, but thank you for the distraction," he said.

"Don't mention it—seriously—to anyone," said Leela.

"You have my word that I will tell no one that I was saved by a little girl casting strange spells," said Captain LeRoy.

"You're so humble for a man who was just saved," I said sarcastically.

"I wouldn't go that far," he replied. "I had them right where I wanted them."

"You were surrounded," said Warrik.

"I prefer to think I was attacking the enemy in all directions," said the captain.

"You certainly are humble," Leela said dryly.

"Too true," the captain agreed. "But let it not be said that I'm ungrateful. Please allow me to escort you the rest of the way to Devour."

"Thank you, Captain, but I think we can manage on our own," said Leela.

"Please, I insist. Consider it the price of my oath to secrecy, if you must."

"Well, since you put it that way, do as you will, Captain," she said.

"Thank you, and please—call me LeRoy. My men call me Captain."

Captain LeRoy gave orders to his officers concerning the last battle and then pulled up alongside our wagon.

"Won't your troops be lonely without their fearless leader?" asked Leela.

"They're brave men, and my second-in-command can get them back to Devour just fine," LeRoy replied.

"So how is it that a child possesses the ability to influence entire battles?" he asked.

"If I had to narrow it down, I'd say it's due to my master's training and hard work," I replied.

"Are you sure it has nothing to do with that strange weapon you were using during the battle?" he pressed.

"That is a product of hard work," I answered.

"That's enough answers, Nisha. He doesn't need you telling him any more," said Leela sharply. "Here's a question for you, Captain—why are there so many skirmishes with Moltura right now?" asked Leela.

"Again, please, call me LeRoy," he said. "It started about a month ago, when the King of Multira died. The king had two sons, and normally succession would go to the eldest, but the younger brother took power by promising to return contested land back to the control of Natura."

LeRoy explained, "We don't know for certain how far the new king claims belongs to Multira, but we do know he wants to take Duvortt."

"Is that why there's a garrison there?" Warrik asked.

"Indeed it is," replied LeRoy. "Now that I've been more than generous in answering your questions, please feel free to return the favor. What brings nobles from Elvas all the way to Duvortt?"

"What makes you so certain we're nobles?" I asked.

"Your clothes and equipment suggest wealthy merchants at the very least. But I recognize the breed of your burrow dog. That breed would only be available to nobles," he said.

I shared a look with Leila. She just shrugged, as if to say *It's your call.*

"We heard rumors that there are dungeons in the far north," I said.

"And what purpose would finding one serve?" asked LeRoy.

"Nobody has seen or heard of any for hundreds of years in Elvas. Wouldn't you be curious to find out if they still existed?" I asked in return.

"I see. So it's a quest of knowledge you're on," LeRoy clarified.

"It's as I said yesterday," I replied.

"Well, I don't claim to be an expert in ancient lore, but I too have heard rumors of dragons still existing in the far north. I have no idea if any are true. There are giant flame salamanders that live near active volcanoes, but I wouldn't exactly call them dragons," said LeRoy.

"Does anyone ever hunt salamanders?" Leila asked.

"I'm not sure about that. You would have better luck asking someone at a hunter's guild," said LeRoy.

As morning shifted into afternoon, the last leg of the journey to Duvortt proved to be the most pleasant. The sun had finally come out, and there wasn't much to occupy the time besides the back-and-forth political conversation between Warrik and LeRoy.

Duvortt, as it turned out, was a walled city. Seeing the captain with us, the guards didn't question us as we entered.

"This is where we part ways," said LeRoy. "I have reports to give, but if you need anything, don't hesitate to reach out to me at the military headquarters."

"I trust some areas of those reports will be vague?" Leila asked with a wry smile.

"On my honor," replied LeRoy as he rode off.

Chapter 18

Siege

It was still early afternoon as we rode into Duvort. With most of the homes and businesses being confined to the area behind the walls, three- and four-story buildings were commonplace. We made our way to an inn and reserved lodging for the next several days.

"What will you do from here?" I asked Warrik.

"I'm not sure yet, but I'm sure I'll see my calling when it comes around," he replied.

"I'm not exactly sure what you mean by that, but good luck. It was a pleasure traveling with you," I said.

"It means he's going to hang out at a pub or the Hunter's Guild until he meets someone he thinks is interesting," Leila interjected.

"That's not the case! If it were, I'd be staying with you—as I'm sure you are the most interesting person in this city," Warrik replied defensively.

"We both know you don't have the commitment to stick around," Leila shot back.

"Don't you two think you should sort your issues out with each other?" I asked.

"I don't have any issues with him," said Leila.

"Nor do I with her," added Warrik.

With that, Warrik turned and walked away.

"Would you tell me what happened between you two if I asked?" I said.

"There isn't much to tell, but I don't feel like discussing it now," Leila replied. "Let's head over to the Hunter's Guild and see what we can learn about fire-breathing lizards."

The Hunter's Guild in Duvort was an old stone building with three floors. The weathering and moss buildup showed that it was much older than the buildings around it. The inside was filled with round wooden tables, and well-rusted iron sconces hung from the walls. Several dozen hunters were sitting around, eating, drinking, and planning.

Leila and I checked the bounty board for anything related to salamanders. After reading through all the bounties with no success, we headed up to the counter to speak with a guild representative. The representative was a man who looked to be in his thirties and had a thick red beard.

"Good afternoon, ladies. Is there anything I can do for you?" he said cordially as we walked up to the counter.

"We're hoping to get information on salamanders. Do you ever get bounties for them?" asked Leila.

"That's a good question. I don't think we've had any bounties for them since I've been working here," said the guild representative.

"Aren't there any valuable materials that can be collected from them?" I asked.

"I believe there are, but salamanders have thick hides and are difficult to take down. You'd need some really good hunters to get the job done. I'd say it's easily an AAA-ranked bounty. I'm not sure about the materials that can be harvested from them, but if I had to guess, they don't cover the cost of the bounty," he explained.

"Why don't you think they're worth the bounty?" I asked.

"Because we never get any bounties for them," he replied.

"Do you have a list of materials you can harvest from one?"

"Another good question. Give me a few minutes to check, and I'll get back to you on that."

He returned about five minutes later.

"I was able to find that salamander hide is a good material for armor, but I couldn't find out anything more."

"Well, that isn't too insightful," I said.

"What I can do is tell you that if you kill one and bring its corpse back, the Guild would be more than willing to break it down and pay for any materials that are valuable. That said, you would be taking the risk to see if it paid for the hunt," he explained.

"Thank you. We'll keep that in mind," said Leila.

"What do you think? Should we hunt one and find out what its materials are?" I asked.

"We can, but I'd like to find someone who has at least had an encounter with a fire salamander first. I also feel that the Guild may be right—if they had something as valuable as a fire rune stone in them, there would be bounties on them," said Leila.

"That's a fair point, but unless we can find some other way to verify, I think it's worth a shot," I replied.

"I have an idea—why don't we put up our own bounty for information based on first-hand accounts?" I said. "It may take a day or two, but someone around here has to have had an encounter."

"That's not a bad idea," said Leila.

"I'll get it posted. With that settled, I'm going to check on the dogs and explore a little," I said to Leila.

"Just stay out of trouble. I'll meet you back here at the inn for dinner," she replied.

"I'll see you then."

I walked out of the guild and headed for the stables. Elvis and Bethlehem were in good spirits when I checked on them. They seemed to be enjoying the freedom from the wagon harnesses. I gave each of them a slice of warm meat I had gotten from the inn's kitchen. Elvis gave a low chuff as I was closing the door.

"It's too late. I'll take you out tomorrow," I promised.

Duvortt was an old city—well, parts of it were. The combination of newer buildings mixed with older ones was a bit jarring to look at. I supposed in its own way, it had some charm. I wandered through the market streets, stopping at a vendor who was selling candy. I bought a few pieces and continued my stroll.

As the sun started going down, I decided it would be nice to watch the sunset from the top of the city wall. The view from the wall was just as beautiful as I had imagined. As the sun dipped below the horizon, my thoughts drifted to everyone back home. I wished Kriss could have been there with me.

But then, faint lines began to materialize on the horizon.

At first, I couldn't tell what they were. Over the next few minutes, the lines grew larger, and individual shapes came into view.

Soldiers. Thousands of them.

Just as I was about to shout for one of the city watch, the warning bells began to ring.

I had to find Leila. We had to get the hell out of Duvort.

I found Leila and Warrik at the inn, waiting for me.

"There you are," said Leila. "Do you know what's happening?"

"Soldiers from Moltura. Thousands of them," I said. "We need to get out of the city."

"What about the city and its people?" I asked.

"We aren't citizens of Alsa, and this isn't our fight," she replied.

Within minutes, we had the dogs hooked up to the wagon and were racing toward the eastern city gate. When we got there, the gate was shut and barred.

"Let us pass!" Leila shouted to the guards.

"We can't open it," one of them replied.

"Why not?" she demanded.

"The enemy sent their mounted units ahead. They're right outside the gate."

"Damn it. Turn us around—head for the south gate," she ordered Warrik.

But it was the same situation there. And at the north gate. The city was completely surrounded.

Soldiers rushed to man the walls while civilians fled to their homes.

"What do we do now?" I asked.

"The military headquarters. Let's go find out how that idiot captain let this happen," said Leila.

The headquarters was chaotic. Soldiers ran back and forth, carrying messages and supplies to and from the walls. In the confusion, no one stopped us at the door. Captain LeRoy stood over a table covered in maps, issuing orders.

Two soldiers stepped in front of us, hands on their swords.

"Let them pass," said LeRoy.

"How did this happen?" Leila demanded. "Didn't you have any scouts to warn you of an invading army?"

"We had scouts," LeRoy said grimly, pointing to a bloody sack filled with round objects the size of melons. "They sent us that as soon as the city was surrounded."

"How many are out there?" she asked.

"Between thirteen and fifteen thousand," he replied.

"And how many do we have?"

"Not nearly enough. Maybe two thousand, if you count the city watch and volunteers."

"Is there any help coming?"

"None that we know of," LeRoy said. "It could be days before Alsa even learns what's happening, then more time to marshal a response—days more to march here."

"So you have to hold out for at least a week?" I asked.

"Optimistically," replied LeRoy.

"How can we help?" I asked.

"You're leaving," the captain replied. "Triple-A hunter—go over to the Hunter's Guild and conscript all the hunters you can in defense of the city."

"I'm not from here. Why would they listen to me?" I asked.

"Your natural charm. And if that fails..." One of the soldiers handed LeRoy a form, and he scribbled something on it. "I hereby conscript Leila Montello into the Alvin Armed Forces to the rank of Lieutenant."

"This is dogshit. You can't just conscript me!" Leila protested.

"Either take it or don't. You're the one who asked if you could help," said LeRoy.

"Fine," replied Leila, snatching the form. "But I'm resigning as soon as this siege is over."

"That's not how conscription works. Now, if you'll excuse me, I have a city to defend."

It was a short ride to the Hunter's Guild. When we stepped inside, it seemed like every hunter in Davort was there—around a hundred or so.

"Who's in charge here?" Leila asked. No one answered. She stepped forward.

"I guess that means I am. I'm Leila Montello, an AAA hunter. Some of you may have heard of me. Captain LeRoy has commissioned me to take charge of any hunter willing to defend the city." She relayed everything LeRoy had told us. "Who's with me?"

A giant of a man with a fuzzy beard and an axe on his back spoke first. "Most of us aren't from here. What interest do we have in risking our lives for this city?"

"I'm not from here either," Leila replied. "But Moltura won't care where you're from, and I doubt they'll stop swinging their swords to ask."

"What exactly do you expect us to do against such numbers?" another hunter in blue plate armor asked.

"We don't have to win. We just have to hold out until the main Alvan forces arrive. I need your help to reinforce the wall."

One by one, the hunters voiced their consent. Out of 115, 111 agreed to fight. The last four stayed seated.

"I won't compel you to fight," Leila said, "but if you hinder us in any way, I'll have you killed."

As Leila began to mobilize her new troops, I stepped up beside her.

"Where do you want me? Up on the wall with my rifle?"

"No," she said.

"But I could help a lot up there!"

"What do you have? About 150 shots?"

"200," I corrected.

"That won't make enough of a difference. I want you to go around the city and bring everyone who doesn't have a safe place to hold out to the guild. This building is old, but its walls are thick and will hold."

"Will you be all right lending Elvis to work?" she asked.

"Work!" I shouted. He looked over. "Take good care of my friend!"

"I promise I'll take the best care I can," he replied.

Leila took her newly formed army to join the rest of the defense. Silence blanketed the city—ominous and unnatural.

What are they waiting for? I wondered as I searched the streets by torchlight. It took only a few hours to check the main roads. I found a few groups—travelers and merchants—and directed them to the guild.

When I was certain I'd found all I could, I went looking for Leila. A few soldiers pointed me to her post above the western gate.

"I found those I could and told them to hold out at the guild," I reported.

"Good work. Now head back there and wait for me."

"Excuse me? You know I can fight."

Leila pulled me close. "I know you can. But you're also a ten-year-old girl. That's all I want the enemy to see."

"I don't care who they see. Let me stay and help!"

"Nisha, you need to listen to me. I'm proud of you, and I know someday you'll do incredible things. But I need you to survive this to do them."

Her words hit me like a ton of bricks. I wrapped my arms around her.

"I'll come for you when it's safe," she said, hugging me back.

"Nisha... if the worst happens, hide or destroy your guns and ammunition. The last thing we need is for a country like Moltura to get them. Promise me."

"I promise," I whispered.

"Good. Now get back to the guild."

I ran. The darkness hid my tears.

Sleep didn't come easily that night. I had paid for my sins, hadn't I? My life as Nisha had been blameless—so why was I being punished again?

No answers came.

As the sky began to lighten, I made my way to the southern gate. Leila was waiting. Several hundred old men, women, and children gathered near the gate.

"I thought there would be more than this," I said.

"Most are leaving through the eastern gate," Leila replied.

"Where's Elvis?"

"He'll get help as quickly as he can and return."

"They thought of that," she said. "No mounts or weapons. Speaking of..."

I unbuckled my gun belt and sword, handing them to her. "The rifle is still in the wagon."

"I'll make sure they don't get it."

The gates began to open, and the refugees started filing out.

"So that's it? We say goodbye?"

"No, Nisha. We say goodbye, and your life keeps going."

I threw my arms around her. "Don't give up. I'll come back with help—even if I have to run to Varlyn and back."

"I'll hold out as long as I can."

"You better. And make sure your boyfriend takes care of Elvis."

"He's not my boyfriend," she said, half-smiling. "But I'll make sure he does."

I was the last to step through the gate before it closed behind me. I turned, took a breath, and began the long walk back to Varlyn.

Chapter 19

A Long Road

The Motaren forces had pulled back from the walls of Duvort, and the road back to Varlyn was clear. After walking several hundred yards, I stopped and looked back. I could see Wark and Leila watching from the top of the wall. For a moment, I was tempted to run back to the gate and demand they let me back inside the city.

But I willed myself to turn around and keep walking.

The city walls of Duvort slowly began to fall out of view, and by midmorning, they were long gone. The trail of refugees—made up of the elderly and the young—began to slow down. Many of the children were as young as three or four. Some small groups stopped to rest along the side of the road.

As more and more refugees began to rest, I kept pushing on toward Varlyn. Before long, I had gone from being at the very back of the group to leading it. I stopped for a moment once I reached the front, pulled out my canteen, and took a few gulps of water.

As I put the cap back on, I felt the ground begin to rumble.

Soldiers on horseback came charging down the road from the direction of Duvort. They wore the uniforms of Motara—there were hundreds of them. As they caught up to the refugees, they pointed their weapons at us and started pushing people into groups.

I knew it. The bastards wouldn't honor their word.

How could we have been so foolish?

There was a tree line about a hundred yards off. I began to sprint for it, ignoring the screams of the other children and the elderly as they were rounded up. Maybe the confusion would help me reach the trees.

I heard the hoofbeats of a horse behind me. I didn't dare look back.

The tree line was only fifty feet away. Just a few more seconds…

My final thoughts of escape were shattered as a net came flying over me. I lost my footing as the cords wrapped around my legs and I crashed to the ground. The man who threw the net jumped off his horse and pinned me down as another soldier rode up, hopped off, and tied my hands together.

Outnumbered and unarmed, there was nothing I could do.

With my hands bound, I was pulled to my feet and led back to where the other refugees—now prisoners—were being held. Motarans didn't speak the same language as the people of Elris and Alza. Our captors began separating the children from the elderly. Cries were heard as grandparents were torn from their grandchildren.

What happened next was a brutal reminder:

I was living in a medieval world.

The Motarans began executing the elderly in front of us.

Screams of terror and agony pierced my very soul. One boy—he looked to be about nine—broke away from the soldiers holding him and threw himself in front of an old woman. The soldiers pulled him back, and another raised his sword.

I looked away.

Half an hour after the executions, wagons with cages were brought up. We were loaded into them. As we were hauled away, I looked at the sobbing children packed tightly around me. I wanted to hold them. I wanted to tell them everything would be all right. I wanted to give them hope.

But I couldn't.

My own hope was so far gone that I couldn't move or speak. I did the only thing I could do—leaned my back against the cage and closed my eyes. I couldn't sleep, but keeping my eyes closed helped pass the time. I did my best to imagine I was anywhere else.

Eventually, the wagon came to a halt. Our captors opened the door and pulled us out, one by one, shackling us together in a long chain. Our hands were left unbound, but there was no chance to run—every time a child tried to speak, a captor would shout and strike them.

Eventually, they gave each of us a slice of bread, a bit of soup, and some water—the first food we'd had since being taken. Blankets were handed out, though not nearly enough. Maybe every other child got one. As the cold night crept in, those lucky enough to have blankets began to share. They quickly learned that sharing body heat helped keep the cold at bay.

As for me, I didn't bother. I lay in the open, letting the cold bite into me, hoping it might be enough to end me. I couldn't sleep. I could barely think. When morning came, they handed out another piece of bread and more water, then loaded us into the wagons again.

That cycle—of cold, hunger, and caged travel—went on for three days.

Eventually, we reached a city.

As we were hauled through the streets, I saw children playing, people shopping—living their normal lives. Some children even laughed and pointed at us as we passed. Their joy, their ignorance, struck like a blade.

At last, the wagons stopped in front of a large building with a gate tall enough for dozens of wagons to pass through. As the last wagon entered, the gate clanged shut behind us.

We were dragged out of the wagons into the center of what looked like a wide, open arena. A fat man with a thick accent stepped forward.

"Welcome," he said. "You are now slaves of the Kingdom of Multura. As you are processed, comply with all instructions, and you will not be punished. There is no rescue coming. If you obey, you will be fed, you will be clothed, and you will not be punished. This can be as painless or as painful as you make it."

With that, he turned and left.

The boys were taken first, led through a door to the right. Then it was our turn—the girls. We were led through a door on the left. Once inside, they removed our shackles one at a time and sorted us by height. Each of us was handed a simple garment—a tunic with a hole at the top for our heads and two more for our arms—and then sent into one of four rooms.

My room had eight girls. A voice shouted, "Change!"

One girl didn't move. I approached her gently and whispered, "It's best to do as they say... for now."

"I don't want to do what they want me to," she replied.

"None of us do. But if we live through today... maybe we can fight back another day."

Something in my words must've reached her. She changed.

Hours later, two women with clubs entered the room. One of them noticed the healing rune still around my neck and yanked it off. Then, we were each handed a thin blanket and taken to another room—this one filled with rows of beds and other girls our age.

They came from all over. Most had pale skin, but some were darker, their faces shaped by distant lands.

"Can anyone tell us where we are?" I asked.

A girl with dark hair and thick eyebrows spoke up. "We are in the city of Kapala."

"What happens to us next?" I asked.

"They will do a medical exam tomorrow to determine your... quality. After that, they'll take you to the market each day until you are sold."

"Do you know how they determine our quality?"

"Mostly by your looks and health."

"And... How long does it take to sell someone?"

She shrugged. "Hard to say. Some are gone in a day. Others... months."

I held out my hand. "I'm Nisha."

She didn't take it. "Don't bother. Introductions don't matter here." Then she pointed. "The beds at the far end are unused."

She turned and walked away.

I found an empty bed and lay down, looking around the room. Light came through barred windows high on the walls. The room was built of mortar and stone. I wondered if I could take down a guard alone—maybe.

But why? I needed information. Time.

The next day, we were brought to another room where the medical exams took place. An old woman who looked like she might drop dead at any moment conducted them, scribbling notes on parchment and handing them off to a nearby guard.

After the exams, they brought us to a room that opened to the street. Iron bars separated us from the world beyond. A guard sat outside, likely to deter theft—or worse.

Soon, two men came to the bars. I couldn't understand what they were saying, but one seemed to be doing all the talking—gesturing, pitching. The other just nodded. After they left, a guard came in and took one of the girls who had arrived with me.

We never saw her again.

When the day ended, we were led back to the sleeping quarters. I found the girl with the bushy eyebrows again.

"Do you speak the local language?" I asked.

"I can," she replied.

"The girl they took today... "How much did she sell for?"

"Eight hundred hearts."

"Is that a lot?"

"That's on the low side."

"Do you know your price?"

She nodded. "Someone offered two thousand harks for me. They were denied."

I took a deep breath.

"I don't suppose you know what my price is, do you?"

"Why does it matter?" she asked.

"I'm just trying to figure out how long I'll be here," I replied.

"Like I said yesterday, there's no way to tell for sure."

"Well, you're a higher price... and from how much you know, I guess you've been here for a while."

"Right. The buyer is also important," she said. Then after a moment, she added, "If I hear your price and you're still here tomorrow, I'll tell you."

The next day, nobody was sold, but I took note of the locks and started to think of ways they could be picked. In a pre-industrial world, there aren't a lot of paper clips or other thin pieces of metal lying around. If I could find something that would work, I might be able to pick the lock on the door we were locked in at night and sneak out.

I was determined to keep my eyes open for anything that might help.

The following day, we were taken out of the display cell—as I had come to think of it. As we walked in, I noticed a tall, thin man with tan skin and a curly mustache. His clothes were much more ornate than those of the people around him.

I wonder who's being sold today, I thought.

There was a lot of back and forth, and at one point, I thought they were pointing and talking about me. My heart dropped. But then I saw them gesture toward another girl, and I relaxed. When the men finally left, a guard came in and took the girl they had pointed at.

Three more guards entered right after. They took the girl with dark hair and thick eyebrows, a girl with brown hair, and... me.

"So, you wanted to know how long?" the girl with the thick eyebrows said as we were being hauled out. "Looks like today."

We were taken to a room I hadn't seen before. There, we were washed, scrubbed, and dressed in white robes. Then, a metal collar was placed around each of our necks and sealed with rune magic.

We were loaded into another caged wagon. The tall, thin man with the curly mustache came over and placed a lock on the cage himself. I felt like I had been hit in the gut. We were probably being taken even farther from home.

Once the wagon started moving, I turned to the girl with the thick eyebrows.

"Do you know where we're going?"

"I have no idea," she replied. "I didn't recognize his accent."

"Since we've been sold to the same buyer... my name is Zora," she added.

"Nice to finally know your name," I said. "Not that I suppose it matters at this point... but how much were we sold for?"

"A lot. 4,000 harks each," she replied.

Interlude One

Fire surrounded the city. The first day had been the most aggressive and extreme, but even so, nine days after the attack, there were now less than 300 men still manning the wall. Though many attempts were made to breach the walls, Leela, with the help of her platoon made up of hunters and mounted units, had been able to quickly reinforce every section of the wall that came close to falling. Despite all those efforts, it was only a matter of time before the city defenders would be completely eroded away by the military invaders.

Tired and exhausted from repelling the last wave, Leela took a respite and posed a question to her golden-haired companion.

"Did you figure out your reason for coming up to confront us yet? I have a few suspicions, but nothing really jumps out at my mind," replied Warrik.

"You mean you really didn't come with me because you wanted to make amends? I see. I'm not sure what I would need to make amends for, but if you wanted to abandon the defense of the wall and find an empty room to spend our last few hours in privacy, I wouldn't say no," replied Warrik.

"You oblivious ass! All these years later, and I bet you still don't know why I'm upset," said Leela.

"If you still want to hold a grudge for some perceived offense, that's up to you," replied Warrik.

The giant hunter who wielded an axe looked from Leela to Warrik. "You two are unbelievable. We don't have time for this. It looks like they're coming back for another assault," said Leela.

131

"It looks like they've got themselves a siege tower," said the axe-wielding hunter as the invading army advanced.

Leela looked over at Warrik. "You think Nisha and the others made it to Varlyn yet?" she asked.

"I'm sure they're close by now," replied Warrik.

"Well, I'm glad our efforts haven't been a complete waste," Leela said. The defenders watched as the invaders moved closer and closer to the city walls. It was undetectable at first to all except the most observant. Masked by the movement of the invading army, the sound and vibration grew louder and stronger. After several minutes, it became too strong to be ignored anymore by the defenders of the city.

"Reinforcements!" someone shouted, but for whom? It couldn't be seen yet. High on the hill to the south of the invaders, several mounted soldiers on borrowed dogs were spotted. Their uniforms and armor were not like those of chainmail worn by the invaders, but of polished plate armor. Even the dogs were armored.

One of the soldiers on top of the hill thrust his sword up in the air and began to charge down the hill towards the invading army. A line of mounted soldiers, both on horses and dogs, soon followed behind those already charging. There were hundreds of them. More lines of mounted soldiers began to pour in from over the hill, and their numbers soon swelled into the thousands.

The mounted soldiers formed a wedge based on the lead soldier and began to cut through the invading forces like a knife. Banners began to be flown by the mounted soldiers, which could be seen by the city defenders as they came. Some of them belonged to Alza, and some belonged to Elvis.

"How could they have gotten here so quickly?" asked Warrik.

"I'm not sure, but the only thing that makes sense is that they were already preparing for it," replied Leela.

Even though the troop count may have been higher on the side of the invaders, they were no match for the heavily armored mounted soldiers. In less than half an hour, the entire invading army had been routed and was now in full retreat.

As the fighting began to die down, some mounted soldiers who were not pursuing the fleeing military forces rode up to the western gate. The lead soldier was the same one who had led the charge against the invaders. The gate was opened, and he rode into the city with his retinue.

The man had dark brown hair and blue eyes. "I'm Duke Andarol Felton of Elris. Who is in command here?" he asked.

A bloody but very much alive Captain LeRoy appeared from the wall. "That would be me, and thank you for arriving when you did. I don't know how much longer we could have held out," said LeRoy.

"I'm Captain LeRoy of the Alvin Armed Forces. You did well to defend the city for as long as you did. We estimated that the city would likely fall within the first day or two," said Duke Andarol.

"Forgive me, my Lord, I don't mean to insult our saviors, but it sounded like you anticipated this attack," said LeRoy.

"Not specifically. We knew that there was a planned invasion, but we didn't know which city would be targeted first. We guessed that it would be Varlyn, as it was less defended; much to my regret, we were wrong," said the Duke.

"My Lord, did you happen to travel here by the road to Orlando?" asked Lady Montello.

"What a surprise to see you here!"

"We did come by way of the road to Varlyn," replied the Duke.

"Did you happen to receive several hundred refugees on your way here?" asked Leela.

"They allowed us to release all the children under 12 and the elderly after the first day," she added.

"I see," said the Duke. "Perhaps it's best if we find somewhere private to debrief."

"Please, my Lord, tell us all here if you will," asked LeRoy.

The Duke was silent for a moment. "There were no children among them, but we came across the corpses of many slain elderly. My guess is that they must have taken the children as slaves," he concluded.

The pain and anger could almost be physically felt through the stone among those standing.

"Captain LeRoy, I may need to hold onto that commission a bit longer," said Leela.

Chapter 20

Potoma

The cage wagon we had been loaded into was much more comfortable than the ones we had arrived in at Kapala. It even had padded seats, but as they say, a cage, no matter how fancy, is still a cage.

"Zora, why do the collars have room circuits?" I asked.

"It allows them to track us down if we escape," she replied. Her statement made me think back to AnnaLisa and how she seemed to always know where Kriss was.

"Do you know how it works?" I asked.

"Not really. I just know that it is linked to a room they carry," she replied.

Our pace was much more leisurely, with periodic stops to rest and eat. Three guards, including the man with the thin mustache, were our escorts. Even though we were just children, it seemed as though their policy was never to have less than two of them with us at all times.

Outside the wagon, I figured it was probably the thin mustache man that had the tracking room, but I couldn't be sure. Each day we were taken further and further from Elris. I thought of Leela, Warrik, and Elvis. I wondered if they were still alive. Most of the time, I tried to imagine that Leela had survived and was already coming to find me. However, there were times when I was beginning to lose all hope. It felt like every time I arrived at a point where I could start to figure things out, things would change, and I'd have to start back at the beginning.

I did try to look for an opportunity to escape, and there were several times I could have gotten one of the guard's weapons, but then what? Hope that my skills were good enough to take on two grown men at the same time? The next part would be figuring out where to go when I had no idea where I was.

We passed through several towns and villages, but it wasn't until about two weeks later that we finally arrived at another big city. There was a massive wall around it, about four floors high. As we passed through the main gate, I could see that the wall was about 50 ft thick. Building it must have been a monumental undertaking. The streets were wide and paved with cobblestone. Many of the pointed circular roofs reminded me of pictures of buildings in Russia.

Autumn was in full swing, and before long, winter would set in. I tried to keep track of how to get back to the main gate, but my mind could only keep track of so many buildings, streets, and turns. Eventually, I just noted that I was somewhere to the east, based on the sun. After riding through the city for over an hour, we passed through another gate. While it was much smaller than the first one, it still had guards at the gate. As we rode past the gate, there were pathways, ponds, and perfectly manicured bushes.

"We must be at a noble's estate," I thought. Eventually, the wagon made a left turn, and a massive building came into view.

"That's not a mansion; that's a palace," I remarked.

"Sorry, I just shrugged. I've never seen one before, so I wouldn't know," Zora said.

The wagon kept traveling until it circled around to the back of the palace and pulled into a gated building. Several more guards joined the ones that had been escorting us. We were taken out of the wagon and led through a series of hallways and doors until we arrived at a large wood and iron door.

I'm not sure what I was expecting, but I wouldn't have guessed a barrack-style room filled with women wearing matching uniforms. We were pushed inside, and then the doors were closed behind us. A young woman came up to us and started speaking in military terms. Zora understood what she said, but the rest of us just stood there.

Then she spoke to Leela. "Welcome to this part of my palace. As of today, you are palace maids in training. I am Tarra. Follow me, and I'll take you to your bed."

She took us past several rows until we got to a section of the room that was filled with girls about our own age. "These are yours," she said, indicating a set of bunk beds. "Inside the chest at the foot of the bed, you should be able to find your uniforms. If anything you need is missing, let me or one of the older girls know. You will be expected to learn more. The quicker you learn it, the easier your life will be. Your training will begin in the morning, so get settled in. There is a bathroom over to your left, and dinner is in a couple of hours. Do any of you have any questions?" asked Tarra.

"I have one," I asked. "Are we really expected to go around the palace cleaning it and not try to escape?"

"You'll be immediately punished if you're seen in places you're not supposed to be. Because of your collar, you'll be hunted down long before you reach the outside wall. And last, if you do make a run for the wall, both you and another maid will be executed," Tarra explained. "Likewise, if you refuse to obey and learn, someone else will be beaten with you," she added. "It was as I said earlier: the quicker you learn, the easier your life will be."

The other two girls who had come with us from Kapala looked as if all life had been drained from their eyes.

"If you have no more questions, I'll leave you for now," said Tarra. With that, she turned and walked away.

I sat down on one of the beds Tarra pointed out to us. Anger began to rise within me. Why the hell hadn't I tried to escape while traveling here? The odds may not have been on my side, but at least I would have had a chance. For that matter, why the hell did I even leave home? I'm sure I could have found a way to deal with Marx if I had explored more options. It felt like everything that had happened since I left home was one bad decision that just kept getting worse and worse at every turn. Doesn't God have any sympathy?

I was never one to believe in my past life, but given that I still remember my old life and the voices I heard after my death, I assumed that there must have at least been something more than mortal existence. So why am I still being punished? Is this how God punishes murderers? Does he give them a wonderful new life only to take it away from them in cruel ways?

I lay my face down on my bed and spoke quietly, "I'm sorry, God, for what I've done, but please stop punishing me. Either take my life or help me fix it, but I can't take anymore."

Someone touched my shoulder, and I turned to see who it was.

"Who are you talking to?" asked Zora.

"God, if he's listening," I replied.

"Who is God?" she asked.

That's right; they were worshiping elemental spirits in this world. They don't know anything about monotheism.

"He's the one who controls everyone's fate," I replied.

"I've never heard of him before, so I don't know," she said.

"How long have you been a slave?" I asked.

"I don't consider myself a slave, but if it is captivity you referred to, I was born into it," she replied.

"Call it whatever you want. I don't think the guards and magical tracking collars care either way," I grumbled. My mother once told me that you become a slave once you've given up hope of ever being free, and I intend to be free one day," she replied.

"And how will you become free one day?" I asked.

"I don't know how it will come, but for now, I will learn," she replied.

"That's surprisingly optimistic, Zora. Will you do me a favor?" I asked.

"What is the favor?" she asked back.

"Will you teach me how to speak more Turian?" I asked.

"Not tonight. Tonight my soul hurts too much, but maybe in the morning," I asked.

"I will do that if you wish," she replied.

The next morning, we were woken up early by Tarra. After breakfast, the iron and wood door that had been closed on us during the evening was open and left that way.

"How else could we go do our job?" she replied. Tarra took myself, Zora, and the two girls that came with us, Lycillia and Alta.

Tarra explained that it would be confusing at first, but we would always be paired with someone that we knew where to go until we could navigate the palace on our own. She first showed us all the other servants' quarters. Our next stop after that was the main kitchen.

The kitchen was impressive, and at any given time, there were at least five or six cooks at work, explained Tarra. "You should never receive a request for food or drinks directly from the Royal household or their guests. It should only ever come to you from their direct servants. That said, if any of them ever do approach you, make sure you pay attention and fulfill their request," she explained further.

Tarra instructed us about when approached by anyone not in uniform, depending on their position or occupation. All the palace workers, servants, and slaves wore uniforms that denoted their positions. Special pins were worn by those with higher authority than others. Under no circumstances were we to ever approach someone not wearing a uniform unless it was specifically ordered or otherwise necessary.

Most of the rules Tarra gave us were simple and easy to follow, but some of them seemed like they would need practice—like where to go when told to go do certain things. Most of the hallways and proud places Tarra told us not to go were places that led to the outside.

"Tarra, are there any times and places we can go outside?" I asked.

"I'll show you at the end," she replied. All the major locations like the ballrooms, dining rooms, libraries—anywhere that was likely to need cleaning—were places we were allowed into. Personal quarters and other similar areas were regulated to servants of higher status.

"Just remember to stay behind the lead girl you are paired with and do everything they do," said Tarra.

By early afternoon, Tarra had finished our tour of the areas we were allowed to go. She started to bring us back to the maids' quarters. There was a door directly opposite in the hallway to the maids' quarters. Tarra opened it, and as we walked through, sunlight hit my eyes. It was a large fenced-in courtyard about half the size of a football field. It was filled with benches and pathways.

"This is our recreation area. Once you're done with your tasks for the day, you are allowed to come here and do whatever you like until we are locked down for the evening," said Tarra. "However, if you are found here before your tasks are done, you will be punished," she added.

"I have added your names to the roster, so starting tomorrow, you will be assigned tasks. You may now do as you will for the rest of the day. Enjoy it because it may be a while before you have this much free time again." With that, Tarra walked off and left us in the recreation room.

As soon as Tarra left, I began to explore the recreation area. On the wall by the door, there were several old books on a shelf that looked like their best days were far behind them. I opened one up and saw that it was written in Turian. The rest of the books were the same.

"Can you read these?" asked Zora as she walked over to the books and opened one.

"They are storybooks made to help children learn to read. They are easy to read," she said.

"Well, do you think you can use them to teach me more Turian?" I asked.

"Will you teach me too?" asked Lycillia.

"I will," said Zora.

For the rest of the afternoon, we went over some of the more basic Turian words and tried our best to memorize them. More and more girls began to enter the recreation room as the day wore on. Before we ended our lesson with Zora, the four of us agreed to try and meet up again the next day for another lesson. With the remaining time, I decided to get in as much exercise as I could. I could tell that my muscles had lost some of their tone since Duvort and vowed to get them back into shape.

The next morning after breakfast, another girl about the same age as Tarra started to assign groups, and her names were called off of a list. We were required to go to our group. The new girls all ended up in different groups, and I had it off with my assigned group. I walked in the back of my group and tried my best to memorize the route we took.

Several times we ran across several people not in uniform, and the lead girl about the rest of us followed her example. Our first stop was to a large supply closet. The lead girl started handing out supplies to other girls in our group. I held out my hands like the other girls, and she placed a basket full of feather dusters in my hands. After we gathered up our supplies, we left the supply closet following the lead girl.

We eventually ended up in the large library Tarra had shown us the day before. We then headed down one of the many rows of bookshelves and stopped at the section where one side had clean books and the other books on the other side looked like they hadn't been touched in years. The lead girl pulled out one of the dusty books and showed me how to carefully clean it, then returned it to the same spot it had been taken from. Each of us moved to a section and began cleaning books.

After a few minutes, I checked my pace, and it was clear that the other girls were cleaning at a much quicker pace. Determined not to be outdone, I sped up my pace, but it wasn't long before the lead girl stopped me and pointed out some books that needed to be re-cleaned.

"Best to do it right the first time," I thought. I got progressively better throughout the day, but by the end of it, I was still far outpaced by the other girls.

The lead girl said something to me in Turian, and I don't know exactly what she said, but I assumed she said something about needing to be faster. We returned the cleaning supplies and headed back to the maids' quarters, and I was the second one back as Lycillia was already there.

"What did you do today?" I asked.

"We washed bed sheets," replied Lycillia.

"That sounds about as fun as dusting books," I said. I pulled off my shoes and socks. "I'm going to get some training in. Will you let me know when Alta and Zora get here, please?"

"I can do that," she replied.

About 30 minutes later, Alta and Zora were both in the rec room, and we began learning more Turian. Before I even realized it, a routine had been established. The groups we had been assigned to stayed the same; occasionally, one girl would be swapped for another for various reasons. Once every week, the cleaning locations would rotate in an effort to maintain fairness, that way, no one group would have to be stuck cleaning the same areas for more than a week.

At the end of every day, our group of four would meet up to learn more, and I found an old broomstick and started going through the forms Leela had taught me. I got better at cleaning, and after a few weeks, I could finally keep up with the other girls.

Something changed in the rec room, too—more girls had joined us learning Turian. Apparently, all the other bilingual girls were too busy to teach, and now Zora had six or seven of us every evening. After two months, I could count and knew how to read simple words in Turian. I struggled with fast-paced conversations, but I could follow simple instructions and converse at a slow pace.

One day, while I was practicing sword forms, one of the girls came up to me and asked if I really knew what I was doing or was just fooling around. I handed her the broomstick and said, "Try to hit me and find out."

"Are you sure?" she asked.

I put both my hands on my back and said, "I'm sure."

She swung at me, and I dodged her attack. "Go faster," I said. She swung and missed several more times, but I easily evaded her blows, stepped in closer, and snatched the broomstick from her hands.

"Wow, you're really fast," she said.

"Thanks," I replied.

"I bet I could hit her," said another girl who had been watching. I tossed her the broomstick and said, "Give it a try. Give it your best shot."

She didn't get any closer to hitting me than the first girl did, and I disarmed her with ease. "Mind if I try?" asked another girl. I was getting a good sweat going and decided this was going to be training for the evening.

Before I knew it, there were a bunch of girls lining up to swing at me like I was some sort of piñata. After about an hour, I was drenched and sweating, but no one had landed a hit on me.

The next day, one of the girls had found another old broom handle, and after Zora's lessons were over, she asked me if I could show her how I moved the way I did the night before. By the end of the third month at Potomac, I could read and write Turian well enough to take notes. Occasionally, I would have to ask someone to explain a word I didn't know, but I could hold a full conversation in Turian.

Several girls had taken up sparring practice with me, and I could now get a decent training session in. If I hadn't been a slave, I could have almost thought I was having fun.

One day, when cleaning tasks were being assigned, a man not wearing a uniform walked into our quarters. Everyone bowed as he walked over to the girls assigning tasks.

"Where's the girl that is skilled with the sword?" All the other girls looked at me, and I stepped forward.

Chapter 21

Alonzo

After I stepped forward, I bowed. From a purely optical standpoint, I could see how training slaves to fight would be frowned upon, but as far as I knew, I hadn't broken any rules, and Tarra had said we should use our free time however we wished. When I looked up from my bow, I could see Alonzo's features better. He had a neatly trimmed red beard, blue eyes, and dirty blonde hair.

"Why are you teaching the other maids to fight?" he asked.

I knew I had to be careful how I answered this question. "Forgive me, my Lord. I train in the evening for exercise. Some of the other maids saw me doing it and asked me to teach them. It was not my intent to be disruptive," I pleaded.

He seemed to be in thought for a moment, then he finally spoke. "I understand. Come with me." He turned and started to walk outside the maids' quarters, and I fell in behind him.

We walked past most of the areas the maids typically cleaned. Eventually, we came to a passageway that was off-limits to the maids and walked through it. The passageway took us outside the palace and into an adjacent building. We finally came to a large set of double doors. When we walked through them, there was a large open room filled with dozens of voices training in different types of martial arts. Some were grappling, some were sparring with their hands and feet, and some were sparring with wooden swords.

We walked over to the section where sword matches were taking place. There was an old man, probably in his sixties, with graying hair and a trimmed gray beard.

"What do you want, Kona, and why have you brought a maid into the dojo? You know they aren't allowed here," said the older man.

"I have special permission to bring this one here. I have instructions for you to test your skills and train her if you find her to be competent," said Kona.

"It is too early in the morning for your jokes. Take her back to the palace before you get her into trouble," said the old man.

"I assure you that this is no joke, Alonzo. The instructions came directly from the third Prince," replied Kona.

"Another one of his pet projects, I presume. Take her back, and I'll deal with the prince," said the old man.

"So he figured you might say that, and he assured me that His Highness insists. Besides, she's been training some of the other maids how to fight, and we can't have that," replied Kona.

Alonzo sighed. "I will hold you responsible when she gets hurt."

"Girl!" Alonzo shouted, "take off your shoes, then grab a training sword from the rack and stand on the far side of the mat."

I slipped off my shoes and did as he instructed.

"Builder!" Alonzo shouted. A young boy of eleven or twelve came running up.

"Yes, Master," said the boy.

"I want you to spar with this girl and do not hold back," said Alonzo.

"Understood, Master," the boy replied. Builder took one of the training swords from the rack and faced me.

"Mates do not belong here," said Builder.

"Begin!" shouted Alonzo.

Builder came at me fast with a flurry of swings. I backed up and gave ground in his eagerness. Once he went too wide and overshot me, I hit his hands with a well-timed slash. The wooden sword cracked hard against his fingers, and he dropped his weapon. Builder looked more surprised than hurt.

"That wasn't fair! You made me think you couldn't fight," he said.

"You assumed I couldn't fight," I replied.

"Again!" shouted Alonzo.

Builder picked up his sword and got back into position. I had speed and timing down now.

"Begin!" Alonzo shouted.

Builder swung; I deflected it and stepped inside his defense, using a hand manipulation technique to wrench his sword from his hand. Once again, Builder looked surprised.

"That's enough," said Alonzo.

"I can beat her, Master! I know it! Please let me try one more time!" asked Builder.

"She has been sparring with you by only disarming you. Don't make yourself look any more foolish," replied Alonzo. Builder bowed to Alonzo and returned to training sword to the rack.

"You see why I brought her here?" said Kona.

"Maybe," Alonzo replied. He grabbed one of the training swords himself and faced me. "It is clear that you were trained well by someone who knew what they were doing. I will find out how thorough your training was," said Alonzo.

He stood in front of me, holding up his sword.

"Ready?" called Kona.

"Begin!" shouted Alonzo.

Alonzo instantly closed the gap between us and attacked. I jumped back and evaded his swing. He was fast, but not as fast as Leela. He quickly recovered and turned his sword back for another pass. As he stepped forward, I dropped low and was able to deflect his swing.

As it began to rise up, another swing was coming directly down on me, and I raised my sword to block it. I realized I had made a mistake; all the training I had couldn't make up for the difference in muscle mass between a ten-year-old girl and an adult male. His swing hit my sword with the force of a ton of bricks. The shock ripped through my arms, and I was forced back down. I used the momentum and rolled back as I fell. I wouldn't be able to block another hit like that.

I jumped back onto my feet and went on the offensive. I got close with a couple of swings, but Alonzo acted as if deflecting my swings took almost no effort on his part. I decided I would tire him out and make him come after me. Unfortunately, even deflecting his hits took a heavy toll on me. I couldn't drag this out; otherwise, he'd definitely win.

I got some distance between us, and then I came with everything I had. I jumped as high as I could and swung down towards Alonzo's head. He deflected it, and I turned to face him again. He was already swinging; there was no room to evade or deflect. All I could do was try to block.

There was a quick flash of light. For a second, I thought I might have been knocked unconscious, but I was still able to see, and Alonzo was holding his training sword next to my neck. I hadn't felt my sword being hit; there was instead a clean slice through my wooden training sword. Half of it was lying on the ground several feet away.

"You're a mage," I said.

"I'm not," replied Alonzo.

"Then how did you do that?" I asked.

"Perhaps I will teach you one day if you prove yourself to be competent enough. What is your name?" he asked.

"My name is Nisha," I replied.

"I will train her. Take her to get some training uniforms," Alonzo said to Kona. "She can start tomorrow."

"I'm sure the prince will be pleased," said Kona.

"I'm sure he'll be pleased," replied Alonzo.

Alonzo took me to another part of the training building, where there was a large closet filled with training uniforms. He found two of the smaller ones and handed them to me.

"My Lord, may I ask you a question?" I asked.

"By all means, and call me Kona. I am but a servant to His Highness," he replied.

"Why does the third Prince want me trying to fight?" I asked.

"Are you not grateful for the opportunity?" he asked.

"I am, but also confused," I replied.

"It isn't for me to say, but I'm sure His Highness will tell you himself at some point," we started heading back to the palace the way we came.

"Be sure to remember how to get back to the training hall," said Kona. "You'll still be staying with the maids, but you will report to Master Alonzo each morning."

"Oh, and Nisha, you aren't allowed to train the maids in combat anymore," said Kona.

It was just before noon when we made it back to the maids' quarters.

"Make sure you're dressed in your training uniform when you leave here in the morning," said Kona.

"You also need this," he handed me a small metal pin in the shape of two crossed swords. "Make sure to wear it on your collar; it will let everyone know to let you pass without issue," he added.

"Until I see you again, good luck with your training," said Kona.

"Thank you," I replied.

With that, he turned and walked off. When I came into the maids' quarters, most of the girls were still out doing their daily tasks. Tarra was still there, and when I walked up to her, she seemed surprised to see me.

"I thought they had taken you to be punished," she said.

I explained everything that had happened and the instructions I had been given. "It certainly is a strange position to be in, but I think I understand," Tarra said. "I think it will be best if you get changed into your training uniform and only wear those from now on to avoid any confusion," she concluded.

I changed into my new uniform and placed the pin on my collar. I went over to the rec room and found a patch of grass under the sun and lay down. As far as slavery goes, this wasn't as bad as I had imagined. However, I knew things could have turned out much worse if I hadn't been bought by the palace.

I thought that it was odd that a slave from the palace had been all the way in Kapala; there must have certainly been closer slave markets. I suppose it was possible that he was there to see what became available as a result of the invasion of Alza. I started thinking of all the other children that had been taken captive and wondered how things were going for them. There were a lot of questions rolling around in my mind: Who is the third Prince, and what does he want with me? The questions in my mind led to more questions, none of which I had answers to.

My stomach finally pulled me out of my spinning mind, and I got up to eat. When I returned to the rec room, Zora was already there. She looked over at me and said, "Your new outfit looks good on you. What happened after you left this morning?" she asked.

"I'll explain everything once everyone else gets here," I replied.

Once Lycillia and Alta and the other girls returned, I explained everything that happened. They said I can't train you to fight anymore, but I was thinking that you could still practice what I taught you on your own, and when I learned something new, I'll come here to train on my own, and you can watch me," I said.

"I'm glad you get to stay here with us, but why wouldn't they have you stay with the rest of the knights in training?" asked Alta.

"Their training to be knights," I asked.

"Well, I don't know for sure, but that's what one of the other girls told me when I saw someone wearing that uniform," she replied.

"I can't say for sure what they do yet," I said. "Start tomorrow. As for why I'm not staying in their quarters, it's because they're all boys," I explained.

"Then why would they allow you to train with them?" asked Zora.

"I don't know, but it has something to do with the third Prince," I replied.

"Promise us you'll be careful. It could be dangerous being the only girl there," said Lycillia.

"I will, but the only one there that could beat me is the instructor," I replied.

The rest of the evening took on an excited tone as the rest of the girls came and asked about my change in attire. Most of them told me how lucky I was or congratulated me, but a few just turned and walked away. It seemed like I had shown that there was a way out of being a maid forever, but for those who were paying attention, they already knew there was another way out, as none of the maids appeared to be over 20.

Chapter 22

Knight in Training

The next morning, I showed up at the training hall. The boys were still coming in, and some of them were starting to form up in front of Master Alonzo. I went to stand next to some of the shorter boys when Alonzo motioned for me to come over to him. I quickly went to him, and he told me to stand next to him. We stood there in silence while the rest of the boys arrived. Once no more were coming in, Alonzo spoke.

"Good morning."

"Good morning, Master!" they all shouted in unison.

"This is Nisha," he said, pointing at me. "Nisha will be training with us for the time being by request of the third Prince."

"Yes, Nisha is a girl. She has already proved to me that she's a capable warrior in her own right. If you want to find out for yourself, you will have an opportunity to spar with her in due time. It is unorthodox, but we are not going to have any issues. Do I make myself clear?"

"Yes, Master!" they shouted back.

"Does anyone wish to complain or have any questions?" Alonzo asked.

None of the boys said anything.

"Good. Now that is out of the way, Nisha, fall in over there," he said, pointing to the end of the formation.

"Raelynn!" shouted Alonzo. "Get them warmed up!"

"Yes, Master," said an older boy who looked like he was about 16 or 17.

The boys started filing out of the back of the training hall, one row at a time, where I fell in. They put me at the very end. When I got outside, I saw an open oval-shaped pathway that looked like a running track. Raelynn led us through a series of stretches. I did my best to follow along, and after about 10 minutes, Raelynn took us out to the stone pathway.

"At your own pace today, but no slacking!" shouted Raelynn. The boys took off. I was faster than some but nowhere near the front. I could hear Leela's words about needing to work twice as hard as the boys to keep up echoing in the back of my mind.

"Okay, today's goal is to not be last, but I will work to be up in the lead, even if I have to work out multiple times a day," I thought to myself as I was running. A boy behind me kicked my feet, causing me to stumble. I was able to catch myself before face-planting, but I was instantly enraged. It was one of those moments, like when you stub your toe, and you're instantly overtaken by irrational feelings of anger and rage.

I started sprinting after the boy who kicked my feet and had every intention of taking him to the ground and beating him half to death. When I caught up to him, I was about to kick his feet out from under him when I was suddenly hit with a flash of realization. I couldn't let them get to me. If I wanted revenge, I'd have to beat them by being better than them.

I used my anger as fuel and then ran past the boy who tried to trip me. After that incident, I made sure to pay close attention to who was around me. I figured that avoidance was the best way to shut down issues before they could happen. When Raelynn finally stopped us, I was firmly in the middle of the pack.

We went back inside the training hall, where we split up into groups, mostly by size.

"How are the groups decided?" I asked one of the boys next to me.

"It goes by how good you can fight," he replied.

"What group is this?" I asked.

"This is the fifth class," he replied.

"And that's low?" I asked for clarification.

"It's the lowest," he replied.

The boys in our group came and stood in a circle. Two boys came up to each other; there was a painted circle on the floor where they stood. The two boys started sparring with their hands and feet.

"What are the rules?" I asked.

"Force them out of the circle, knock them out, or make them submit," replied the boy.

"Sounds simple enough," I replied.

The first fight ended when one boy, who was backed against the edge of the circle, grabbed the other boy's leg and spun him out of bounds. The boy who won stayed inside the circle, and another boy stepped in. The second match ended when the winner of the first round was thrown to the ground, and after being punched in the face a couple of times, he tapped his hand against the floor.

The winner of the second round was also the winner of the third round, and again, he stayed in the circle. So you just keep fighting until you're eliminated?" I asked.

"Or until you win five times in a row and move up to the fourth class," the boy explained.

After his third win, it took a moment for another boy to enter the circle with the winner. After a few minutes, the three-time champion stumbled his opponent out of the circle and was again the winner. Either nobody wanted to end his winning streak, or the other boys were afraid to lose, but nobody was stepping up.

I stepped inside the circle. "This is just great. If I win, they will say it was only because he was worn out," I thought. We squared off against each other. The now four-time champion threw a jab at me. He was easy to dodge, and I caught his third strike with my hand, pulled his arm around to his back, and pinned him to the ground. He refused to submit, so I brought his wrist higher and higher on his back.

"Submit, or I'll break your arm," I said.

"No, go ahead and break it," he said defiantly.

"Have it your way," I replied. I let go of his arm and got off his back. As he started to stand up, I brought my knee against his jaw and knocked him out cold. I stood up and looked around. "Who's next?" I asked.

Nobody spoke up. Nobody stepped forward. Master Alonzo came over to our group. "I thought we agreed there would be no issue," he said.

"What's the matter? Are you afraid to beat a girl or be beaten by a girl?" he asked.

None of the boys spoke.

Alonzo sighed. "Come with me, Nisha," said Alonzo. He took me to the next group of boys. Most of them looked to be a few years older than me.

"Do any of you have any issue fighting a girl?" asked Alonzo. Again, none of the boys from the fourth class group said anything.

"Very well then," said Alonzo. He walked over to the same spot he had taken as the boys came in that morning and issued a loud, sharp whistle. All the boys stopped and came over to their master.

"I thought we agreed we weren't going to have any issues. Am I mistaken?"

"No, Master!" they shouted back.

"Let's try this again. Do any of you have the courage to fight a girl?" asked Alonzo. "Step forward if you do."

Four boys came forward. One of them was the boy I had knocked unconscious earlier. Two of them looked like they were from the third or second class, and the last was definitely one of the older boys.

"You four hold back. The rest of you go back to training," after the rest of the boys left, Alonzo motioned for the remaining boys to come forward.

"Why am I not surprised that it is only you four that have enough courage? The rest of these fools are too afraid to lose face by being beaten or by beating a girl, but their pride will cost them a valuable training experience. Nisha has been trained differently than the rest of you. No doubt there will be plenty you can teach her, and she to you," explained Alonzo.

"What is it you would have us do, Master?" asked the oldest boy.

"As the oldest boy, from here on out, the five of you will be your own class. Godwin, you have more than enough experience to lead it," Alonzo said, implicating the oldest boy.

"How will we advance if it's just the five of us in our own class?" asked one of the middle-aged boys.

"After you train for a while, you'll be able to fight your old groups for advancement," explained Alonzo. "After you finish warming up with everyone else in the morning, you'll separate into your own group for training. I suggest you get to it. Follow me," said Godwin.

We went to an empty section of the training hall. It looked like Master Alonzo will have a training session for a while, so let's introduce ourselves, said Godwin.

"My name is Godwin. I'm 17, and I'm a sponsored knight."

"My name is Leon. I'm 15, and I'm also a sponsored knight."

"My name is Dartan. I'm 15 and also a sponsored knight."

"My name is Cordell. I'm 11 and also a sponsored knight."

Next, it was my turn. "My name is Nisha. I'm 10, and until this morning, I was a maid in the palace. Before that, I was a hunter in another country. As of now, I don't know what title I have."

"What is a sponsored knight?" I asked.

"It means we weren't born with a silver spoon up our butts like the rest of these snobs," explained Leon.

"No more cursing," said Godwin.

"But he's right. Most of the other knights in training were born into nobility, whereas a sponsored knight is a commoner who shows promise and skill. A noble will then sponsor them to come here and train to increase their reputation," Godwin explained.

"Can nobles not fight girls in this country?" I asked.

"Win or lose, their precious egos couldn't handle the fallout," said Leon.

"That's enough chatting for now," said Godwin. "Let's get back to training before Master Alonzo comes and yells at us. I need to see where all of your skills are today so that I can make a training plan for tomorrow."

So Godwin was the first up for hand-to-hand. Given that the rest of the group hadn't been there for our previous match, Cordell and I fought first. Cordell was a lot quicker when he wasn't all worn out, but it still took less than a minute for me to get him to tap out. He was a lot more reasonable without advancement on the line.

Next, Leon and Dartan fought. They were both evenly skilled, but after ten minutes of back and forth, Leon finally made Dartan tap. After that, I fought Leon, and the results were strange. Leon couldn't corner me or hold me down, but every time I tried to trip him or hold him, he just used his superior strength to break free. I did tag him with a couple of punches, but he was stout enough to take my hits.

After about fifteen minutes, Godwin decided he had seen enough and called an end to it. After that, we had more duels with training swords. I'll spare the details, but none of them were a match for me. Godwin held his own for a bit, but eventually, I was able to pick him apart.

"You're amazing with the sword! How did you come by such skill?" asked Godwin.

"Lots of hard work. My master trained me nearly every day for six years," I replied.

"Your master must be very talented," said Godwin.

"She is—or was. I'm not sure if she's still alive," I replied.

"I'm sure someone of her skill doesn't go down easy," said Leon.

"Thanks, I appreciate you saying that," I replied.

The rest of the day was spent figuring out how we matched up in various other skills like knife throwing and archery. Let's just say that I can hit the target, but I'm no Robin Hood," Godwin finally said.

He said he had seen enough and called an end to our training for the day. By the time we were dismissed from the training hall, every muscle in my body was sore. Unfortunately, I knew it was only going to get worse before it got better. I still needed to come up with my own plan on how to fit in an extra training session during the day.

It was that walk back to the maids' quarters, with aching muscles, that I began to feel like I had a knot in my stomach for everything that had happened that day. I had fun, yet how could that be? I was a long way from home, I was being held against my will, and I was being toyed with by an unknown puppet master. Shouldn't I be using my new permission to leave the designated areas for the maids to escape?

I was certain I had eyes on me, but it felt like I had betrayed the sacrifice that Leela, Warrik, and the rest of the people in Duvort had made to try to get us to safety. With everything that had happened, all that had been lost, and all those who had been taken as slaves, having fun didn't feel right.

Interlude Two

When something good happens in any world, news about it seems to travel at a snail's pace. Conversely, when something bad happens, news about it travels at the speed of a racing barrel dog. The terrible news about the war crime of executing and kidnapping refugees outside of Duvortce covered the whole northeastern continent. In only a couple of weeks, not only had the group of refugees heading south been intercepted, but the much larger group heading east into Alza's interior had been as well.

Although most of the refugees had been citizens of Alza, it was now publicly known that some of the refugees, including the daughter of a well-known count, were citizens of Elris. The call to arms had fallen across both countries as vengeance against Multira was demanded. At the head of the combined forces invading Multira was Duke Andarol Felton, who was about to have his leading commanders initiate an attack on the city of Kapala.

The cold of winter was in full swing, and four months had passed since the attack on Duvortce. The ranks had swollen since then as more soldiers had joined up, and experienced commanders were in short supply. Colonel LeRoy was walking through the half-frozen mud on his way to a meeting at Duke Andarol's tent. His troops were ready to begin the attack when given the order, but one last meeting was called before the final call was given.

As LeRoy walked past the guards to the Duke's tent, they saluted him, which he promptly returned. The Duke was waiting inside the tent with his other top officers.

"I apologize for summoning you at such short notice like this, but we received some intelligence that you should all be made aware of before the attacks," said the Duke.

"Now that everyone is here, Colonel Leela, would you relay what you told me to everyone else?" asked the Duke.

"My spies in the city have told me that they have pressed all the able-bodied slaves into service, most of them running supplies. Be cautious with those surrendering, as they may be slaves or even the missing refugees," said Leela. "They also have heavy scorpions placed on the walls that will likely pose issues for your siege engines," she added.

"I'm sure you have a plan to deal with them for me, currently," replied LeRoy.

"I do, but it will take time, so just be sure to take precautions on your end," said Leela.

With that out of the way, does anyone have any questions?" asked Daryl.

Nobody spoke.

With that out of the way, Leela began the attack on their defenses.

"When you're ready," said the Duke as the officers left the tent. Leela came up to LeRoy. "How long will it take you to make your modifications?" she asked.

"About 30 minutes," he replied.

"All right, I'll buy you that time, but don't be late," she said. With that, they headed their separate ways.

LeRoy had six siege towers and several battering rams ready to roll up to the walls of Kapala. When given a signal, he called his officers to him, and shortly after giving instructions, modifications began on two of the siege towers.

It was mid-morning when Leela had her soldiers with the tower shields advance towards the city walls. Directly behind the shield units were archers that would fire on the city walls. The soldiers on the walls had the advantage and began to lose their arrows as mages began casting spells. After sustaining some losses, the shield and bow units were finally close enough to return fire.

Leela hopped up on Beslim, where Warrik was sitting on Elvis, and a hundred other mounted units were waiting.

"Do you think they'll come through on time?" asked Warrik.

"They'd better, otherwise this will go down as one of the dumbest charges in history," replied Leela.

She poured mana into a rune that would send a signal to a corresponding room. She snapped her reins, and Beslim took off on a sprint. Hot on her heels were the rest of the mounted units, charging directly at the locked city gate.

Arrows and fire blasts came down at them as they came closer to the gate. Leela pulled out her gun and shot one of the mages casting spells. The charging units were now less than 100 yards from the gate. If they slowed down, they would be easier targets for the soldiers on the walls.

Just as it became almost certain that Leela would run Beslim headlong into a shut gate, it began to open. Leela's infiltrators had done their job and opened the gate. She turned and ran Beslim up the stairs to the wall. The burrow dog was knocking and tossing soldiers off the wall.

Leela found the first heavy scorpion and began taking out the crew running it. A few moments later, as LeRoy's siege towers came close to the walls, the modified ones lowered their boarding ramps to reveal two crews, one on each tower. The crews were manning strange metal tubes that they aimed, and then with a loud bang, took out two of the heavy scorpions.

The rest of the siege towers soon made contact with the wall. More and more troops poured into the city through the towers and open gates. Leela, Warrik, and the rest of the mounted soldiers kept clearing out the defenses on the wall. By the end of the day, a siege that was predicted to take more than a month was over in less than a day.

As predicted, most of those pressed into defending the city surrendered as soon as they could. There was some fighting inside the city, but it was quickly suppressed by overwhelming forces. With the city taken, Leela started riding over to the slave market.

"You shouldn't get your hopes up too much," Warrik said. "I know what I might find," she replied. "She's been gone over four months now. It may be more about what you don't find," Warrik added.

The proprietor of the slave market was a bit resistant to answer questions at first. After being informed that slavery was a crime to his new overlords and that he could be held to account, he became more than helpful. In the end, less than half of the refugee children were recovered; most had been sold and sent outside the city.

Leela, through an interpreter, questioned all of the slaves present after the attack on Duvortce. She finally met a slave girl after several days, who said that a girl matching the show's description had been sold with three other girls a few days after arriving.

Leela matched the timeline with the sales records and found that four of the new acquisitions had been sold around that time. She let out a frustrated sigh. "I really will have to rip this entire kingdom down brick by brick," she said.

"Did you find who she was sold to?" asked Warrik.

"She was sold to a palace slave merchant from the capital," she replied.

Chapter 23

The Third Prince

I always felt like I could come up with a plan for just about anything, but that was back when I had access to many more resources and people. I had recently hit some hard walls, and I was feeling like I was at my limit. For example, I had started running in the evening after being dismissed from the training hall. While I did initially get faster, my shorter legs and lower lung capacity held me back from keeping up with the fastest runners. I wasn't getting any better at fighting hand-to-hand or with swords.

It wasn't as if I wasn't learning anything. In fact, the boys in our special class had been teaching me lots of new techniques that were useful. However, as much as I learned from them, they learned from me. If anything had changed since our class was formed two months ago, it was that the boys had gotten better at fighting against me because of the techniques I had taught them. Leon and Dartan had moved up to first class, and Cordell had moved up to third. Every time I fought against the boys, they became more and more difficult to beat in hand-to-hand combat. Leon, Dartan, and Godwin became more adept at catching me, and I had to become more and more creative to beat them with swords. But I knew it was only a matter of time before one of them beat me.

The only place I seemed to be improving significantly was archery, and that was mostly due to the fact that I hadn't spent much time with it before. Master Alonzo would come by from time to time and watch us spar, but he never said anything.

One day, after being dismissed from the training hall, Master Alonzo caught me and told me to stay back. It was just the two of us still there.

"You seem to be losing your edge. Why is that?" he asked.

"It's because the boys are getting better, and I'm not," I replied.

"You're partly right. They are learning more from you than you are from them. As the gap in skill closes, their natural advantages in strength and physical abilities become more of a deciding factor," he explained.

"Then what am I supposed to do? Just keep teaching them everything I know until eventually they beat me?" I asked with a bitter tone.

"Stop running after training. You've done what you can until your legs and lungs grow more. Instead, come train with me and increase your skill set," Alonzo offered.

"I understand, Master. When can we start?"

"We can start right now," he replied.

I automatically went to grab a training sword from the rack, but he stopped me. "We won't need those for today's lesson," he said.

I came back and stood in front of him. Alonzo pulled out a healing rune—more specifically, my healing rune that Kriss had given me.

"How do you have that? I thought it was lost back at Kapala," I said.

"When the palace buys a slave, they buy their belongings as well. It is an option the slave market provides. It can be profound to return a personal item to a slave," said Alonzo. "However, I'm not returning this to you for any profound reason. Do you remember when we first sparred?" he asked.

"I sliced your sword with a training sword," I added.

"I was able to do that through mana control," he said. "It's actually a misconception that mages have more mana than other people. What they have is the ability to manifest it outside their bodies," he explained.

I picked up what he was putting down. "And mana control allows you to focus the mana inside your body?" I asked.

"I knew you would understand," he replied. "And that allows you to make a clean cut with something that shouldn't cut?" I asked.

"That's exactly right, but it can do so much more," he replied. He pulled out a knife and handed it to me. "See that it is sharp," he said.

I ran the end of my thumb along the edge and felt that it was indeed sharp. "Swing the blade at me," he said.

I swung the knife at him, and he caught the blade edge in his palm and pulled the knife from me. Alonzo held up his hand and showed that there was no cut. "Mana control can make your skin hard as stone. It can make your muscles as strong as iron. It can even help you move your body at incredible speed. With proper mana control, you can even cut through the mana cast by a mage," Alonzo explained.

"I believe you, Master, but why doesn't everyone use it?" I asked.

"There are some people who use it and do not even realize it. Even fewer people know it is possible. But the people who learn about this ability—only a small number even learn to use it, and even far fewer master it," he explained.

"Why is it so difficult to master?" I asked.

"Because to use it, you have to visualize what others would say is impossible and believe that it is possible." Suddenly, even more of Leela's old words came back to me, and I wondered if she had been one of those who used it without realizing it.

"So how do I learn the skill, Master?"

He handed me my healing rune and said, "For now, practice feeling the mana inside your body. Get to a point where you can recall how it feels and how it flows into this rune without thinking," he said. "That is all for today," he finished.

"Thank you, Master," I said as he turned and walked away.

As I walked back to the maids' quarters, I twirled the healing rune around in my hand. In a way, I felt like I had been reunited with an old friend. I passed under a large archway that was supported by two massive stone pillars, and as I stepped past it, I saw a man leaning back against one of the pillars.

"This is convenient," said Kona. "You got here quicker than I had expected."

"You were waiting for me?" I asked.

"Yes, His Highness, the third Prince of Multira, wants to meet with you, so please follow me," he said.

I fell in behind Kona, and we made our way to a section of the palace I had never been to before. We began to climb a circular staircase, and after ascending five floors, we came into a hallway lined with doors. Kona stopped at one of the doors in the hall and knocked on it before walking right in. Sticking right behind him, I took a look around the room. At the far end of the room, there was a large stained glass window. There were stacks of books all around the room, and sitting behind a large desk under the stained glass window was a man with white hair, busy writing on a piece of paper. Judging from what I could see of his face, he looked like he was in his early twenties.

"My Lord, I have brought Nisha here as you have requested," Kona said.

"Give me a minute; I'm almost finished with this report," he replied.

After about another minute of writing, he stopped writing and put down his quill as he looked up.

"Kona, introduce him. Nisha, this is His Highness, Garland, the third Prince of Multira."

As I looked up, my eyes met his red ones. "You stand out too much. How am I supposed to use you if you stand out too much?" said the prince.

"I might be able to answer that question if I knew what His Highness intended to use me for," I replied.

"You may want to leave for a while. I plan on discussing treason for a bit with our young friend here," said the prince.

"As I have stated before, Your Highness, when your boots swing, mine will as well," replied Kona.

"Fine, but don't say I didn't try to warn you," said the prince.

"Have a seat," said the prince, pointing at one of the chairs in front of his desk.

I sat down. "Prince, what do you know about the recent transition of power that took place last year?" he asked.

"I know that your grandfather died and your father took the throne over his older brother by taking land from Alza," I replied.

"An extremely simplistic view," said the prince, "but accurate. When my grandfather, King Letrius, died, my uncle Hildred was favored to take the throne. My father, Torland, took the throne by greatly overpromising. It wasn't just the contested lands he promised; he promised to take all of Alza. Its citizens were to become slaves, and its cities plundered," the prince explained.

Emboldened by the tone of the room, I spoke up. "Is that why the soldiers at Duvortce lied and committed a war crime?"

"Yes," replied the prince. "They thought that by the end of the war, there would be nobody to hold them accountable."

"That seems really short-sighted," I replied.

"The entire situation was so misguided," said the prince.

"Does that mean that the war is still going on?" I asked.

"It is. Multira is losing—calculating forces, supplies, population, and other figures. I predict that Multira will fall in about two years. Right now, you're probably wondering why I'm telling you all this. It's because I want your help," said the prince.

"Forgive me, Your Highness, but why would I help a country that enslaved me?" I asked, failing to hold back my anger.

"You misunderstand me. I want you to help me bring down this country even faster," he replied.

"Why would you want to hasten the destruction of your own country?" I asked.

"As much as I love my country, it has been on the decline for the last several generations. The way a despot like my father came into power is a manifestation of the depths to which it has fallen. Sometimes it's best to wipe the slate clean," he explained.

"There are close to a million people living in the city, and my father would sacrifice every one of them before surrendering or giving up power."

"I'm a ten-year-old child. How am I supposed to change that?" I asked.

"Your job would be quite simple. I need you to kill certain people for me," he replied.

"Don't you have people for that?" I asked.

"I have people that can kill, but I don't have an innocent-looking assassin that nobody would ever see coming," he replied.

"And what if I can't bring myself to kill?" I asked.

"Master Alonzo thinks you already have," he replied.

"And the people I killed? That would lead to you taking power?" I asked.

"It would lead to a peaceful surrender. Whatever happens to me after that is irrelevant. If you agree to help me, I'll give you four months to master your training with Master Alonzo and then a month with Janna to learn how to blend in at social events," said the prince.

"Four months isn't long enough! I just started today. And who is Janna?" I asked.

"Nice to meet you," said a voice right next to me. I nearly jumped out of my skin. I turned and looked to see the source of the voice. It was a woman with brown hair wearing a blue dress.

"How long were you standing there?" I asked.

"I came in the room right after you did," she replied.

"As you can see, she's very good at her craft," said the prince.

"So let me get this straight: You want me to learn from Master Alonzo in four months a skill that, by his own admission, is extremely difficult? After that, spend one month learning how to be a spy so that I can kill people you say need to die? Why should I trust you?" I asked.

"If you're smart, you'll never trust anyone. But I don't see what you have to lose by giving it a shot," he replied.

"I have an idea, Your Highness. Why not give Nisha tomorrow off? Let Janna take her into town while she thinks it over. This will also give you time to sort things out with Master Alonzo," said Kona.

"That's a good idea," agreed the prince. "What say you, Nisha?" he asked.

"This has to be a trick," I replied.

"No trick," said Janna.

"Then I'll consider your offer," I replied.

"Good. That reminds me, you won't blend in well with that around your neck," the prince said. He took out a key from his desk and tossed it over to Janna.

Janna unlocked the tracking collar and took it off my neck. For a moment, I almost broke down with tears of gratitude until I realized that I was probably their goal. I stifled the tears and denied them the victory.

"If you decide to accept, there is one other thing I need you to do. I need you to keep the techniques you learn from Master Alonzo a secret. I also need you to start losing to the knights in training. Like I said when you came in here, you stand out too much," said the prince.

"You mean for me to intentionally lose?" I asked.

"Well, don't make it obvious. I'm sure that Master Alonzo will see it, but if the boys think that they can beat you, then there won't be as much attention surrounding you as there is right now. Basically, I need you to appear to be more normal—something you obviously have a difficult time doing," said the prince.

"Why me? Why use a child to do what you could have Janna here do?" I asked.

"Janna is good at what she does, and she can kill when she needs to. But you are already mostly trained, and you are a killer. I use the assets that are available to me, and a skilled killer that my enemies will never suspect is an asset that I can definitely use," said the prince.

"Now, if you'll pardon me, I have to work," he said.

"I need to get back too. Leave your answer with Janna tomorrow." With that, he picked up his quill again and got back to writing.

"Come with me," said Janna. She took my hand and led me out of the room.

Chapter 24

Outing

Janna led me down the hallway from the room where the prince was working. At the third door down, she stopped and opened it, leading me inside. The room had a large bed made up with blankets and pillows. Laying across the bed was a green dress that looked about my size.

"This will be your room from now on. The clothes and everything in it are for you to use. My room is across the hall if you ever need anything. If I'm not there, which is often, just leave a note under the door or look for Kona. His door is to the left of mine. If there is an emergency, the prince can usually be found in his office," Janna explained.

"What happens if I refuse this offer? Will this all be taken back from me?" I asked.

"The prince has made it clear that these are to be your quarters from now on, regardless of what you decide. But I'm confident you'll say yes," replied Janna.

"You'll need this as well." She held out a pin with an engraved face of a large cat and three silver lines at the bottom. "This is the prince's signet. It will grant you access to meals from the kitchen, the bathhouse, and most of the palace," Janna explained.

"Can I still go down to the maids' quarters to visit my friends?"

"You can, but from now on, it would be best to keep your visits limited to once or twice a week, as it doesn't look well to have the princess's sponsored knight down there too often," she explained.

"I'll come by in the morning to take you out," she said. After Janna had explained everything, she turned and walked out of the room.

My sudden change of fate left me with many thoughts. There was a window in my room, and I didn't have a tracking collar on anymore. Better yet, I had a pin and clothes that would probably let me walk right out the front gate. I could almost taste my freedom. Tomorrow, I would be walking around a crowded city and could probably slip away without any problems.

Just to be absolutely sure, I went and checked the dress on the bed for any hidden runes. I couldn't find anything on it and finally decided it would make me stand out less than the training uniform. I clipped the prince's signet pin to my uniform and went down to the kitchen.

When I got there, one of the chefs pointed out the window for special orders. I went over to it, and the man behind the counter looked at the pin and asked me what I wanted.

"What can I order?" I asked.

"Anything you want," he replied.

"Fried egg sandwich with bacon and cheese," I replied.

"Take a seat; I'll bring it out when it's ready," he said.

I know what he's doing—he's trying to spoil me into agreeing, I thought to myself. Fifteen minutes later, the man who took my order brought out my food along with a drink of warm cider.

"Let me know if you need anything else," he said.

I took a bite of the sandwich, and my deprived taste buds slapped my brain with pure joy. I still won't let him win me over that easily, I thought. Tears rolled down my face.

After dinner, I decided to check out the bathhouse. It was still somewhat early in the evening, and there weren't many people there. There were several large tubs, the size of hot tubs from my previous life that had steam rolling off of them. As I climbed in and the hot water hit my skin, I thought that, as good as the sandwich was, it didn't mean much compared to the hot bath.

"I won't be bought," I kept reminding myself over and over. By the time I got back to my new room, I felt content in a way I hadn't in a long time. I started thinking about the girls back at the maids' quarters, and a sudden bolt of guilt hit me. I didn't deserve this special treatment any more than the rest of them did. Probably even less so in many cases, like Zora, who was taking the time to teach the other girls a valuable skill.

It was too late to go see them that night, but I promised myself I'd visit them after. No, I was planning on escaping tomorrow, wasn't I? I thought to myself as I lay down on the bed in my room. Every muscle in my body was finally able to relax, as it was the first soft bed I had lain on since Varlyn.

"I'm going to enjoy this, but it doesn't mean I have to like it," I said to myself.

"Time to get ready," said Janna. She stood over me, her sudden appearance startling me, but I was soon thrown off by something else. "Wasn't your hair a different color yesterday?" I asked.

"It was," she replied. Her hair had been brown the day before, but now it was bright red.

"Your eyes seem different, too. Did you use eye lenses to change their color?" I asked.

"Eye lenses? What are those?" she asked.

"Small round pieces of glass that go over your eyes," I replied.

"That sounds painful. I'm a Triad," she explained.

"I've never heard of that before. What's a Triad?"

"Some people are born with the ability to be mages, but most aren't. Some people are born as a Triad and have the ability to use mana to change their appearance—about one in every half million, according to what the prince tells me."

Just then, Janna changed her hair from red to blonde and then back to red again as a demonstration. "That's amazing! But isn't it dangerous showing me this?" I asked.

"I have several different identities I use throughout the palace. Today, I will be Tina, the prince's escort, taking you out of the palace. It's important that you call me by the right name, so that's why I'm showing you now. Hurry up and get dressed," she said.

At the back of the palace, where I had been offloaded as a slave, there was a carriage waiting for us. It felt strange getting a ride that didn't involve chains. The carriage took off as soon as we were inside.

"So how will you try to bribe me today?" I asked.

"Oh, that's such a harsh way to think of this! His Highness's goodwill," she replied playfully.

"I won't give anything away, so you'll just have to be patient," she added.

"I can make a run for it, you know," I said.

"I'll make you a deal: give me today to convince you to work for Prince Garland. If I can't convince you by the end, I'll have the carriage take you anywhere you want, and I'll give you enough money to get back home," said Janna.

"But only if I have your word that you'll give me a day," she added. She held out her hand. I felt that the offer was too good to be true, but I could play along for a day. Janna held her hand out, and I shook it.

"Potoma is the coastal city, and as our carriage took us closer to the ports, the smell of the ocean became more pronounced. As we came over the top of a large hill, I could see most of the city.

"Janna, can we stop here for a minute?" I asked.

She signaled the driver to stop, and he pulled the carriage off to the side of the road.

"What's wrong?" asked Janna.

"Nothing specific. I just want a moment here," I replied.

I hopped out of the carriage and took in the sights and smells. The ships with their tall white sails were floating about in the harbor. Carts, wagons, carriages, and people could be seen traversing the streets.

"It felt strange seeing people move about freely," I said to Janna.

"Haven't you seen it before?" she asked.

"Many times, but I guess not seeing it for a while reminded me how beautiful it is," I replied.

I felt this way once before—after being reborn. I had spent the last decade of my previous life incarcerated. I guess that after enough time, even the most traumatic experiences begin to fade. Not completely, but enough that it takes a reminder to fill them again.

After looking over the city for a few minutes, I climbed back inside the carriage. "I'm good now," I said to Janna.

"I think we should start with food first," said Janna.

The carriage took us to a part of the city that looked like a shopping plaza. Once we stopped, Janna hopped out of the carriage, and I followed her. We came to a shop that had tables and chairs set up under an awning. Janna sat down, and I took a chair directly across from her.

"This place has some of the best food in the city. Would you trust me to order for you?" asked Janna.

"It's your day. Surprise me," I said.

"Has anyone ever told you that the way you speak doesn't match the way you look?" asked Janna.

"I've been told that before," I replied.

A man in a white shirt came over to us, and Janna gave him our order.

"What do you think of the city so far?" asked Janna.

"At first glance, it looks like a civilized place to live. You wouldn't expect it to be filled with war criminals and slavers," I replied.

"I wouldn't argue that it doesn't harbor its fair share of those. Would you judge the capital of Elris by its worst inhabitants?" asked Janna.

"No, but if I did, its reputation would still be cleaner than that of Potoma," I replied.

"Is that your angle? To convince me that not all the people here in the city are bad?" I asked.

"No, I just thought it was only fair to point out that the worst elements should not represent everyone from the same city," she replied.

"Do you really believe that the third prince will do what he said and surrender if he comes to power?" I asked.

"I do," replied Janna.

"How can you trust him so much?" I asked.

"The prince isn't like his father and older brothers. He's never sought power for his own sake," she replied.

I was about to argue further when our food finally arrived. It was a large piece of cake with thinly sliced fruit of some kind on top of it.

"This is dessert, not breakfast," I stated.

"Calm down; it's time for dessert," she said with a smile.

Somewhere, the oddly familiar saying caught me off guard, and I couldn't help but laugh a little.

"I know you've been through a lot recently, but you should really take a moment to enjoy things," said Janna.

"The girls who came to Potoma with me can't enjoy this with me," I protested.

"Then try to enjoy it for them until you can bring them here with you," replied Janna. "Besides, it's already served, so you might as well enjoy it," she added.

I reluctantly took a bite of it. It tasted like cheesecake and was absolutely delicious. "It tastes really good! What is it called?" I asked.

"Well, you can name yours whatever you like," she joked, "but the dish is called cheesecake. It's a specialty dish from Berosa," she explained.

It must have been one of his creations, I thought to myself. I felt nostalgic eating something sweet from my past life. I never cared for sweets back then, but as Nisha, I was pretty fond of them. They were far less plentiful in this world, though.

"I could be mistaken, but is that a smile on your face?" asked Janna.

"No, it must be your imagination," I protested.

I decided that motives aside, I liked Janna, but I still didn't trust her. After we finished eating, Janna paid our bill, and we got back into the carriage.

"What place are you going to try to spoil me at next?" I asked.

"Just be patient," she said. "You'll see soon enough," replied Janna.

As we continued down the road, we passed a wagon with a slave cage on it. The cage was empty, and soon we passed another one. Soon, there were rows and rows of slave wagons. The carriage pulled up to a building that was much larger than the surrounding ones by about five or six times. Janna climbed out of the carriage and motioned for me to follow her.

There was a massive archway that led into a building filled with people coming and going. Some of the people in the archway were wearing slave collars. I recognized the stench from my time in Kapala.

"Why are you taking me into the slave market?" I asked.

"I think you need to see this," said Janna.

As we finished passing through the archway, the building opened up into a large circular arena where the slaves would be. In a normal arena, there were hundreds of display cages filled with thousands of slaves—both female and male—of all ages. The scale of this slave market put the one in Kapala to shame by multiple orders of magnitude.

As we walked past the cages filled with young boys about five to seven years old, I could see that the light and hope had gone out of them all. "Are all of these slaves coming from the war?" I asked.

"Very few are coming from that. Most are captured from other countries, born as slaves, or sold back after being owned once before," explained Janna. "You see, all of this cruelty and suffering is what the prince wishes to end," she said.

Janna stopped in front of a cage of young women in their late teens and early twenties. The side of the cage listed a price of $500. "You see, these ones have lost value due to illness, deformity, or other reasons," explained Janna. "This is where the prince found me," she said.

I looked at her face, and all I saw was a cold, empty stare as she looked at the cage. Her pleasant demeanor from earlier had completely vanished. "What do you suppose will happen to all these slaves—the ones throughout the city, the ones that the palace owns—if the city comes under siege?" I asked.

"You have a chance to help all of them if you accept the prince's offer," Janna said.

I swallowed a large lump that formed in my throat. "I get your point, but I'm still just one person—one child. What could I possibly do that you or Master Alonzo couldn't?" I asked.

"The men and women who control this country are cowards. They're guarded and cautious around adult men, and especially around unknown pretty women. But to them, a small child of 10 or 11 is nothing to fear. It's something they believe they could control. You could walk right past their defenses," Janna explained.

"It sounds a lot like a one-way trip to me," I replied.

"It could be, and that's a risk you'll have to accept. However, with proper planning, I think you could take down many of those causing the suffering in this city or this country," said Janna.

I looked around at all the cages, at all the people being treated like cattle. "You win. If I have a chance to help these people and those like them, I'll agree to help. I can't guarantee that I'll be able to master the training from Master Alonzo," I said.

"You seem like a reliable person. I'm sure you'll figure it out," said Janna. "I think you have more faith in me than I do. Four months to master something that few people ever do is a tall order," I said.

"I think you should try to have a bit more faith in yourself," replied Janna.

As we began to walk out of the slave market, I became lost in thought for a moment. "There's something I don't understand. Why does the prince want me to start losing my fights with the other knights in training? I know he said it's because I stand out too much, but he wants me to become more obscure. But as his sponsored knight, won't it tarnish his standing and reputation if I'm looked at as incompetent?" I asked.

"That may be an issue, and I don't know the answer myself. What I can tell you is that the prince has already taken that into his calculations," explained Janna.

"I really hope you're right about him; otherwise, this will all end in disaster," I said.

"Try to have faith," Janna replied.

Chapter 25

Losing

After coming back to the palace from my outing with Janna, we reported back to the prince and told him that I had agreed to join his cause. "There's a lot at stake, so make sure to do your best," he stated.

As I was getting ready for bed that evening, I remembered that I was supposed to be working on the lesson assigned by Master Alonzo—something I had neglected to do the night before. I pulled out my healing rune and started feeding it mana. Feeling the flow into the rune was easy; it was almost second nature to me. In a way, it felt like the mana was being pulled out of me.

I dared to rest my fingertips where I could feel the flow the strongest and tried to trace it back up my arm into my body. I could feel it up to about my wrist before the sensation became too diffused to feel anymore. I tried feeling it the other way, and I could sense some sort of sensation in the stone. I focused on the sensation I could feel in my fingers and hands as I fed the rune.

I put it down. Without the rune in my hands, I imagined the flow of mana there, but nothing was there. Remembering that visualization was important to the process, I imagined that I still had the rune in my hands and that I was feeding it mana. I felt the slightest stirring in my fingers. The feeling was so faint that I almost wondered if I was just imagining it.

Real or not, I kept up the practice and tried to focus on the flow of mana. It was slow, but after about fifteen minutes, the stirring in my fingers became stronger until I was certain that the feeling wasn't imaginary. Finally satisfied with my progress, I ended my practice and went to sleep.

The next morning, as I was standing in the training hall, I had all but forgotten about my training session on mana flow and was now focused on how to start losing gracefully with grappling and hand-to-hand fighting. It would be simple, as I didn't usually win anyway. I typically just evaded them until a draw was called. All I had to do was let them catch me.

As for sword training, I had always won, but the gap for victory was closing as they became more accustomed to my fighting style and learned my techniques. I would need to make it appear as if that gap had finally closed. My first opponent in hand-to-hand fighting was Dartan. I had beaten him several times with joint manipulation techniques, but as he learned to break away from me, it happened less and less often.

Godwin signaled for us to begin, and Dartan shot after me. I evaded his first attack. A sudden thought entered my head: did I need to lose all my matches from here on out, or just enough to make it appear that I had lost whatever edge I had? The prince hadn't specified, and I couldn't just go ask Master Alonzo during training. I decided to play it safe for the day and only lose half my fights.

I took a swing at Dartan, and he held my arm out for just an instant longer than he should have. Dartan latched onto my arm and tossed me out of the circle. We bowed to each other after his victory.

"What happened there? It looked like you were distracted or lost in thought, the way you paused," said Dartan.

"Oh, crap," I thought to myself. I shrugged. "I guess I was a little... I'll focus more next time," I replied. I needed to be careful not to let it look too obvious.

My next fight was with Cordell, and it was an easy win for me, as his physical advantages weren't as pronounced as the older boys. After we finished hand-to-hand training and moved on to sword training, things became a bit more complex. I had never lost before, so it would need to feel absolutely real for whoever took the first win from me.

My first opponent was Leon. Leon was a technical fighter and was quick to pick up on what was working and what wasn't. I decided to slightly reduce my counters. I figured that would be the perfect handicap to make his win believable—or so I thought. Leon seemed to be having an off day and kept leaving himself wide open. If I didn't press the advantage, it would have been too obvious.

"Off day?" I asked.

"Maybe. I'm not too sure what's going on," replied Leon.

That seemed a little too unlike him to believe, but I supposed anything was possible. I still had Godwin to fight, and losing to him should be straightforward. He had me beat by a wide margin in most categories, and defeating him was a challenge on more than one occasion. He had nearly defeated me; it was only through quick thinking and improvising that I had been able to clutch the win from him during those fights.

The match began, and as our swords began to clash against each other, it became more of a dance than a fight. I began to wonder if he was taking it easy on me as he passed up multiple opportunities to press on openings.

Godwin lowered his training sword. "What's going on with you today?" asked Godwin.

"I'm not sure what you mean," I replied dumbly.

"You haven't taken a single fight seriously today. It's like you've only halfway here," he said. I noticed something was off, too.

"It was like the fire you normally have inside of you went out," said Leon. "Did something happen when you were gone yesterday?"

"Not really, but I suppose I have a lot on my mind lately," I replied.

"What's it about?" asked Dartan.

"If it's all the same to you, I'd rather not talk about it," I replied.

"Come on, we're a special team. You can tell us about it," said Leon.

I tried to think of a way out when suddenly an old memory from my past life popped into my mind. "It's girl troubles," I finally replied.

"It was a complete lie, of course," I thought to myself.

"I have boy troubles all the time," said Cordell.

Leon smacked Cordell on the back of the head. "What was that for?" asked Cordell.

"Just shut your mouth! I'll explain it to you later," said Leon.

"This is going to keep being an issue because if I'm going to defeat you, I want it to be when you're at your best," said Godwin.

"I'll get things sorted out by tomorrow," I replied.

"Glad to hear it. That's enough training for today; you are dismissed," Godwin said.

I won't lie; that kind of power is dangerous. Boys will do just about anything to avoid talking about girl issues. As good as it felt, I needed to be careful not to abuse that power, I thought to myself.

As the training hall cleared out, Master Alonzo was waiting for me. "Were you able to pick up on the flow of mana inside your body?" he asked.

"A little, but it was really faint—like a whisper. I couldn't feel much past my hands," I admitted.

"Flow is easy to feel, especially at the point where it is moving into or out of your body. It is much more difficult to feel the mana pulled inside your body. If it helps, think of it like a pool of water. The inlet and outlet are easy to detect, but unless something disturbs the pool and makes waves or ripples, it will sit motionless. With enough practice, it becomes possible to feel small currents in the mana within your body, but that can take many years of practice," he explained.

"The prince has told me that he's giving you four months to master this training, so we will need to take a more direct approach."

"What is the direct approach?" I asked.

"By disturbing the mana pool within your body directly, you'll be able to feel the ripples and gain sensation of your mana flow," he replied.

"How do we disturb the mana pool, Master?"

"If you are hit by someone using mana control, there will be a disruption in your mana pool. The disruption will only be slight, so it is important to shut out all other sensations, including pain. Focus only on the disruption," explained Alonzo.

"So I get hit really hard, and that allows me to feel the mana inside of me?" I asked.

"Try to think of it like body hardening. It will be difficult to handle at first, but you can build up resistance to it," said Alonzo.

"This is really going to hurt, isn't it?" I asked.

"That's up to you. Pain is in the mind, and the quicker you can sense your mana flow, the less you'll need to endure," he explained.

"Are you willing to go through with it?"

"Yes, I'm ready, Master."

"Close your eyes. Let it be a surprise. As much as you can, remember to ignore the pain," he instructed.

I closed my eyes, and a few seconds later, a foot hit me square in the chest and sent me flying. The force of the kick knocked the air out of my lungs. I knew I was supposed to ignore the pain, but as my back bounced off the ground and my lungs fought to get air back inside them, all I could feel was pain.

When I finally started breathing again, I sat up. "Were you able to sense anything?" he asked.

"Only the shock and the pain," I replied.

"Take a moment to practice with your healing rune. Hold it up to your chest and feed it mana."

I held my healing rune next to the place Master Alonzo had hit me and began feeding it mana. I felt the flow going into it and tried to trace the flow back up my hands. The sensation still just separated at my wrist, but the flow of mana going into the rune was increasing and decreasing slightly.

"I still can't feel my mana pool, but I did feel the rate of mana fluctuating as it was feeding the rune," I reported.

"I can't say that we're any closer, but at least we're on the right path," said Alonzo.

"What do you mean by that? Isn't this how you learned?"

"Master, absolutely not. The way I learned was the slow way, by gradually learning to feel the currents," he replied.

"Have you ever taught someone this way before?" I asked.

"No, this method is based on my hypothesis," he replied.

"So I'm probably getting kicked around for nothing?" I asked.

"Not for nothing. We should at least discover if it's a viable method," he replied.

"Thank you, Master. That will make the pain so much easier to endure," I said sarcastically.

"That's enough complaining. Are you ready to try again?"

"Yeah," I replied.

I closed my eyes and said, "I'm ready."

This time, I was struck from behind and face-planted. I tried again to push past the pain, but by the time I could sense my mana, all I could feel was the flow and fluctuation. As I got back to my feet, I started pouring mana into the healing rune and was struck by an idea.

I closed my eyes again and was pouring mana into the rune when I shouted, "Master, hit me again!" As the blow hit me, I felt a wave surge clear through my body, like I was sensing a new dimension to myself for the first time. The wave bounced through me a couple of times before it vanished.

I got back up to my feet. Master Alonzo was staring at me as if he was asking a question. "I felt it, Master! I can't fully describe it; it was like seeing it for the first time, but I could only hold it open for a second," I explained.

"That sounds about right. For me, it was like slowly learning to open my eyes for the first time," he explained. "Remember that sensation and try to visualize it when you practice tonight. I think we've covered enough for today," he said.

"Master, before you leave, I need to discuss something with you," I said.

"What is it?" he asked.

"The prince has instructed me to start losing to the boys so that I don't draw too much attention to myself. I tried holding back so that they could win, but they know how I fight and can tell that I was throwing the fights."

"I see, so that's what was going on today. I was wondering what was wrong with you," said Alonzo.

"Before I give you an answer, I want you to consider something. Those boys have had to earn everything they were ever given, so I want you to imagine how insulting it was to throw off the fight and give them something they hadn't earned."

Looking at it from that perspective, I realized how condescending it must have been to them. "As for what to do about it, I suggest that you try the honest approach," he added.

"I can't tell them why the prince ordered me to start losing," I replied.

"I don't mean that you should tell them everything, but I think that if you explain to them that your sponsor wants you to stand out less, they may be more willing to help you out. Also, as long as you don't use any of the new techniques I'm teaching you, it won't be long until they can win on their own talent," he explained.

"I appreciate the advice, Master. What should I tell them if they ask why my sponsor doesn't want me standing out?" I asked.

"His Highness typically keeps to himself. It won't be hard to imagine that he wants his servants to have a low profile as well," he said.

"Thank you, Master," I replied.

"If you don't have anything else to ask, I'll see you tomorrow," said Alonzo.

I had to be warming up. The next day, we split into our classes as normal. I walked up to Godwin. "Can I have a minute to speak before we begin?"

"That's fine," he said.

"I need to apologize for yesterday," I said.

"Oh, don't even mention it. Things happen," said Leon.

"No, I do need to apologize because I lied to you," I said.

"What are you talking about?" asked Godwin.

"I lied about why I was throwing the fights," I said.

"You mean it wasn't girl problems?" asked Cordell.

"No, it wasn't," I replied. "Please just hear me out."

"I hope this better be good because that was dirty," said Leon.

"My sponsor wants me to have a low profile, and to do that, he said I should start losing fights so that I'll have less attention on me."

"Why does it matter how much you stand out? I think you deserve to be recognized," said Leon. "I would still be a slave working as a maid if it wasn't for the third prince."

"But he wants his servants to be less noticeable," I replied.

"Well, I don't know if he'll get that when it comes to you," said Godwin, "but you should have told us this yesterday."

"I know, and that's why I'm asking for your forgiveness," I replied.

"Let us beat you fair and square, and we'll call it forgotten," said Leon.

"He's right. Besides, we know that the only reason we're even getting close to winning is because we're older and stronger. If we were all the same size, we wouldn't stand a chance," said Dartan.

"Just be honest with us, and we'll help you out," said Godwin.

"Thanks for understanding," I replied, knowing I had to keep Alonzo's training a secret.

Chapter 26

Breakthrough

Ever since the discovery of how to fill my mana pool with Master Alonzo, progress had stopped. Although I could now sense my mana pool momentarily, it was nothing more than fleeting glimpses. A week had passed since I first felt it, and my training sessions felt more like piñata control than mana control. I could ignore the pain better, but that was about the only thing getting better.

On a positive note, the boys in the special class and I had worked out a system for losing fights: a deep bow before the fight, take the fight seriously, whereas a short moment could be thrown. A few of the boys from the other classes saw my recent losses as grounds to make snide comments at me, but they quickly stopped after Leon challenged them to a duel and destroyed them.

I'm not going to lie; it felt kind of nice having a friend stand up for me like that. I also managed to get down to the maids' quarters from time to time. Oddly enough, there were now more people who resented me in the maids' quarters than with the knights in training. Even some of the girls I used to spar with would no longer talk to me. Still, it wasn't all bad. Zora told me that most of the girls had become inspired by my recent rise in status. Seeing my tracking collar removed and the third prince's signet pin on me had given them hope of one day rising above their station.

"Did you ever find out what happens to the older girls?" I asked after noticing that I hadn't seen Theresa since I moved out of the maids' quarters.

"It isn't as bad as some of us, I guess. Most ended up working here in the palace as part of the staff. I've heard that some go to work for other nobles, but I've also heard that some are resold as slaves," Zora explained.

"That still isn't right. I'll find a way to get you out before something like that happens," I said.

"Don't worry about me; I'll be fine," said Zora.

"I will worry about you and the rest of the maids," I replied.

"What will you do, break us all out of the palace?" asked Zora in a playful tone.

"If it comes down to that, I just might," I replied with a straight face.

As I laid in bed that night, trying to practice mana control, I stopped for a moment to consider everything I had learned so far. Flow was easy to feel, and when my mana pool was full, the flow rate would fluctuate. When Master Alonzo disrupted my mana flow, I could feel it, but only for a few moments. When I closed my eyes, I could recreate the flow through visualization, so why couldn't I recreate the sensation of my mana pool?

It was like a familiar concept that my mind couldn't quite wrap itself around. The thought suddenly came to me, and I wondered if I could somehow disrupt my own mana pool. I took my healing rune and smacked it against my forehead. It wasn't much, but the slightest stirring happened. I hit myself again, but even harder. It was enough to make my mana pool reveal itself to me.

I held on to the sensation for as long as I could, but like every time before, it vanished. I repeated the process again, but this time I immediately hit myself over and over again. I must have looked like a mad person smacking my forehead repeatedly, but the result was worth it. My mana pool stayed visible to me, and I began to feel it out. It was like swimming through a sea of light, and the process of hitting myself with the runestone was making waves throughout my body.

Apart from the waves, I could feel a gentle current that I hadn't been able to feel before. After a few minutes, I stopped hitting myself with the rune, and for the first time, the pool remained visible to me. It slowly faded away over the course of a few minutes, but it had definitely been present much longer than ever before. I repeated this process a few more times and discovered that the more I kept hitting myself, the longer the disruption in my mana pool stayed. Eventually, I had to call it quits; even though the healing rune was healing the skin when I hit myself, the area I was hitting was getting more tender.

The next day, I shared my discovery with Master Alonzo. I told him how many smaller but more frequent disruptions allowed me to sense my mana pool for a longer period of time.

"I see. So it's more like using repeated motion to rock a boat instead of one solid motion," he said.

"Exactly. So how do we keep rocking the boat?" I asked.

"It sounds like you came up with the solution last night, but I can see how having someone else help would free you up to focus on your mana pool. I'll try using mana control to generate the disruption. I'll start off with a lower intensity and increase it until you can feel it working," said Alonzo.

He took out a training sword from the rack and started tapping my shoulder with it. I closed my eyes and began to focus.

"I'm going to increase the intensity. Let me know when you sense your mana pool," he said.

By the time my shoulder began to sting, I told Master Alonzo that I could feel my mana pool. I then began to block out the pain and focus on sensing the mana.

"I feel it! What do I do with it now?" I asked.

"Try to play with it. Swirl it around. Direct its movement," he replied.

I began to visualize it swirling, and soon the current began to form. I tried to force the current into my hands or feet, but it had a mind of its own and became unwieldy. Master Alonzo stopped tapping my shoulder, and the waves began to die down.

I discovered that I could keep the sensation going as long as I visualized the current.

"I feel it, but I can't make it do what I want," I said.

"It's part of you, so think of it like moving your arms and legs," he replied.

"How do I do that?" I asked.

"The same way you learn to walk: build the muscles, learn to stand, find your balance, take baby steps," he said.

After an hour of training and getting no further with control, Master Alonzo called an end to our training.

"How are you feeling?" he asked.

"My shoulder stings, but I'm finally getting to a point where it's easier to sense my mana pool," I replied.

"That's good. Don't become frustrated; you've already come further in just a few days than I did in years," he said.

By the end of the first month of my training with Master Alonzo, I could independently sense my mana pool. I was learning to manipulate its movements, but not to any practical degree. I was standing in front of a wooden training dummy that I had been punching with my bare fist for the past ten minutes.

According to Master Alonzo, all I needed to do was feed mana into my fist, then visualize my fist becoming as solid as a rock. Then I could punch the dummy all I wanted without breaking any bones or skin. My swollen red knuckles meant that I probably wasn't doing something right.

"Master, I've heard that seeing is believing. Can you show me that this is possible?"

"I already showed you once, and I'm not destroying another dummy simply because of your lack of vision," he replied. "You need to know that your fist is solid. Clear out all doubts," he added.

"That's what I'm doing," I replied.

"The dummy says you are not! Now try it again," said Alonzo.

I cleared my mind, focused my mana into my hand, and punched the dummy. My hand started bleeding as one of the knuckles split.

"What motion are you feeling before you hit?" asked Alonzo.

"Mostly frustration, but I tried to clear out all emotions and focus only on visualization," I replied.

"The ability to visualize can lean heavily on emotion," said Alonzo.

"What motion should I have when punching a dummy?" I asked.

"I don't know; it is different for everyone. But make it an emotion you felt when you were successful at something," said Alonzo.

"So positive emotion?" I asked.

"I don't know. Some are only successful when they're angry or upset," he replied.

I closed my eyes and thought about the first time I rode Elvis. It was one of my most cherished memories. I opened my eyes, cleared my thoughts, and put mana into my fist. I once again visualized my fist being as hard as a rock. I punched the dummy as hard as I could, and when my fist made contact, a reverberating shockwave was sent up my arm. I started shaking my whole arm as it stung.

Master Alonzo was laughing, as if he had just witnessed the funniest event in history. I knew what happened, but it didn't make it any less annoying.

"Why didn't you warn me?" I asked.

"I figured someone as smart as you would know you'd need to put some mana into your muscles as well. You're kind of an idiot for how smart you are. But look, your hand is fine and left an imprint in the wood," he said.

I had indeed left the shape of two of my knuckles in the wood, and my hand wasn't bleeding.

"You're doing great! Do what you did last time; just put some mana into your arm muscles as well as your hand."

It took a few minutes to clear my head of Master Alonzo's laughter. Once I had a clear head, I thought of Elvis again and brought mana into my hand and arm muscles. I braced my feet, then visualized my arm as strong as Elvis's legs and my hand as hard as stone, and punched the dummy as hard as I could. The base of the dummy snapped in half, and the top part went flying across the room.

I now had another happy moment to recall.

"I knew you'd figure it out! Now let's move on to the next lesson," said Alonzo.

Interlude 3

Richette was by no means one of the largest cities in Multira, but its population was still close to 100,000. After the victory over Kapala, when the city fell in less than a day, expectations among the combined forces of Alza and Elris were high. Richette was the next obstacle in carving a path to the capital.

Unfortunately for the combined forces, Multira had also learned from the battle of Kapala. Everyone inside the city was scrutinized for potential betrayal. To compound issues, Richette had a major academy. After the initial siege, it became clear to the combined forces that Richette would not be as easy prey as the last city had been. Over 50,000 troops surrounded the city, and after three months of fighting, the walls had still not been breached.

To discuss the stalemate they currently faced, the 22nd meeting was called between Duke Andarol and his commanding officers. As they came together inside the Duke's tent, he asked for a progress report.

"My sharpshooters have taken out two more mages, but it's becoming more difficult to get clear shots at them. They have figured out that whatever keeps killing them requires a direct line of sight," reported General LeRoy.

"And what about you, General? Any progress using mages or the cannon crews to blast through the walls?" Andarol asked.

"It's still a stalemate. As fast as we can blast through, they repair the walls with earth magic," replied LeRoy.

"We can't simply starve them into submission. Reports from inside the city suggest that they have enough supplies to hold out for over a year. That's a year of resources and time we cannot afford to spend on one city. I need ideas," said Andarol.

"One of my mages suggests that we might be able to tunnel under the wall using earth magic. The problem is that it would be easy for the enemy to detect a project of that scale. The solution is to draw their attention away from the area we would tunnel under," explained LeRoy.

"Do you think you could provide a distraction big enough to facilitate

190

this project?" Andarol asked.

"We would need to pull back forces from sections of the city. They might think that they're reinforcing for another attack, but if it were me in their position, I'd be very suspicious," replied LeRoy.

"I'd say it might be possible," Andarol said. "Mark that as a backup plan. Then what else have you got?" he asked.

"We could gather up a few dozen alley cats under the cover of darkness and catapult them over the wall. That could create a big enough distraction for an assault," said LeRoy.

"By the elements! You must have dropped on your head as a child! Is this a serious plan, or are you just jesting?" asked Andarol.

"I'm absolutely serious, my Lord! We already have twelve of them caged up. My estimation is that we would need between thirty to forty of them to create a large enough distraction. What I mean by catapulting is that mages would use air magic to toss them up over the wall. They've already been practicing and think they can do it without killing the cats," explained LeRoy.

"Do you think you can round up enough cats to pull it off?" Andarol asked.

"There should be more than enough based on how long it took to catch the ones we have," replied LeRoy.

"My Lord, you can't be serious considering this lunacy!" exclaimed Lila.

"We've been stuck here for three months at this point. I'll try just about anything. If you have a better idea, I'm all ears," said Andarol.

Lila started rubbing her temples. "All right, I guess we're doing this. What do you need me to do?" she asked.

"Round up your hunters. I have a couple of mages that can cast sleeping spells. We'll both spend the next week rounding up all the dangerous wildlife we can, to include enduras and saber bears," said LeRoy.

"You seriously want us to go after enduras? Some of them can weigh over two tons!" said Lila.

"My mages told me they could get them over the wall," said LeRoy.

"Once we have enough animals, I'll need you to do a nighttime assault while we clear out any watchmen and send them over the wall," he added.

"This is so stupid," Lila admitted.

"I'll admit it's highly unconventional, but you have your orders. Get to it," said Andarol.

A little over a week later, forty-three alley cats, twelve saber bears, and three enduras—think of an oversized badger—had been rounded up. About a dozen men lost their lives trapping the enduras.

"I hope this wild plan of yours works," said Lila.

"Sorry about your men, but if this works, they'll save thousands that we would lose in a direct siege," replied LeRoy.

"Will it work?" asked Lila.

"My gut says it might," replied LeRoy.

"Elements help us," said Lila.

The assault began at 2 in the morning. Troops had been pulled from all around the city; the cannon crews began firing first, supported by mages casting spells. Large berms of dirt had been brought up by earth magic, and as one force was blasting them apart, another inside the city was putting them back together. It looked like an unending cycle that would only end when one side ran out of mana.

On the far side of the city, guards had been pulled to reinforce the side being assaulted. All that remained were a few watchmen. LeRoy and his troops advanced under the cover of darkness. When they got closer to the wall, the sharpshooters that had been borrowed from Lila started taking out the remaining watchmen.

"I could end this war in less than a month if I had an army of those," thought LeRoy.

With the wall cleared, he quickly advanced up to the wall. No doubt the sound of the gunshots had alerted more troops who would be there shortly.

It seemed to work in unison to lift all the sedated animals up over the wall. Some of them would probably be killed before they woke up, but it was time. As some of them were beginning to stir, when the last of the animals were over the wall, LeRoy's troops fell back to safety.

About fifteen minutes after the animals had been sent over the walls, the screams of terrified soldiers could be heard. LeRoy, with a force of over 20,000 soldiers, began his assault on the city. The chaos inside the city worked, and very little resistance was brought against LeRoy's assault. Within several hours, the stalemate had been broken, and the city of Richette was overrun by the forces of Elris and Alza.

By noon, with the city's defenses divided, the assault force finally broke through the walls. By that evening, the two forces met up inside the city.

"I think you owe me an apology," said LeRoy.

"It was still a stupid idea," replied Lila.

"Look where you are," said LeRoy.

"I'll admit that it worked, and I apologize for the insults I directed at you. I can only imagine what historians will write about this," replied Lila.

"All right, then. I was successful," said LeRoy.

At that moment, Warrik came riding up to the duo. "Where have you been, Master Warrik?" asked LeRoy.

Warrik had fresh scratches on the side of his face. "I was cleaning up your mess. You got lucky that most of the animals were dead by the time you reached the wall."

"What was your plan if they were still alive?" asked Warrik.

"I would have conscripted them," replied LeRoy with a wide grin on his face.

"I still can't tell if you're an idiot or a genius," said Lila.

"It's a fine line," replied LeRoy.

Chapter 27

All About Mana Control

They say that nothing in life is free, and that is particularly true when it comes to using mana control. The amount of mana you seem to use is proportional to the energy requirements of the demands you place upon it. For example, strengthening my legs to jump four feet into the air uses significantly less mana than jumping eight feet. Likewise, using mana to block an attack increases the demand; the harder the hit is, the more mana it takes.

One of the results of all this was that the number of direct attacks I could block from Master Alonzo went from one to between four to eight, depending on how much he enhanced his own strength. Mana fatigue is a concept well known among mages; the lower the mana pool becomes, the more exhausted and lethargic they feel, until eventually, they can't manifest any more magic or cast spells.

The mana expenditure for mana control is more directly linked to the source than through manifestation. As a result, mana fatigue could happen much faster through mana control than through spell casting. The first time this happened to me, I was blocking a direct attack from Master Alonzo. I had overextended myself and immediately collapsed to the ground, unable to move for a few minutes. When I finally began to recover, every muscle and bone in my body ached.

This lesson taught me the importance of sensing and keeping track of my mana pool. Mana control could also send mana into objects I was in physical contact with by visualizing it as an extension of my body. This was how Master Alonzo had cut through my training sword during our first duel. Just as I learned that I could harden my fist, I could also enhance the strength of any weapon I held. In theory, I could defend myself against an opponent with a metal blade if all I had was a stick—or even my bare hands.

In reality, that would be a very short fight before I ran out of mana. Another way to explain it is that mana has the ability to enhance the existing properties of the user or object. A sharp steel blade will use much less mana to cut through something solid than a mana-enhanced wooden sword. The lesson this teaches is that you need to be careful about what you enhance and how much mana you use on it. I could block a sword with my bare hand once or twice, but unless I wanted to end up incapacitated on the floor, I better find something more solid than my hand to defend myself.

Where I had really come into my own with mana enhancement was my speed. By the end of four months, I could become adept enough with mana control that I could keep pace with Master Alonzo, and I had even managed to get a couple of wins against him. Sparring with Master Alonzo became the only time I could really cut loose; it was one of the few outlets I had for my building frustration.

My mastery of mana control had come with a cost. During the morning warm-up when I ran, I could have easily used mana control to be first every time I started with the boys in my class. I was frustrated to not be able to reach out and take the tool I had access to for an easy victory. It was like being armed with my guns again and not being able to use them. I had to keep reminding myself that it wasn't a complete waste because it forced me to focus on my technique.

I had become more proficient at countering the natural advantages of the boys. Our serious fights were now about 50/50 on who would win, except with Cordell, whom I still beat every time. Cordell, Dartan, Leon, and Godwin were now at the top of first class. With the exception of Cordell, he was stuck much the same way I was, with his body being the limiting factor. Still, he had managed to make it to the top of second class, and as he grew, it was only a matter of time before he would get his five wins to be in first class.

Those of noble birth that made up the rest of the knights in training knew or suspected that it was the techniques and skills that the special class learned from me that had helped them rise to the top. However, I think it was simply too much for their pride to admit. In their minds, I was still nothing more than a girl—nothing more than a slave. Rumors began to circulate that my class was receiving special training from Master Alonzo.

It was true that one of us was, but it had nothing to do with them getting their noble butts kicked by my classmates. It brought forth a sense of pride when I watched my detractors being defeated by my friends.

After training had ended for the day, Dartan came up to me and, for what felt like the hundredth time, asked, "When are you going to tell us what kind of training you've been doing with Master Alonzo?"

"I've told you before, I'm not allowed to talk about it," I replied.

At that moment, Master Alonzo walked up to our class. "I want all of you to stay back today and observe my training with Nisha," he said.

"Master, will the third prince approve of it?" I asked.

"He's already approved of it thanks to the training techniques you helped develop. I think I can train others without needing years to develop a sense of their mana pool. Seeing is believing; well, that should be covered after today's demonstration, so don't hold back," he said.

After the training hall was all but empty, our group moved to a secluded area where Master Alonzo and I had been training. We had moved far beyond wooden training swords that couldn't keep up with the level of mana control we both used in training sessions, and now kept steel blades on hand for our practice.

I picked up two blades and tossed one to Master Alonzo as our special audience watched in silence. Alonzo and I bowed to each other, then we picked our blades up. We stood still for a moment, as if the room had been frozen in time. I made the first move. I pushed mana into my legs, and in an instant, I closed the distance between us. Sparks flew as our blades clashed. Without mana control, they would have broken.

I dashed around Master Alonzo, striking and probing for any weaknesses. His feet stayed planted as he read and countered all of my moves. He stood as an immovable object, and I needed to become an unstoppable force to overcome him. I dashed from one side to the other, trying to take him off balance. Our swords rang and cried out against the abuse we were subjecting them to.

It was a gamble, but I visualized my sword being sharp. I thought of the edge coming down to the thickness of a single atom. I felt an immense strain of mana flow into the blade as I swung it. Master Alonzo blocked it with his blade, and a bright light shot out from the point where our blades made contact. I tried to pull my sword back, but it was stuck. Our blades had fused together where they had made contact. Upon closer inspection, it looked like our blades had passed halfway through each other before being fused together.

"That's enough," said Alonzo as he took the two swords apart.

"What happened?" I asked. "I thought of the most solid thing I could think of."

"Metal," he said. "You must have thought of something very sharp."

"Master, what did we just see?" asked Godwin.

"You saw what is possible," replied Alonzo.

"I don't know what I saw. Your swords were moving way too fast," said Cordell.

"You've been toying with us every time we fought! You could have easily beaten us, but instead you held back and let us think we actually did win," said Leon. He sounded genuinely hurt by this new revelation.

"You did win fairly. I just didn't use the techniques you just saw," I replied.

"No, it doesn't mean anything now if it wasn't all you had," he replied.

"She was under strict orders not to display any of the training she was learning from me. If you want to become good enough to beat her, then come learn what I have taught her," said Alonzo.

"Are you really offering to teach us what you've taught Nisha?" asked Godwin.

"It would be easy for you to learn. Some of the concepts may be too difficult for you to understand. It won't be like the training you're used to," replied Alonzo.

Godwin yielded, and the other three boys followed his lead. "I would be grateful for you to try, Master. I pledge to give it my all," said Godwin.

"Me too!" said Cordell.

"I'll give it my all as well, Master," said Dartan.

"I will learn this training, and then I want another fight with Nisha," said Leon.

"I won't accept a win unless she gives it everything she has, just as she did with you, Master," he added.

"I never meant to deceive you, Leon, but I promise I'll give it everything I have during our next fight," I said.

"That reminds me, that might be a while. Someone was going to tell you, and I asked His Highness if I could be the one to tell you—you're leaving the palace tomorrow," said Alonzo.

"Where am I going?" I asked after a moment of shock.

"You'll be going to work for the prince. Where and doing what, I can't say, but I figured it would be best to tell you all now," said Alonzo.

"What will happen to them?" I asked, pointing at the rest of my class.

"Will they just go back to the other classes?"

"No, they'll stay as their own class. His Highness has taken over their sponsorship," replied Master Alonzo.

"Does that mean he has a plan for them, too?" I asked.

"He always has a plan for everything, so I'm sure he does," replied Alonzo.

I looked at my classmates and said, "I think that means we'll meet again, but I'm not sure."

"Obviously, we'll meet again! I still have to have a proper duel with you," said Leon.

"Don't you mean you still have to confess your love for Nisha?" asked Dartan.

"Oh, you're funny. It's too bad you don't fight as you joke," replied Leon.

"I'm hurt! I'm not worthy of your affection," I said jokingly.

"Jess, no!" replied Leon sharply.

I thought we had something special, I replied. Leon's face went bright red, and silence was all he could muster.

"That's enough torture! Say your goodbyes. I'm sure you have other people you want to see before you leave," said Alonzo.

He was right. I still needed to get down to the maids' quarters before lockdown. I said my final goodbyes and headed off to the recreation room next to the maids' quarters. When I got there, Zora was already teaching some of the other girls how to speak Moturan. As I came in, she looked at the expression on my face. She told her class to keep practicing some words she had just taught them, and came over to me.

"Did something happen?" she asked.

"I've been told that I'm leaving the palace tomorrow," I replied.

"Do you know where you're going?" she asked.

"No, but I think I know who I'll be with and some of what I'll be doing," I replied.

"Well then, may the elements guide you," she said.

"I'll come back and set you free," I said.

"I don't know how or when. Ever since I was taken from my mother, people are only in my life for a short time before they leave," said Zora.

I took off my healing rune and handed it to her. "This was given to me by a very dear friend. I want you to hold on to it for me until I come back for it," I said.

"You know that the maids can't have jewelry," she replied.

"Then keep it hidden and know that I'm coming back," I said.

"I'll be waiting," she said as she accepted the rune.

Chapter 28

Molturan Nobility

The next morning, after I said goodbye to my friends at the palace, I found myself in a mansion close to the heart of Potoma. Jenna had brought me to this place, and on the prince's orders, would spend the next month teaching me how to blend in with the Molturan nobility.

"You know, I actually am a noble in my home country," I told the prince.

He shook his head. "Be that as it may, you still stand out way too much," he replied.

The official story is that I was the adopted daughter of the third prince. Adopted family members in Multira were a bit like pets; they couldn't have any official titles conferred upon them or take the inheritance of their adoptive family. This was to ensure that nobody of low birth could ever become a proper noble.

The closest an adopted family member could get to nobility would be through marriage, where they could give birth to children with the proper noble lineage. This was a rare occurrence, as most nobles would accept marriage offers from proper nobles. The true fate of an adopted noble was to be given, traded, and collected by other nobles to curry favor or to build alliances. Honestly, there were any number of reasons an adopted noble could go from one noble to another.

"So I'm basically still a slave? I just got an education and get to dress nice?" I asked Jenna after she explained the life of an adopted noble to me.

"I suppose you could look at it that way, but some nobles actually do care for their adopted family members," she replied.

"You mean that they care for their pets?" I corrected.

"That may be, but if you hold on to that hostility while socializing with them, they will pick up on your resentment," said Jenna.

"Aren't I supposed to be there to kill them?" I asked.

"Some of them. In order to do that, you can't have them looking at you with suspicion or resentment," replied Jenna.

"So what am I supposed to do? Become friends with them?" I asked.

"That is exactly what you need to do," replied Jenna.

"It won't be enough just to blend in," I asked.

"And how exactly will you blend in if you come off as aggressive or indifferent? You need to talk about the things they like to talk about, do the things they like to do, and be what they expect you to be," said Jenna.

"And what do they expect me to be?" I asked.

"They expect you to be nice and pleasant. You need to be charming enough to all who meet you, to see why His Highness adopted you," explained Jenna.

"I thought the goal was not to stand out," I said.

"I'm not suggesting you stand out. I'm suggesting you become someone these people want to be around. Think of it like you're wearing a mask. On the outside, they'll see nothing but a charming young lady whom they want to be around. Underneath the mask, you can despise them all you want," she explained.

"Okay, I think I understand what you're getting at. I can't just look the part; I need to be able to stand up to scrutiny," I said.

"That's exactly it! I'm glad you're such a fast learner," said Jenna.

"So where do we start?" I asked.

"How are your dancing skills?" she asked.

My dancing wasn't bad, but after being out of practice for nearly a year, I had built up a bit of rust. The next week was spent brushing off all the rust and practicing different styles that were common in Multira. After my dancing was considered satisfactory by Jenna, we moved on to dressing properly for specific occasions.

There really wasn't much to it, as Jenna said she'd be sure I was dressed properly. I think what she mostly wanted was an excuse to go shopping for clothes and to dress me up like a doll. Customs and courtesies were next; they didn't take long to learn. But what did take time was memorizing the names and relations of all the important nobles in the capital.

The last week was spent going over everything Jenna had taught me and familiarizing myself with the current events and trends within the kingdom. After a month of training, Jenna decided I was ready to make my debut. The first prince, Garland's older brother, Harold, was hosting a party at his estate, and I was to accompany Garland to the party.

The night was to be a dry run, but even still, Jenna thought it would be a good idea to bring concealed weapons so that I would be familiar with the practice. The dress I was wearing had two hidden pockets that blended in with the seams on the sides. Strapped to my thighs were two twelve-inch blades. My hair was also done up with metal hairpins that were sharpened to deadly points.

"You look absolutely splendid!" said Jenna as she placed a necklace on me. Jenna's hair was bright red tonight.

"I see you're going as Tina tonight," I said.

"Of course! We'll be arriving with His Highness tonight, and most of his peers are familiar with his escort," she explained.

A knock on the door from one of the servants broke our conversation. The servant informed us that a carriage had arrived for us. As we approached the waiting carriage, a door was opened, and Prince Garland held out his hand to me.

"You two look like radiant flowers this evening," he said.

"I'm so glad to hear you say that, as you did pay a considerable amount for the petals that adorn us," replied Jenna.

"I trust you stayed within the budget I gave you," said the prince.

"Don't I always?" asked Jenna.

The prince just sighed and sat back in his seat as the carriage began to move. Jenna sat next to him, wrapping her arms around him and leaning against him.

"What are you doing?" he asked.

"I'm enjoying the moment while I can, so please don't ruin it," she replied.

Garland surrendered and let Jenna have her way. "How's the war going?" I asked.

"About how I predicted. But two of the generals from Alza have proven to be more competent than I had accounted for, and have caused me to step up my timetable," he replied.

"Then is it really wise for the Royals to be throwing parties as their country is being defeated?" I asked.

"Part of the curse of being a tyrant is that nobody has the courage to give you any bad news. My father and most of the leading nobles believe that they will still win," he replied.

"So they just ignore the fact that they keep losing?" I asked.

"It's reality, not part of their decisions," I said.

"They're told that the losses are strategic withdrawals. As for your second question, they can't see reality. Even if they could, they would just lie to themselves," replied Garland.

"Shush! You two are ruining the moment for me with all your chatter! You can talk later," said Jenna.

"Did she just shush the prince?" I asked.

"I suggest you do as she says," said Garland.

Upon arriving at Prince Harold's estate, we were announced as "Third Prince Garland and his guests."

"So even the herald doesn't acknowledge adoption as family," I said.

"Remember to behave," said Jenna.

His introductions took place, and Garland introduced me as his adopted daughter. My mind was immediately put to work memorizing faces and putting them with the names Jenna had forced me to memorize.

Fortunately for me, I could ignore most of the people I was introduced to— I only had to memorize once from the list Jenna had given me.

"She's such a delightful thing! Wherever did you find her?" asked Baron Lozano. He was a banker and one of the notable people I had to remember.

"I plucked her from the maid staff at the palace. Apparently, they didn't realize she was educated far beyond her station," replied the prince.

"Well, at least that part is true," I thought.

After about an hour of socializing, music started playing, and Prince Garland asked me to dance with him. The idea was to show that I was not just a pet, but a well-trained pet as well. I remembered what Jenna had been telling me and put on my mask.

Prince Garland was a graceful dancer, and if we had been in another ballroom in another country, when not filled with people I detested, I could have had fun. Still, I smiled as if I was having fun. I pulled out all the stops and made sure that I put on the best display that I could.

When the music finally stopped, I could hear the sound of applause. "You're a very good dancer," said Garland, conscious of the ears around us.

"I'm too kind, Your Highness. All I did was follow your lead," I said.

"What a marvelous display, brother! You were always gifted with your feet," said a man walking up to us.

"As I have told you many times before, it is only through diligence and hard work that I have skill," replied Garland.

"Well, hard work and diligence are their own gifts. Who is your lovely companion here?" he asked.

"This is my adopted daughter, Nisha. Nisha, this is my oldest brother, Prince Harold," I said as I took a deep bow.

"It's a pleasure to meet you, Your Highness," I said.

"The pleasure is mine," said Harold.

The contrast between Harold and Garland was stark. Where Garland was thin with a pale complexion, Harold was round with dark hair and a dark complexion. As Harold walked away, I had to ask, "Is he really your brother?"

"Half-brother," he corrected. "My mother wasn't an adopted noble."

"Is that why he is so disdainful?" I asked.

"We can talk about it another time, but not here," said Garland as I began to leave the dance floor.

The music picked up again, and an old man with gray hair asked me to dance with him. I put on my best fake smile and told him I would be delighted. Every time I tried to make my escape from the dance floor, someone else was standing right there to ask me to dance.

Being ever willing to ingratiate myself to these people, I pushed through. About an hour later, Jenna came to my rescue and pulled me from the dance floor.

"You're covered in sweat. You can turn people down and take a break," she said.

"I thought the whole point of tonight was to win these people over," I said.

"Trust me, you've done that and then some. Now take a break for a bit," she said.

"So what should I do for the rest of the evening?" I asked.

"Well, go make more friends. Maybe if they like us well enough, they'll even invite us to spend time with them," she replied.

What that translated into was more socializing and introductions. By the end of the evening, I felt as if I had been introduced to every noble family in Multira.

"Did you two enjoy the evening?" asked Garland on our carriage ride home.

"As much as one can enjoy being in a pit of snakes," I replied.

"Come on, Nisha, it wasn't all that bad. I could tell you had a bit of fun dancing with Jenna," said Garland.

"Maybe I did a little," I admitted.

"So who's the first target? I know that part of tonight's purpose was to introduce me to their faces," I said.

"I suppose that it was a bit obvious. Your first target is my brother, the first prince," said Garland.

Chapter 29

Tools of the Trade

"You're serious? The first in line to the throne is our first target? Won't that be a bit on the nose and put the rest of the nobles on guard if we kill him first?" I asked.

"My brother has his fair share of enemies; his death won't create a whole lot of suspicion," replied Garland.

"I'm not sure what I imagined, but I didn't think it would be someone that high up the Royal line," I said.

"Don't try to put too much thought into it. Tonight we'll go over it. Tomorrow, now try to be quiet and let Jenna get some sleep," he said.

Jenna was snuggled up against his side with her eyes closed. I was fairly certain that she was wide awake, but I decided to keep my suspicions to myself.

The next morning, Prince Garland called Jenna and me to a room that looked like a study. We had returned to the mansion Jenna and I had been staying at for the past month.

"What's the plan?" I asked.

"Jenna, Nisha has been invited to a garden party at Prince Harold's estate two days from now. There will be lots of other guests there as well. Naturally, if the prince is killed at a social event, the last one to be suspected will be the ten-year-old girl," explained Garland.

"I'm almost eleven," I challenged.

"That's irrelevant to the point. My brother is a notorious drug user and often sneaks away from social events to indulge his habit. When he slips away, this is where you act. Harold will be surrounded by no less than two guards. The more overpowering you make the scene look, the less you'll be considered a suspect," said Garland.

"What if someone notices I'm gone when it happens?" I asked.

"I'll have someone there to help divert any suspicions away from you," he replied. "Worst-case scenario, if you can escape, just injure yourself in a convincing way. It won't be too difficult to believe that the assassin didn't want to kill a child. I also have the construction documents for his mansion, so you may be able to just slip away using a secret exit," he added.

"Why didn't you start with that?" I asked.

"Because there is no guarantee where the opportune moment will take place," he replied. "Secret passageways are always made the same way, and these have big houses. Once you know what to look for, they are easy to use," he added.

Garland walked over to a bookshelf and pulled the top of a book. The bookshelf cracked open like a door.

"How will I know what to look for?" I asked.

"It tells you what to look for on the documents, obviously. Try to keep up, Nisha," said Garland. He stepped through the open bookshelf, and Jenna and I followed right behind him.

In the next room, the walls and shelves were covered in every weapon a medieval assassin could want. There were stashed plates of all shapes and sizes. One item I took particular note of was a gauntlet with a small crossbow on it.

"You might find that a bit too difficult to smuggle into the garden party," said Garland.

"Well, if it was just a bit smaller, maybe I could hide it somewhere," I replied.

"I think your eyes are bigger than your stomach—or arms in this case," said Jenna. "You need something that can do a lot of damage in a very short order," said Garland.

"I realize that, but this is your brother we're talking about killing, and you're basically telling me I need to pick a more brutal way to do it," I replied.

"Not basically. I'm telling you to make it more brutal. If you knew even part of the atrocities he's committed, you would agree," said Garland. "The reason for the brutality has nothing to do with how I feel and everything with nobody thinking that it could come from an innocent-looking girl," he explained.

"Then I'll need something long to keep the blood off me—something sharp and something that I can conceal. A sword would be ideal if I could hide it, or if there happened to be one on hand," I said.

Garland walked across the room and opened a case. "Then I think this might suit your needs," he said.

Garland pulled out what looked like a long cross with a handle. "I believe it's Dwarven make, but I don't know enough to be sure of that," said Garland. The object was about sixteen inches long.

"Turn around," he instructed. Once I turned, I felt it press against my back. "What do you think?" he asked.

"I think I can get something made that will hold it in place and allow her to reach it," said Jenna.

"Okay, you can face me again," he said. I turned back around and looked at the object. Prince Garland twisted the end of the handle, and a blade sprung out from the end, giving it the overall length of a short sword.

"That's amazing! I've never seen a switch sword before," I said.

"A what?" asked Garland.

"A sword with a blade that extends with the press of a switch," I explained.

"I suppose that's an accurate description, but as far as I know, it's just called a hidden blade," said Garland.

"I'll bet the Dwarves had a better name for it," I replied.

"Probably, but I don't know what it is. From what I understand, there are only a couple of tribes left on the continent, so it might be difficult to find one to ask," explained Garland.

He handed the sword to me. As I swung it about, nothing was loose; nothing rattled. Despite being made of multiple parts, the entire sword felt as if it was one solid piece.

"Pull the end of the handle," instructed Garland. As I pulled the end of the handle, the blade began to retract against the spring. With a smooth, steady pull, the blade came back into place until I heard a click and the blade locked into the retracted position. I tested it a few more times, twisting the handle and retracting the blade. The tolerance that the blade was made to was far beyond what any smith or artificer I had ever met could produce.

"Where can I find a Dwarven tribe?" I asked.

"Some say to the far south, but I don't know for certain," replied Garland. "With that level of precision, I could make solid case ammunition. I could make automatic weapons once I was done with the war. I had to go find a Dwarf and try," I thought to myself.

"Why are you gaining so much over that?" asked Jenna.

"It's just so well made," I explained. I knew there was no way I could explain it all to her, so I just left her with the impression that I was excited by strange things.

"So will it work for you?" asked Garland.

"Not that I need it, but I could reinforce it with mana, and it already has a razor edge. It will work perfectly if Jenna can find a way to hide it on me," I replied.

It was a bit on the heavy side for its size, but it was perfect for the purpose I needed it for. "How much does something like this cost?" I asked.

"More than this house and most of the things inside it combined," explained Garland.

"So if I break it—"

"Try your best not to," Garland cut me off before I could finish my question. "The construction documents are over on that table," said Garland, pointing at the far side of the room. "I suggest you spend the next couple of days going over them, as it may save your life," he added.

In short order, the day of the garden party arrived. Jenna had fashioned an internal holder for the switch sword that held it along my spine. A slit in the back of my dress that was cleverly disguised behind a bow allowed me to reach the handle. With enough lace and a few extra add-ons, nobody would suspect that I was armed.

"How does it feel?" asked Jenna.

"Good. Are you sure it won't fall out?" I asked.

"Unless you plan on hanging upside down with hooks, the hook should hold it securely," she replied.

The carriage that was going to take me to Prince Harold's estate arrived. Today, I would be all on my own. Just as I was about to get inside the carriage, Jenna grabbed my hand.

"Listen, I know you can do this and that Prince Garland is counting on you to do it, but I want you to promise me that you'll be smart. If anything seems strange or off, I want you to be smart and call it off," she said.

"Part of this whole agreement of being an assassin is that I'm somewhat disposable," I replied.

"Not to me. Now promise me," she said.

"All right, I promise."

When I arrived at the first prince's estate, it was mid-afternoon. A series of ushers were waiting by the front entrance to escort guests to the party area, and I soon found myself surrounded by many of the same familiar faces that I had seen a few nights before.

"There's a war going on, and it seems like all these people do is go to parties. No wonder they're losing the war," I thought. It felt a little strange on my own, with no escort. A few people I had met the other night stopped and greeted me, but otherwise, I was a complete wallflower.

When I spotted Prince Harold, I was about to reintroduce myself to him when a group of girls my age walked up to me.

"You're the third prince's adopted daughter, aren't you?" asked a girl in a blue dress. Her clothes, hair, and accessories were all superior to the girls around her. I had to resist the urge to just walk off, but I suppressed it and introduced myself.

"I took a short bow. As you have said, I'm Prince Garland's adopted daughter, Nisha. It's a pleasure to meet you," I added.

"I see. So the third prince finally got himself a pet. I'm Anita, daughter of Count Osteen," she replied.

"I haven't had the pleasure of meeting the count yet, but I've heard that he's one of the wealthiest nobles in the kingdom," I said.

"Your accent is different. Where are you from?" she asked.

"My place of birth is a mystery, but I've lived in several different countries," I lied.

"How interesting! Why don't you come sit with me and my friends and get to know each other better?" she asked.

"I couldn't possibly impose on your generosity," I said, trying to break away.

"Oh, please!" she answered.

Anita had her own table reserved, and as we got there, there was one last chair for us. "The T-shirt give your chair to Nisha and go find another one," said Anita, without arguing. One of the girls in her group got up and left. I could see that she had them well-trained.

"What do you think of the party so far?" asked Anita.

"It's been pleasant so far," I replied.

"This is a horrible garden party! Whoever the first prince hired to do the arrangements should be fired immediately," she stated.

"I could see what she was doing; she was disagreeing with my responses to see if I would change or take back what I said to agree with her. I was tempted to play along. Convincing her that I'd be an obedient subordinate could possibly get me access to more nobles."

I noticed that Prince Harold was leaving the room, and I had to step away from the nasty little rich girl.

"Goodness, something isn't agreeing with me," I said. I made a point to get up quickly and leave before Anita could reply.

I followed the prince as he left the party with his guards. I kept track of my distance and made sure to check behind me. Once I was certain nobody had been observing me, I took note of the room Prince Harold had gone into. One of the guards was left outside the room. Well, that might be an issue, I thought.

On the plus side, the room the prince had gone into did have a hidden entrance. I walked up to the guard outside the door and introduced myself. "Hello! I'm the adopted daughter of the third prince. My father instructed me to give Prince Harold a message when I left the party," I said.

"What's the message?" asked the guard.

"Well, it wouldn't be proper to say it out loud, but I could whisper it," I said regarding Garland.

I whispered the message into his ear. "I understand," he replied, opening the door for me.

As I walked through the door, I saw Prince Harold putting something inside his jacket pocket.

"How did you get in here?" asked Harold.

"Forgive me, my prince; the guard let me in," I replied.

"I remember you. You're that girl Garland showed up with the other day," said Harold.

"Prince Garland sent me here to present you with a gift," I said.

"And what is this gift?" he asked.

"I am the gift," I replied.

"I see. That actually makes more sense than my younger brother wishes to ingratiate himself to me rather than start collecting pets. Well, come over here so I can examine you better," he said.

"Careful, Your Highness. Let me check her for weapons first," said the guard.

"Nonsense! She's just a small girl. Come now!" instructed Harold.

At the prince's order, the guard backed down. Once I was several feet from the guard, I began to focus mana into my arms and legs. In one fluid motion, I pulled my blade and decapitated the guard. Whether it was because he was high or some combination of both, Harold didn't move. I dashed toward him and slit his throat as he stood there bleeding out.

"You should have listened to your guard," I said.

Harold collapsed to the ground, and I hurried back to the door. I waited for the guard outside to come in, but a few seconds later, the door was still closed. Did he not hear the bodies falling? I had to kill him; he had seen my face. Panic began to set in. Maybe he had run for help, I thought.

Calm down. Maybe it wasn't loud enough, I thought to myself. I grabbed a bottle of alcohol from the table the prince had been sitting at and returned to the door. I threw the bottle on the ground, and an instant later, the guard from outside came in. I closed the door behind him with the heel of my foot as I thrust my blade into the back of his head.

I locked the door using a key I found on the first guard and used the secret exit to leave the room. I was careful not to let anyone see me as I returned to the party. The chair I had left at Anita's table was still empty, and I sat back in it.

"I'm terribly sorry about that, but I feel so much better now," I said. Everything in the room with the prince had happened so fast that I had just assumed that everything else would unfold quickly. It took over two hours before the prince and his guards were found. Apparently, it wasn't uncommon for him to vanish for extended periods during social events.

For two hours, I listened to Anita go on and on about how everything was just dreadful. I did my best to be agreeable and win her favor, but at the end of two hours, my responses were limited to one or two words. Finally, shouting broke the boredom, and I was actually relieved.

An important-looking man came into the party and demanded that everyone remain at the party. I could have left early, but I intentionally stayed behind so that I would be ruled out as a suspect. Some men in military uniforms eventually showed up and began sorting everyone into two groups. One looked at me and put me in the group that was allowed to leave the estate.

It was late in the evening when the carriage finally made it back to Prince Garland's mansion. Jenna and Garland were both waiting for me.

"Come on in, and we'll discuss what happened inside," said Garland.

"Can we do it tomorrow?" I asked. "Mana control uses a lot of energy," I complained.

I actually hadn't used a lot, but between what I did use, the adrenaline, and Anita, I was drained.

"We'll keep it brief for tonight," said Garland. "I hope you come to realize how effective it is with you helping us. Their pride would never allow the investigators to consider someone like you to be the culprit."

"You are! I'm just the tool you use," I corrected.

"That's beside the point," he said. "I can see the value I bring to the table. I apologize for being so skeptical in the beginning," I replied.

"Good. Now, did anyone see you go into the room with Harold?" asked Garland.

"Just the guard posted outside, but I was able to take him out," I replied.

"Did anyone see you leave the party?" he asked.

"Just Anita, Count Osteen's daughter, and her friends. I told them the food hadn't agreed with me. I was gone for about fifteen minutes, and it took over two hours for Harold to be found," I explained.

"From your explanation and the other reports, I don't think anyone will be looking at you," said Garland. "Were there any issues at all?" he asked.

"Only that it took so long to find him, and I had to endure two hours of a rich girl complaining about how everything was just dreadful."

"At least that part sounds like a typical garden party," said Jenna. "How about you? How are you holding up?" she asked.

"Just tired. I feel fine. It wasn't the first time I've had to kill a person, but it was the first time it was up close with a blade. I'm not sure how I'll feel about it twenty years from now, but I'll be able to sleep tonight," I explained.

"Will be well. I'll be close by if you need anything," said Jenna.

"I appreciate that. I'm going to get some sleep now," I said.

As I slept that night, I had a strange dream about the assassination. My mind took me through the same sequence of events that took place with Prince Harold. When I looked at the head of the decapitated guard, it had changed. After hitting the floor, when I looked at it closer, it was no longer the face of the guard; the face had been replaced with Renisha's face.

I tried to run away, but I ran into Prince Harold, whose face had been replaced with Clovis's. As I turned and tried to get away, my face smacked into something. As my mind shifted from dream to reality, I opened my eyes and saw Jenna rubbing her forehead.

"What's going on?" I asked.

"You were making a lot of noise in your sleep. I came to check on you, and when I tried to wake you up, you head-butted me," explained Jenna.

"Oh, I hadn't realized that I was making a lot of noise," I said.

"It's not a big deal. I'm sure my face will recover. So Jenna, what were you dreaming about anyway?" asked Jenna.

I took a deep breath and thought about it. "I'd rather not talk about it," I replied.

"Was it about the assassination?" asked Jenna.

I didn't respond; I just looked off into nothing. What could I say? There was no way to explain it in a way that made sense. "I've killed before, but yesterday was different," I finally said. "They weren't trying to kill me or someone else," I added. "Harold had more than his fair share of innocent blood on his hands," replied Jenna.

"I know that, but knowing that doesn't make me feel better," I said.

Jenna didn't try to push it any further. She just put her arms around me and held me for a while. "Thanks, Jenna. I think I needed that," I said.

After a while, she replied, "Don't mention it. I'll give you all that you need."

"So what are you doing today?" I asked, more to change the tone of the room than anything else.

"First, get cleaned up and get dressed. Then come meet me in the dining room," she said.

Interlude 4

"I see it, but I still don't understand it. Why have they come out to fight us head-on?" asked Leela.

"Probably because they assume they have some advantage. It might have something to do with not wanting to lose control of the country's primary source of grain," said LeRoy.

"What's this place called again?" I asked.

"They call it Golden Valley. Fields of wheat stretch in all directions, only broken up by fences and the occasional farmhouse or windmill," he replied.

"I'll be honest. It would be nice to not have to attack a fortified city for once," said Leela.

"It's just a lot faster to open melee than it is in a siege," said LeRoy.

"Then we'll just have to make sure they're the ones dying at a faster rate," replied Leela.

The beating sound of giant paw pads and hoofbeats grew as Wark and some of the hunters, recruited back in Dvor, came riding up to her and LeRoy.

"So how does it look?" asked Leela.

"Numerically, it might turn into a slugfest. We estimate their numbers to be around 70,000 to 73,000 troops. We're sitting at about—what?— 65,000?" Wark replied.

"So that gives them an advantage?" Leela asked.

"One that they may think will carry them to victory, no doubt. However, we did note that about a fourth of theirs appears to be ill-equipped peasants forced into service, whereas most of our troops are properly armed and trained," said Captain Gabbana, one of Leela's officers.

"You're right about the armament, but my reports on many of our newer recruits are that they have little if any formal training," replied LeRoy. "Is there any chance we might have enough time to teach them some basic drills?" asked Leela.

"Not likely. The enemy is marshalling just a few miles away. We suspect that they will be on the move by tomorrow," replied Wark.

"That gives us a few more advantages. If they intend to come to us, I'll have the mage core use earth magic to start warming the terrain to our advantage," said LeRoy.

"And what do we do if they stop advancing?" asked Wark.

"Then we do nothing and maintain control of the valley. Their interest is definitely in taking back the valley. They'll keep coming," explained LeRoy.

"Well, it sounds like we both have our work cut out for us," said Leela as she hopped up on Beezlem.

"Where are you headed off to?" asked Wark.

"Their supply lines are probably strung out from here to Potoma. It will be the perfect opportunity for some raiding," explained Leela. "You stay here and defend, and I'll make sure that they're tired and hungry when they get here," she added.

"I see, so you intend to leave me with cleanup again," said LeRoy.

"I'll be back in time to help out," said Leela. And with that, the two generals parted ways.

The night was warm, and a well-equipped army of over 3,000 mounted soldiers was on the move. The army was split into five groups, each with their own targeted sections of the road. Out of the 3,000, only 274 were mounted on borrowed dogs. The group of borrowed dogs, being the fastest, took the furthest targets.

The entire raid had been timed so that once the furthest group attacked, they could start heading back and supplement each additional raid group they attacked. If all went according to plan, all 3,000 troops, minus casualties, would regroup and return to the main army just before sunrise.

"General, it's time to see Captain," said Leela.

"All right, remember to keep moving and don't stop. If you get lost, home is to the east. If you can't tell which way is east, well then you're in shit out of luck," said Leela. Her joke elicited a few muffled laughs.

"All right, let's move!" she ordered.

In addition to being armed with swords and other weapons, the raiders on the borrowed dogs had another weapon that normal cavalry didn't. A well-trained borrowed dog could cause just as much damage with their mouths, if not more, than their riders could.

As the raiding party closed in on the torches that lit up the supply lines, the dogs began to speed up faster and faster. They ran, and by the time they were at full sprint, the panicked soldiers that no doubt could hear the thunderous paw pads were still unsure of which direction the attack was coming from.

Like a dark wave rolling over the beach, the raiding party slammed through the supply line. Wagons and carts were overturned, and torches were instantly snuffed out as they dropped to the ground. The screams of the men being taken out by swords and other weapons were overshadowed by the screams of agony coming from those being turned into chew toys.

The supply line, which had started out as a seemingly continuous line of lights, now had growing dark spots as the raiding party zigged and zagged through it like a sewing needle. It was hard to see if any riders had fallen behind in the dark, but the momentum held.

Before long, the group of dogs met up with the first group on horseback that had begun its own bloody path through the supply line. The combined effect of the two groups was almost complete decimation of the supply line. As the raiding party continued east, by the time the first two groups met the third, the decimation was complete.

At the time the party hit the fourth and fifth groups, it was basically a road-clearing operation. Just before the sun began to creep back into the valley, the raiding party crossed back into allied territory.

"Report!" Leela ordered to her group commanders as the numbers came back in. Over 90% of the raiding party had been accounted for, and a few stragglers were still coming in.

"How effective do you think it was?" asked Leela.

"I'd say that their advance will be halted for a while, but we won't know the full extent of the damage for a while," explained Wark.

"Obviously, we'll know more later. Can't you just give me your personal opinion when I ask for it?" asked Leela.

"I thought I just did," he replied.

Leela pressed her hand against her forehead. "By the elements, it's like I'm speaking a foreign language when I talk to you," she said.

As more stragglers came in, the official number was less than 200 riders lost. The reports had been right about the advance being halted. By mid-morning, Duke Androl and Daryl had called a staff meeting. Apart from Leela and LeRoy, several other commanders from the combined forces were in attendance.

"It's now official: Elris and Alza have come together. Instead of being called the combined forces, we have an official name," said Daryl. He paused for a moment.

"Are you going to tell us what it is?" asked the female mage.

"Why, certainly, Colonel Lomya. I'm so glad you asked. We are now the Central Allied Forces," said Daryl.

"It seriously took them almost a year to come up with that?" asked Leela.

"It wasn't the top priority. What is a priority is that we still have a battle on our hands. General LeRoy's raid last night was effective, but it has made Multira even more determined to take back the Golden Valley, as they will probably have no other way to feed their army," explained Daryl.

"General LeRoy, how are our defenses looking?" asked Daryl.

"We've done about all we can with the mage core altering the terrain. I certainly have my engineering team setting up hostile defenses. We will definitely have a strong advantage," explained LeRoy.

"Colonel Lomya, history has shown us that battles are often altered by a handful or even one skilled mage. Parents have any surprises for us in that regard?" asked Daryl.

"I know that they have a couple of reputable mages among their number, but not in the numbers they would need to assure victory. As a matter of fact, with General's sharpshooters taking out mages, we should have a distinct advantage in that area," said Lomya.

"The sharpshooters are few in number and can't be everywhere at the same time. I'll need rapid updates to know where to send them," said Leela.

"It sounds like everyone knows what to expect and what their responsibilities are, so in the name of the Central Allied Forces, I call this meeting adjourned," said Daryl.

The following morning, thousands upon thousands of troops lined up on both the eastern and western sides of the Golden Valley. There was no bluffing on who would attack first. From the east, Multira advanced, rows upon rows of soldiers slowly marching forward towards the Central Allied Forces. Several large gaps were left open between the foot soldiers.

When all but a few hundred yards separated the two hostile forces, mounted units from Moltura began to rush through the gaps left open by the foot soldiers. At the moment the mounted units passed the foot soldiers, catapults, cannons, mages, archers, and sharpshooters all opened fire on the advancing army.

Most of the mounted units broke through the barrage, only to be diverted into trenches and pits with spikes that had been made by the mages and engineering corps. The ones that made it through all the diversions were met by a solid defensive line set up by the Central Alliance.

"The military strategy seems to be to overwhelm individual points within the wall of the Central Allied Forces. It looks like they're about to break through LeRoy's line," said Leela.

"I suppose it's time we go help him out," said LeRoy.

Like an arm from the North, Louis's mounted troops began to cut through the Multiran forces that were pushing through LeRoy's defenses. The flanking maneuver had worked, and the push from Moltura had been halted. Unfortunately, the hostile terrain that had been working for the Central Allied Forces was now working against them, and Leela's flanking attack had now begun to grind to a halt.

Leela's mounted units were taking out a lot of the enemy troops, but being completely surrounded, they began to suffer rapid losses. An explosion knocked Leela from Beezlem. For a moment, she wasn't sure what happened. When she got up off the ground, she shook the dirt from her eyes. She couldn't see Beezlem anywhere.

"It couldn't have been cannon fire; that must have been explosion magic," she thought, seeing a downed enemy soldier. Several Multiran troops rushed at Leela, only to be quickly cut down.

The hunter-turned-general was now back on the hunt. She was looking for the mage that had hit her. After slicing through a few more soldiers, she found the mage. He was chanting, and in the next moment, shards of ice went flying toward Leela.

She avoided the spell and began to sprint toward the mage. The mage got off another spell; this time, it was fire. With pure focus, Leela cut through the spell with her sword. She was now only twenty feet away from the mage. Panic struck the mage as he knew he couldn't fire another spell before she would get to him.

Before Leela could close the distance, an armored borrowed dog snatched up the mage and began to crush him between its massive jaws. The mage's screams of terror were quickly silenced as he was crushed to death.

Sitting atop the borrowed dog was LeRoy. "Quit fooling around! We have a battle to win," said LeRoy.

Leela's blood instantly shot to boiling temperature. LeRoy whistled, and a soldier leading Beezlem rode up. "I think he lost something," said LeRoy as a soldier handed Beezlem over to her.

Leela decided that she would yell at LeRoy later. For now, he was right; they still had a battle to win.

She took a quick inventory of Beezlem, and other than a few scratches, he looked fine. She hopped up on his back and headed back to round up her troops. Once they established back with her troops, with the support of LeRoy, who no longer had to hold defensive lines, they began to push back the Multiran troops.

By early afternoon, Multira was in full retreat. The fields of golden wheat were now stained red with blood. The casualties on both sides were unknown but were high. The Central Alliance forces had pushed the militia out of the Golden Valley, but they had to end the pursuit once the Multiran army reached their established defensive lines.

By the end of the day, both armies were regrouping.

"Where do you estimate so far?" asked Duke Androl as Daryl.

"It's still early, but our accounts put us over 14,000 killed or injured. Multira must have lost between 20,000 to 30,000, but that's a bit harder to assess than our own numbers," explained LeRoy.

"How are you doing, General?" asked Daryl.

"General LeRoy says we almost lost you today," said Daryl.

"I assure you that General LeRoy is full of shit, my Lord. However, he did bring me my dog back after I rescued his defensive line from collapsing," she replied.

"I see. I'm glad you're all right," said Daryl.

The next morning, scouts from the Central Allied Forces reported that the main Multiran army had pulled back. Moltura's plans for taking back the Golden Valley had been shattered. LeRoy's estimate of 20,000 to 30,000 Multiran casualties had been conservative. It was later discovered that Multira had lost over 40,000 troops at the Battle of the Golden Valley.

Chapter 30

Capital Unrest

Although news was restricted by the Royal government, word was starting to spread. In spite of all the propaganda pushed on the city of Potoma, the truth was beginning to seep through the cracks. Prices for everyday goods had nearly doubled over the last year; tax hikes were at an all-time high. Casualty reports could only be covered up so much. Weeping mothers were an all-too-common sight. Worse yet were the families that had just stopped receiving letters from their loved ones in the military. The unknown is often a worse curse.

The Battle of Golden Valley was being hailed as a victory, but those who knew the truth were too numerous to suppress the rumors. Amidst all the confusion, nobles with notable power and influence seemed to keep meeting untimely deaths. The local authorities were now certain that an organized group of assassins was responsible, but most theories pointed towards Elris and Alza. Only a small minority was willing to consider that those responsible for the killings were much more local.

Today was a bit different from my previous executions. Normally, I would simply use my appearance and timing of isolation to get close to my targets. The rumors circulating were that the killer must have been a large man with a heavy blade. Four more nobles had been executed in a similar fashion to Prince Harold.

Today would be different. Prince Garland had the wrist crossbow modified so that it would fit on my smaller-than-average wrist. Through visualization and mana control, I had proven to Garland that I could reliably take down a target 150 yards away. This new ability was achieved by strengthening the string and other components of the crossbow with mana. It couldn't change the game entirely for us, but it did open up new possibilities for how we eliminated targets.

Today's target was Baron Tobias. Up until a few years ago, Tobias had not even been a noble but rather a smuggler who had the connections and ability to facilitate whatever illicit products the wealthy desired. For his services, he had been granted a barony. His services had made him influential among certain circles, and Garland had calculated that influence needed to be removed.

As I was waiting and had a window overlooking the gambling den across the street, Tobias walked outside. He would be about 110 yards away. With all the other buildings and activity on the streets, it would give me plenty of time to walk out the front door as if nothing had happened. Jenna was waiting with me, since it might seem odd for a child to be walking around a tavern by themselves in this part of town.

"Are you sure you saw him go in there?" I asked Jenna.

"We've been waiting for hours now," I added.

"People tend to stay for a while when they go to gamble," said Jenna.

"I realize that, but I can think of other ways I'd rather spend my birthday," I replied.

"You mean spending it with me isn't good enough?" asked Jenna.

"Not like this, but I do realize that it could be worse; at least I'm not locked in a cage," I said.

"Well, if it will cheer you up, I'll take you to get something delicious to eat afterward," said Jenna.

"That will only be possible if he comes back out before the sun goes down," I replied.

"In that case, I'll make you something when we get back to the mansion," she said.

"Now try to be a bit more positive," said Jenna.

"I can't make any promises, but I'll try," I replied.

Twenty minutes later, Baron Tobias stepped outside the gambling den. "About damn time," I said. I lined up my crossbow and used mana control to visualize the bolt going through the baron's head. I pulled the trigger, and a second later, the baron dropped to the ground. I took off the crossbow and put it in an elegant handbag. As both Jenna and I were dressed in fine clothing, nobody even gave us a second look as we left the tavern and rounded the street corner that led to our carriage.

"So where are we going to eat?" I asked.

"How would you like some cheesecake?" asked Jenna.

When Jenna and I made it back to the mansion, Prince Garland and Kona were waiting for us.

"I thought you would be waiting for my report back at the palace," said Jenna.

"The timetable got pushed up again. The defeat at Golden Valley changed it. We now only have about a month before the forces from Elris and Alza reach the capital," explained Garland.

"Have we cleared out enough opposition for you to take the throne?" I asked.

"Not even close," said Kona.

"So all that work over the past month was for nothing? All the training from Master Alonzo and Jenna was for what?" I asked.

"Not a complete loss. The nobles you have taken out will make my transition into power less contested. As for taking control, we're moving to Plan B," explained Garland.

"What's Plan B?" I asked.

"I'll explain later. For now, grab all the weapons and armor you would want for an assault and get it packed inside the carriage. We're going back to the palace," said Garland.

Once back at the palace, Garland called for a meeting in his study. I had just finished putting the weapons and armor I had brought from the mansion away in my old room when Jenna found me and brought me into the prince's study. In addition to Garland, Jenna, and myself, Master Alonzo was there too.

"My dear friends, as you no doubt already know, the forces from Elris and Alza will be at the gates of the capital in about a month. I was planning on a simpler transition to power, but with this recent development, my next option will be much more direct than my usual methods. Before I explain more, I need you all to understand that by sticking around, there will be no more opportunities for walking away. There is a good chance that what I'm about to propose will end with all of our deaths," explained Garland.

"I kind of always figured it would end that way anyway," said Alonzo.

"What about you, Nisha?" asked Garland.

"You've been having me execute political rivals for the past month, and now you're asking me if I want to run? I'd say it's a bit too late for that. Besides, I already brought all the equipment up to my room," I said.

"Don't even bother wasting your time asking me," said Jenna.

"A sentiment I fully endorse," said Kona.

"Very well then. You seem to all have your minds made up on that point. Plan B is simple: we start a riot in the capital, then take the palace by force," explained Garland.

"It's so simple! Why didn't we just start with that plan?" I asked.

"Have you seen the number of guards this place has? We would need an army to take this palace by force," I ranted.

"Like I said, there's a good chance it will end with our deaths. However, it wouldn't suggest it if there wasn't a way to pull it off. My agents are already set to start riots. The city is at a boiling point already, so it won't take much. As for an army, I already have one inside the palace. Well, the start of one anyway. I have a dozen Royal guards plus you four, Master Alonzo. How many knights in training can you reliably count on?" asked Garland.

"For maybe more, once the rest are forced to choose a side," replied Alonzo.

"That will have to do," said Garland. "That's only about twenty people against hundreds. What do you expect us to do?" I asked.

"We don't have to fight all of them; we just have to take out the ones in the throne room. Once I depose my father, I'll simply ask the rest to make a choice between me or the rioting population outside the gate," said Garland.

"What about the second prince? Won't he take issue with your rise to power?" I asked.

"Prince Jasper has been out of the country for several years. It's highly unlikely he would return now," explained Kona.

"It isn't like he's a crowd favorite anyway," added Alonzo.

"Well, nobody tells me things like that!" I protested.

"So then, how many guards are usually in the throne room?" I asked.

"Anywhere between twenty to fifty," said Garland.

"There is a pretty big difference between twenty and fifty," I replied.

"Indeed there is, which is why I'll need Master Alonzo to make a distraction to help ensure it's on the lower side," said Garland.

"That doesn't seem fair to Master Alonzo," I said.

"Don't worry about me; I'll be fine," said Alonzo.

"Master, I know how good you are, but that's a lot of guards to take on by yourself," I said.

"It's like I said: I'll be fine. Just focus on helping out the prince in the throne room," said Alonzo.

"Well then, when will all this take place?" asked Jenna.

"I'll put the message out tonight. By tomorrow, the city should be in revolt, and that's when we'll enact our plan," explained Garland.

"Is that even enough time?" I asked.

"It should be plenty. Sorry, Nisha, but you're the only one who has had the opportunity to prepare for this. That's why I told you to bring arms from the mansion," explained Garland. "It's getting late, so I suggest you use the time left to get some sleep or make any other preparations you need to," he added.

Chapter 31

Hostile Takeover

Speed was my most powerful asset in combat, and my armor reflected that. Racer's shin guards and a thick leather chest plate were what I had grabbed for armor. A wonderfully balanced shortsword, some daggers, and my switch sword as backup were my weapons. The wrist-mounted crossbow wasn't practical for use with melee weapons. What I wouldn't give for my guns back, I thought. Numbers and prolonged fights worked against mana control, and today there would be an overabundance of both. I would need to focus on conserving mana and picking moments of opportunity to make effective attacks.

Another thing I wished I had on hand was my healing rune, but there had been no time to slip down to the maids' quarters to get it. Besides, I had a promise to keep, and if all went according to plan, Zora and the rest of the maids would be free by the end of the day.

After going over my gear one last time, I left my room in the palace and met up with Prince Garland in his study.

"You're early. I wasn't planning on moving for a few more hours," said Garland.

"I must have missed the message explaining what time we were going to take over the palace," I said sarcastically.

"Did you at least get some good sleep?" asked Garland.

"How is anyone supposed to get any sleep tonight before a revolution?" I asked.

"I don't know what you're complaining about, but I slept wonderfully," said Jenna. She was still wearing a nightgown and stood up from behind the prince's desk. She leaned over and kissed Garland's cheek. "I'm going to get ready," she said, slipping out the door.

Feeling tired and burned out, I sat down on the sofa. "Wake me up when you're ready to do this for real," I said. I couldn't believe how casual they were being about it all, I thought to myself as I closed my eyes.

Jenna shook my shoulder. "It's time to wake up," she said. I was slightly confused for a moment, but soon remembered where I was. I wiped the drool from my mouth and sat up. Surprisingly, I actually felt a bit rested.

Jenna, Kona, and Garland were armed and wearing armor. "Has it started?" I asked.

"Reports are coming in from the city that the citizens are making their way to the palace. We figured it would be best to let you get as much sleep as possible, but now it's time for us to act," explained Garland.

Garland got up and walked toward the door to his study. Jenna and Kona were right on his heels, and I quickly fell in behind him. When we got out to the hallway, the guards who worked directly for Garland were waiting for us.

"Gentlemen, if today is our last, I want you to know that it's been a pleasure working with all of you," said Garland.

"The pleasure has been ours, Your Highness," replied one of the guards.

"All right, let's get to it!"

As we made our way through the palace, guards and servants were running about. By some miracle, I ran into Lycillia, one of the girls who had been sold with me at Kabbalah.

"Where are you headed?" I asked.

"We're not sure. Nobody has been around to give us instructions," she said.

"Get all the maids you can and take them back to their quarters. Once you get everyone there, barricade the door until I get down there," I instructed.

"Why? What's going on?" she asked.

"I'll explain later. Just get the maids back to their quarters," I said. I pulled my signet pin off my chest. "Use this if anyone tries to stop you," I added.

I caught back up to Prince Garland and we kept working our way toward the throne room. When we were about to round the last corner to the throne room, Garland stopped us.

"Kona and Nisha, come with me. The rest of you wait here with Jenna for my signal," said Garland.

The three of us stepped toward the massive double doors that led to the throne room. We were stopped by the guards at the door.

"Stay where you are! By the king's order, nobody is allowed entry to the throne room at the moment," said the guard.

"I understand the severity of the situation, but I have urgent news concerning the riots in the city that needs to be relayed to my father," said Garland.

"Get the message to me, and I'll relate it to the king," said the guard.

"It's rather extensive in length, and I'll accept any and all punishment for violating the king's orders," said Garland.

That last part about accepting responsibility seemed to be what sold Garland's story to the guard. He stepped aside and pushed the door open for us.

As we made our way inside the throne room, King Torland was talking to a man wearing blue robes with gold seams. The throne was elevated about three feet higher than the rest of the room and was carved out of stone.

"Father, I bring ill news about those responsible for the riots," said Garland.

"How did you get past the guards? I ordered this room to be sealed," said King Torland.

I was trying to get a count of the guards in the room. Some were hiding in the shadows, so it was more difficult to count. I hadn't finished, but it was well over forty.

"It is, as I was saying, the news I bring is urgent—" At just that moment, the throne room door swung open. The guards were slumped over on the floor, and Master Alonzo was standing over their bodies. Godwin, Leon, Dartan, and Cordell were with him too, along with about five other knights in training.

"Torland, your reign of tyranny is overshadowed!" Alonzo stepped inside the throne room and cut down two more guards. Garland grabbed my arm and pulled me to the side of the room as the guards inside the throne room began to swarm Master Alonzo and the knights in training.

"Fall back, child!" Alonzo shouted as they dashed out of the throne room. Over half the guards went after him. Garland looked at me as he held a signal ruin in his hands.

"This is our chance," he said.

I threw a dagger at King Torland, but one of his guards caught it with his neck. The fight was on. Until Jenna could get to the room, it was just the three of us against over twenty guards. To add to the pressure, we had to kill Torland before the other guards could return to the throne room.

The remaining guards began to close in on us. Garland and Kona had drawn their swords and began to split up. I pushed mana into my feet and arms as the first guard swung at me. He must have thought I'd go down easy because I parried his attack with ease and stabbed him in the heart. As he went down, two more blades were being swung at me, and I jumped back as they cut through the air where I had been.

Kona was being pushed into a corner by three guards, and I rushed to draw away some of their attention. I caught two of them in the back of the legs, and Kona was able to evade. The three of us were doing all we could to remain dynamic and elusive targets. Garland was as good with a blade as he was at dancing, and he had taken out two guards by himself, but he was now evading multiple guards.

Jenna and the prince's guards entered the throne room not a moment too late; it was as if the three of us were close to being cornered. We were still outnumbered, but the distraction was all I needed to dash through four more guards and slice them apart with a blade made beyond razor-sharp with mana control.

The sudden drop in mana hit me like I had just sprinted a mile. I was stressed, but still all right. Another guard swung at me, and I pinned his blade against the pillar. With my other hand, I pulled out my switch sword and put it to his chest, running him through with the push of a button. I had to use mana control, as the spring on the blade wouldn't have had enough power on its own.

There were no more guards around me for an instant, and with my other dagger, I poured mana into my arm and visualized it sinking into King Torland, sending it flying. This one hit its mark and sunk into the side of his ribs. That was it; I had hit my limit. If I tried to use mana control one more time, I'd end up as a lump on the floor.

I looked around the room to see who needed help, but the fighting had stopped. One of the dozen men Garland had brought with him was left standing. Kona was laying motionless on the floor, and Jenna was holding her side as blood leaked out onto her hand.

"Garland, come!" I shouted.

Garland came running over to where we were. It was clear that there was nothing that could be done for Kona, and Garland held his hand. Soon, Kona's eyes rolled into the back of his head, and his breathing stopped. A tear rolled down Garland's face, but he quickly wiped it away.

Garland ordered his remaining guards to seize Minister Vargas, then he picked up his father's head and set it by his foot as he sat on the throne. A few minutes later, the guards who had chased after Master Alonzo began to return. I was fearing the worst, but then I saw Master Alonzo being led back with the knights in training that had been with him. Their hands were bound, and some were bleeding, but they were all still on their feet.

"Gentlemen, you have a decision to make. There is an angry mob outside the palace demanding justice. I intend to deliver them to Minister Vargas and my father's head. You can be remembered as heroes that helped overthrow a tyrant, or you can remain loyal to a dead king and fall prey to an angry mob," said Garland.

One by one, the guards began to kneel. "It looks like you're the new king," said Jenna.

233

"For now. There are still the citizens to address and a foreign army on its way," replied Garland.

"I'll be back. There is something I need to do," I said.

Garland looked at me and nodded. I felt exhausted, but my enthusiasm gave my legs extra strength as I sprinted off towards the maids' quarters. When I got there, the door was shut tight, and I banged on it.

"Zora! I need Zora!" I said.

I could hear on the other side of the door as beds were being pushed back. Zora was standing behind the door as it was opened.

"King Torland is dead, and the former third prince, Garland, is now king. There is currently an angry mob outside the palace walls, so I would hold off on leaving just yet. But as of this moment, you are all free," I stated.

"Some of us have nowhere left to go," said one girl.

"We can sort that stuff out later. For now, just relax and do whatever you want to do for a change," I said.

"Zora, I'll be back, but I need that," I said.

So I pulled it off around her neck and held it out to me.

"Thank you for keeping your promise. That hasn't happened to me before," she said.

I gave her a hug. "Thank you for being there for me when I had nobody else," I said.

"You were there for me too," she replied.

"I've got to go, but I'll come back down as soon as I can," I said.

When I got back up to the throne room, I used the healing rune and what little mana I had left, trying to heal Jenna. A moment later, a mage showed up and performed a healing spell on her, healing her completely.

"You couldn't have gotten here just a minute earlier," I asked the mage as I sat completely exhausted. The mage just gave me a confused look.

"It's not his fault," said Jenna. "Thank you both," she added.

"I suppose it's time to go address the crowd," said King Garland as he got up to perform from the throne. "Open up the main gates! I'll address them from the main balcony," he said.

Chapter 32

Reforms

King Garland stood on the palace balcony as the crowd of angry citizens pushed through the gates. The rest of the palace guards had been sent out to stop anyone from trying to rush into the palace. As the crowd came closer to the balcony, Garland held up his father's head. One by one, the citizens began to look up and point to others to look at the display. Once he had their attention, he set King Torland's head on the edge of the balcony.

"My fair citizens of Multira," Garland began, "I understand your anger and frustration. All my life, I have watched as my father and his father before him abused the position of power they found themselves in. In order to bring that abuse to an end, many of my friends have given their lives this evening to that cause."

Many of you are no doubt aware that Multira has been losing the war that my father started with Alza and Elris. By this point, the crowd below was hanging on to every word Garland spoke.

"In less than a month, the Central Allied Forces, as they are now calling themselves, will be at the gates of Potomac and force the city to be under siege. It will be a battle that we won't win. My plan, if you allow me to occupy the position of power that my father squandered, is to pull our remaining forces back to the Potomac. After that, I'll do everything I can to sue for peace, even if it means giving up the throne."

"Why should we trust a child of King Torland?" shouted someone from the crowd, probably one of Garland's agents.

"That's a more than fair question. If I cannot broker peace with the Central Allied Forces and the city falls under siege, my personal guards have orders to remove my head and place it next to my father's. Some of the reforms may be difficult for some of you to accept. I intend to outlaw slavery and return those taken from Alza and Elris, as it will no doubt be one of their demands for peace. So what say you? Will you give me the opportunity to right the wrongs of my forefathers? Will you allow me to hold those responsible for the current situation accountable? If you have someone better suited for the task, please send them forward."

Murmuring and hushed voices took over the crowd for a moment, then a shout went out. "I say we give him a chance!" someone shouted.

"Long live King Garland!" shouted another.

"Hail King Garland!" was soon chanted among the crowd.

"What was his plan if his speech failed?" I whispered to Jenna.

"He had them the moment he came out with Torland's head," she replied.

After Garland's speech, I asked if I could be dismissed for the evening, and Garland granted my request. I went by the kitchen and put in a couple of special requests for food to be brought down to the maids' quarters. It was nothing fancy, just tea and sweet biscuits.

When I got to the maids' quarters, I explained what had happened. "If any of you have families in the city or wish to leave tonight, you are now free to do so. Prince— I mean King Garland will arrange for the rest of you to be sent wherever you wish as soon as transportation is available. As for all who will still be here tonight, the kitchen is bringing down tea and biscuits," I said.

"So does that mean the mighty Nisha will be spending the night down here with us?" asked Astora.

"It does. I figured it'd be the best way to answer any more questions the other maids might have and try to find out where they need to go," I replied.

"So it wasn't because you missed us?" Astora asked.

"Of course I missed you! That was the next point I was about to make," I said with a grin.

A half hour later, a cart from the kitchen arrived with the tea and biscuits. There were many questions I still didn't have the answers to, like how long it would be before they could get rides back home and even the condition of their homes. I learned that the majority of the girls were native to Multira; they had been found on the streets, sold, or born into slavery. Many of the foreign girls had a similar story. In short, most had no home to go back to.

"Well, how about this: tomorrow, I'll go talk to King Garland about keeping all who want on as maids but under a paid employment contract and better working and living conditions," I said.

The girls liked that idea, and it seemed to settle things. Employment for those who wished and transportation for those who needed it. The girls trying to get back to Elris and Alza would need to wait until things could be resolved with the war, but I was able to calm them by reminding them that I was also from Elris.

The next morning, I took a list of requests I had written down from the maids and Zora with me to see the king. I was stopped by a guard as I came to the entrance of the throne room.

"Seriously, you don't recognize me?" I asked.

"I do recognize you, but since the king hasn't granted any specific authorization for you, I'll need to first relay your request," the guard replied.

"Very well. Could you please let his majesty know that the Royal assassin would like a word with him concerning the situation of the palace maids?" I said as eloquently as I could.

"Very well, I'll relay your message," said the guard.

A few minutes later, the guard returned and opened the throne room door for us. The throne room looked completely different than it did the day before. A curtain had been brought in that obscured the throne, and right in front of the curtain was a large desk that had been brought in, in addition to King Garland's desk. Several other tables were seated by administrative workers signing and preparing documents.

"A Royal assassin isn't your official title," said Garland.

"Then what is it?" I asked.

"Officially, it's the king's daughter," said Garland.

"You mean the king's pet, who cannot inherit or possess property or titles?" I corrected.

"That's on the list of reforms to fix," Garland said.

"Are you sure that's a good idea? If you allow adopted nobles to inherit titles and property, many of them will end up as strays," I replied. "It's best for everyone to know where they really stand."

"So who's your friend?" asked Garland.

"This is my assistant, Zora. I asked her to come with me to represent the interests of the maids," I said.

"Hang on a second. Does that mean I'm the princess of Multira?" asked Zora.

"Like I said, it's on the list of reforms."

"Now tell me what I can do for the maids," said Garland.

I pulled up the list of who needed transportation back to their home countries or other parts of the kingdom and read it off to Garland while he took notes. "The rest have nowhere to go and wish to remain as maids but underpaid employment and better working and living conditions," I explained.

"I think we can do that. I'll have the transportation officer meet with the maids and have any employment contract drawn up for those who wish to stay," said Garland. "Anything else?" he asked.

"Yes, a signet pin for me and my assistant sent to my room, and access to you so I don't have to wait on the guards all the time," I said.

Garland took a few more notes. "Anything else?" he asked again.

"Salary," I replied.

Garland rolled his eyes. "Just ask Jenna if you need anything," he said.

"you can't blame me for trying," I said.

"If that's all, I've got a mountain of paperwork to get back to," said Garland.

I stepped up to Garland and wrapped my arms around him. "Thank you for all you've done for me. I'm sorry about Kona. I know how important he was to you," I said.

"It's fine, and there will be a time for mourning later," he replied.

I let go and stepped back. "Is there anything I can do for the king?" I asked.

"Not at the moment, but you can check with Jenna and see if she has anything for you to do," he said.

"Then by your majesty's leave," I said.

"That's enough; go bother someone else now," he said.

Zora and I started to walk off. Something strange happened. "Thank you, sir," I said.

"You're welcome, your majesty," Garland replied with a smile before I went looking for Jenna. I took Zora up to my room and told her to pick one of the outfits from the closet to change into.

"What's wrong with the clothes I'm wearing?" she asked.

"You're no longer a maid, so it doesn't make sense for you to wear a maid outfit anymore," I explained.

"If I'm not a maid, then what am I?" she asked.

"You're free, but I'd like to offer you a job as my assistant if you'll take it," I said.

"What will I do?" she asked.

"I don't know; I'll let you know as soon as I know what my title and responsibilities are," I replied.

"All right, I accept," said Zora.

"Good. Now pick an outfit and get changed," I said.

Zora picked a casual red and blue outfit and kept looking at herself in the mirror. "It's so fancy!" she said.

"It's not that fancy, but I'm glad you like it," I replied.

Just then, a knock came from the door. I opened it, and a servant handed me two boxes.

"These are from the king," said the servant.

"Thank you," I replied, taking the boxes. I set them on the bed and opened them up. They were signet pins. They had the same cat as the third prince's signet, but were much larger with gold and silver inlay.

"That was fast," I said. I took one of the pins and placed it on Zora, then I put the other one on myself.

"So what do we do now?" asked Zora.

"First, we'll go down to the kitchen and get something to eat. After that, I guess we'll go find Jenna and figure out what it is we do," I replied.

Sometimes fake smiles greeted us as Zora and I ran into Jenna down in the kitchen. I had to help Zora place her order because she had no idea what to request. After ordering some sandwiches, we sat down with Jenna to discuss what my new role was in the kingdom.

"His majesty said that I'm no longer the Royal assassin, so what is the role of the princess of Multira?" I asked.

Jenna gave a slight chuckle. "You have any idea how silly that sounds?" she asked.

"What makes it silly? Is it because I couldn't be a princess?" I asked.

"No, it's because of all the technical issues with the statement. Not to mention that the king may very well not be the king in less than a month. You'll have a very short reign as princess," explained Jenna.

"The king said he was going to issue a reform to allow adopted nobles to inherit property and titles. Technicalities aside, I'm the closest thing Multira has to a princess at the moment. So with that settled, the king said to come find you to see how I can help," I said.

"That actually works out really well for me because I have the perfect job for you," said Jenna.

"So Jenna, what have you got for me?" I asked.

"Public relations," replied Jenna.

"Damn it! I don't have to go to any more garden parties, do I?" I asked.

"Fortunately for you, we don't have the time or resources to waste on things like that. I have a list of places that supplies are being distributed to— these are provisional housing for all the freed slaves and orphans throughout the capital. It would be good optics for us to send a representative from the palace to help oversee the distribution. It's the perfect job for our resident princess," explained Jenna.

"Will you be coming along with us?" I asked.

"No, you'll be on your own, but I'm confident you can sort out any issues that come up on your own. Even though the king has outlawed slavery, he's still tasking me like one. I have far too much to deal with to join you," said Jenna.

"That's unfortunate. It would be nice to have you come along with us. Zora hasn't explored the capital yet. I'm sure we'll manage without you, though. To be honest, if we run into issues, it might be difficult to have strangers taking instructions from children. Can I take Master Alonzo with me?" I asked.

"If he's free, but I'm pretty sure the king has him tasked out as well," said Jenna.

Jenna gave us the list of places we needed to make appearances at, and once we finished our meal, Zora and I said goodbye to her and went to the training hall to look for Master Alonzo.

When we got to the training hall, Master Alonzo was overseeing matches between the knights in training. The training hall had a much different atmosphere than it had before. The knights in training weren't fighting just within their classes. In addition, they weren't wearing training uniforms but actual Multiran military uniforms.

I waited until the next break between matches to get Master Alonzo's attention. I waved him over, and he stepped away from the fighting circle.

"Hello, Master. I'm sorry I haven't been able to see you since the fight in the throne room. I wanted to ask you what happened to you," I said.

"I'm a bit busy to give a full account at the moment, but the short version is that I drew the guards away only to buy time. Then we surrendered," he explained.

"It's good to see you. Who's your friend?" asked Alonzo.

"This is Zora. I asked her to come with me to represent the interests of the maids," I said.

"It's nice to meet you," said Zora.

"Likewise. Now what is it that I can do for you two young ladies?" asked Alonzo.

I explained to him our task from Jenna and how it would help to resolve conflicts to have an authoritative figure with us, as most adults might be reluctant to listen to an unknown eleven-year-old girl.

"Explaining who you are would resolve most of your issues, but it's not always practical," I said.

"I see your problem, and I wish I could help. The king has tasked me with integrating the knights in training into the military, so I'm busy commissioning them according to their skills and leadership abilities," explained Alonzo.

"I was wondering what was going on. If I can't take you, mind if we possibly get one of the older boys, like Godwin, to come with us?" I asked.

"Godwin has already been assigned to commission. That does have me thinking. Now that, as the king's adopted daughter, you're the closest thing to a princess this country has at the moment, you need your own escort," said Alonzo.

"You know I don't need protection," I replied.

"You never know what might happen in unpredictable times like these. What I have in mind helps both of us out. People will be more likely to listen to you if you have a military escort, and signing them to you will keep them close enough that I can keep training them," said Alonzo.

"Set Alonzo, you mean—" I started.

"Alonzo cut me off before I could finish. "Exactly!" Leon, Dartan, and Cordell shouted.

The three of them came running over to us. Once they got to us, Master Alonzo began giving them instructions.

"The three of you are, at this moment, the guards for his Majesty's daughter."

"Wait, you mean Nisha is now the princess?" asked Cordell.

"It's complicated," I replied.

"Regardless, the three of you will be assigned to her as her escort. Now go to the arms room and equip yourself with the weapons and armor you need, and meet us back here," instructed Alonzo.

The three of them quickly sprinted off, and a few minutes later, they came back wearing swords and leather plate armor.

"All right, make sure you take care of her," said Alonzo before walking back to the fighting circle.

"We're yours to command, my lady," said Leon.

"Stop being weird; we're still friends! Besides, as far as I know, there hasn't been anything signed that allows me to inherit titles or property, so when it's just us around, please just call me Nisha," I said.

"What do we call her?" asked Cordell, pointing at Zora.

"Right. This is my friend Zora. She's also my assistant, which makes you co-workers. These are Leon, Dartan, and Cordell. They were willing to train with me when none of the other knights in training would," I explained.

"It's a pleasure to meet you," said Zora.

"Likewise," said Leon.

"All right, let's get going. We have places to be," I said.

Chapter 33

Temporary Housing

On our ride into the city, I looked over the list again to see where we needed to go. "So, Zora, the first place we need to visit is the old slave market. From what I understand, the former slave traders are no longer in charge, and due to its size, renovating it into temporary housing was the quickest and cheapest option. Will you be okay going into a place like that?"

"I'll be fine. Besides, I never went there when it was a slave market," she said.

"All right, I just wanted to be sure. We're going to be meeting with the government officials who have been placed in charge and making sure that things are running smoothly between them and the former slaves," I explained.

"Do you expect there to be many problems?" asked Dartan.

"Wherever there are a lot of sudden changes, there are going to be problems. Until recently, the people living there were slaves—most of them are children and uneducated adults. You throw in clothing and food supplies, and there are bound to be countless issues with distribution, hoarding, and exploitation. What we're going to find out is if those issues are being managed properly," I explained.

"You really think about everything, don't you?" asked Cordell.

"Not really. I just understand the basic issues. That's why I have an assistant to help me think of everything else," I replied.

As we pulled up to the old slave market, I noticed all the slave carts had already been pulled away. *That was quick. I wonder what they did with them,* I thought to myself.

Once the carriage stopped, our escort exited first, and Leon held the door open for me and Zora. There was a man wearing some sort of military uniform, but it was a different color than the ones I normally saw around the palace. His black hair was starting to show signs of gray.

"Good afternoon. I'm Inspector Kadima. Are you the palace representative?" he asked.

"I am. I'm His Majesty's adopted daughter, Nisha. Are you in charge here? It was my understanding that I was going to be meeting with one of the city council members," I said.

"You were, but I already had to arrest him for selling off supplies sent over to feed the former slaves," explained Kadima.

"Oh my! Are things really that bad already?" I asked.

"That seems to be the worst of it, but without a replacement on hand, I've been left in charge of things for the time being," said Kadima.

"Well, Inspector, please show me around," I said.

"Right this way," he said.

The inside of the housing unit was a chaotic mess. The gates that locked the former display cages were either pulled off or chained open. Slabs of wood and other forms of sheeting were being fixed to the bars to provide some level of cover. Half the people inside the arena-style building were working on making the units livable, while the other half—mostly the younger children—were sitting around looking confused.

"Who's in charge of distributing food?" I asked.

"That would be our volunteers from the House of Lumen up on the second floor," said Kadima.

"Are they being fair with the distribution?" I asked.

"I've been getting too many complaints, so I hope so," replied Kadima. "Can you please take us up there? I'd like to talk with them directly if you don't mind."

"Not at all," replied Kadima.

Kadima took us up to the second floor to an area that had one of the sales turned into a makeshift kitchen. There were men and women working in it, wearing white and black clothing that was reminiscent of religious attire from my old world. Kadima introduced me to a man wearing a black robe with a white shirt.

"This is Brother Simon of the House of Lumen," said Kadima.

"Hello, I'm Nisha, the representative of the palace," I said.

"It's a pleasure to meet you," said Simon.

"I came to see if the food and supplies were going to those who need them," I explained.

"We're doing what we can to try to ensure that they are, but there are so many former slaves and only a few of us. It's almost impossible to know what happens once things are distributed," explained Simon.

"So what would help you out the most?" I asked.

"I'm sure more issues will show up as things progress, but for now, we could use all the help we can get with preparing dinner," said Simon.

"I'm not a cook, but I can cut up vegetables and do other simple tasks," I said.

"Oh, I didn't mean for you to get involved," he said.

"Nonsense! Just tell me what I can do to help out," I insisted as I began to roll up my sleeves.

Kadima left us with the brothers and sisters of the House of Lumen, and thirty minutes later, I had learned that cutting up vegetables was not as easy as it looked. Zora was amazed by my attempts, but I had been pulled off that task and set to stirring a large pot and setting out bowls.

Leon came up to me. "Don't be too hard on yourself. Cutting up food so that it's all the same size isn't as simple as it seems," he said.

"Shut up! It's not like I've had a lot of practice doing it. Give me a bit more time, and I'm sure I'll get the hang of it," I retorted.

"What's going on?" asked Simon as he brought up more bowls.

"Oh, the princess is just upset that she finally found something she's not good at," said Leon.

"Oh my goodness! I didn't realize you were the princess," said Simon.

"I'm not! I'm just the king's adopted daughter. It's hardly the same thing as a princess. Don't worry about it. I was butchering those poor vegetables and deserved to be pulled off that task," I said.

"Even still, I hope you'll forgive me if I've overstepped my boundaries," he said.

"Once again, don't worry about it. Leon is just being an ass. Just let me know if you need any dishes cleaned, and I'll have him take care of that," I said.

"I think we've got that covered, but I'll let you know if something else comes up," said Simon.

After about an hour of cleaning, prepping, stirring, and setting up, dinner was finally ready to serve. Simon rang a bell, and hundreds of former slaves began lining up. Some of the adults began to crowd the front of the line, and my blood began to boil as I started walking towards them. My escort came up and pulled me back just as I was about to speak.

"Tell us what the issue is, and we'll handle it," said Leon.

I took a deep breath to calm down, but it didn't work. "Children eat first!" I shouted.

Dartan and Leon started sorting out the situation, and any resistance from the adults melted away at the directive of the armed guards. Once the line issue was sorted out, I grabbed a ladle and went to the serving line to help out.

Twenty minutes later, everyone was served, and there was still enough for seconds. I grabbed a bowl and a piece of bread and found a spot to sit down. Simon came by to thank me for helping out.

"I should be the one thanking you. That's a lot of work, and I'm not sure if these people would be eating right now if it wasn't for your services," he said.

"I'll be honest, I'm not familiar with the teachings of the House of Lumen. What is it that your faith teaches?" I asked.

"It's simple: treat others how you want them to treat you, and everything— all life is connected through the field of light," said Simon.

"What is the field of light?" I inquired further.

"It is a source of everything—everything living, everything dead, everything that has been, and everything that will be," explained Simon.

"That sounds straightforward enough," I replied. "What is it that you believe?"

"A lot the same. I believe that you should treat others the same way you want them to treat you. Apart from that, I suppose that I believe that God has a plan for all of us, but I'm still not sure what his plan for me is yet," I said.

"Who is God?" asked Simon.

"He's the one who controls everyone's fate," explained Zora as she walked up.

"Oh, that's right! I completely forgot we had that conversation," I said.

"But she's right," I added.

"That's interesting. I've never heard of this religion before. Can you tell me more about it?" asked Simon.

"Well, I wouldn't call it a religion, just my personal beliefs," I explained.

"And this God is a man?" Simon asked.

"I think so. He sounded like it to me, but I think he also works with a woman. I believe that God cleans our souls as we pass from one life to the next," I said.

"Are you saying that we live multiple lives?" asked Simon.

At this point, more of the brothers and sisters, as well as former slaves, had gathered around to listen to Simon's and my conversation. I wasn't sure what to say or if I should say anything more. I finally decided to keep going.

"I'm not trying to convince you of anything. I'm just telling you what I believe. I don't know if we live multiple lives or that our souls are on a journey, but I can tell you that part of us does go from one life to the next."

"How do you know this?" asked Simon.

I tried to think of a good way to answer without lying. "Don't read too much into what I'm about to say, but God, for whatever reason, didn't cleanse my soul completely from the sins of my past life. At least that's what I think happened."

"Why would he do that?" asked Simon.

"I wish I knew. Maybe to punish me or teach me a lesson. I'll let you know if I ever figure it out," I said.

"Maybe it was so that you could teach others," suggested Zora.

"So that I could teach them what exactly? How not to be? We have more than enough evil in any world to demonstrate that," I said.

"Well, letting out more anger than I intended to... or to teach them how to be better," offered Zora.

"That's a stretch. I can't imagine that God, in his infinite wisdom, let me remember the sins I committed in my past life just to come tell other people about it. That seems a bit silly to me."

"Look, I'm not sure what you find so interesting about this. It's just things that I believe," I explained.

"Please tell us a bit more," said one of the sisters.

I let out a sigh. "Fine, but this is the last I'll say about it. I don't remember if I heard this or if it was a dream, but the woman that God works with was saying that I was broken or missing something. Then God said, 'I can fix it. I can still use this one.' I'm pretty sure they were talking about me."

All around me, blank faces stared at me. *Yes, I know it sounds strange, but that's what I remember*, I thought to myself.

"Oh shit! I said way too much," I thought. I figured that I needed to start backtracking as fast as I could before I was burned at the stake for heresy or worse.

"Look, people believe all sorts of strange things. It's not like I'm trying to change anything you believe," I said.

"You haven't changed anything that the House of Lumen teaches, but

I do believe that you had a divine experience," said Simon.

"I could just be crazy or making it up. Doesn't it sound ridiculous to you?" I asked.

"Your beliefs and explanations seem unusual, but I don't think you came here to help out and lie to us," said Simon.

"I didn't come here to change what anyone believes, and I feel like I've said too much already," I said.

"I wouldn't be too concerned about it if I were you. Honestly, I'm just happy to learn that a member of the royal family believes in divine retribution at all," said Simon.

I couldn't help but let out a short laugh. "I'm glad that's your takeaway from our conversation," I replied.

"Trust me, I got much more than that out of it," Simon said. From the looks of others around us, I thought some of them did, too.

"I'll be honest, it was all confusing to me," said Cordell.

"You get confused by everything," replied Dart.

"I'm glad I'm not the one who's confused by it," said Cordell.

"Then, for the sake of simplicity, let's just say that my beliefs I've expressed here today are from a strange dream," I said.

"I don't believe that convictions are the result of strange dreams," said Simon.

"Fine, but just promise me that none of you will make a big deal out of anything I've said today."

After receiving a couple of nods, I figured that was as good as I was going to get. We said our goodbyes to the members of the House of Lumen and to the former slaves.

As we were leaving the temporary housing complex, Inspector Kadima came by and asked a strange question.

"Forgive me for overstepping if I am in any way, but I was hoping you might be able to answer a question I've had for a while," said Kadima.

"I will if I can. What is it?" I asked.

"Was the third prince, or as he was at the time, any of his household involved with the assassination of Prince Harold and the other influential nobles?" asked Kadima.

"Whatever gave you that impression?" I asked back.

"A certain member of the third prince's household was seen in the vicinity of some of the assassinations."

"Well, it isn't proof. It is strange," said Kadima.

"Well, Inspector, you don't miss much, but the answer to your question is a state secret that I'm not at liberty to disclose," I replied.

"I figured that might be the case, but I thought it was worth asking anyway," said Kadima.

"I'll be sure to let the king know about the hard work you and the volunteers are doing here."

"I can only hope that the rest of my visits go as well as my visit today went," I said.

"Thank you. I'll try my best not to disappoint you," replied Kadima.

Chapter 34

Envoy

Several weeks had passed since King Garland took the throne of Multira. During that time, he had recalled what was left of the military and reinforced it with as many volunteers as he could gather. Refugees poured into the capital from the surrounding towns and villages in preparation for an assault from the Central Allied Forces. Most of the new reforms Garland had passed made him popular among the poor and lower class, but they had also won him many enemies among the nobles. Several attempts at assassination had already been thwarted, including a kidnapping and extortion attempt on the king's adopted daughter, who, while not technically a princess, now had the right to inherit lands and titles.

"Did you have to kill the kidnapper?" asked Garland.

"He had a knife to my assistant's neck. I had to stop him somehow," I argued.

"I'm not saying it was the wrong thing to do, but we can't interrogate a corpse," said Garland.

"If it happens again, I'll see if I can take them alive," I replied.

"How are things going with peace negotiations?" I asked.

"They keep returning my envoys. The commander of the Central Allied Forces says he won't settle for anything less than total surrender without conditions. That is something I can't accept just yet—for the sake of the people. If we were forced to pay an unjust amount of retributions, for example, it would be as bad as placing the entire country in slavery," explained Garland.

"Then you just need to get them to negotiate," I prompted.

"For starters, but ultimately I need them to agree to some basic conditions," Garland said.

"Send me as your envoy then," I suggested.

"I can't send you. They wouldn't listen to a child," said Garland.

"Do you remember when I told you I was a noble from Ellris? I wasn't lying. My father's count, Dylan, is close friends with King Hallid. My best friend back home is his daughter, Krisstina. Someone among the army is bound to know who I am. I'll convince them to hear you out," I explained.

"If that's the case, then they'll just take you back home as you're part of the reason they came this far," said Garland.

"I'll make it difficult for them to claim my rescue," I said.

"How?" asked Garland.

"Make me the official princess of Moltura," I replied.

"That's ridiculous! They probably wouldn't even recognize the title," Garland said.

"Probably not, but you're right about it being ridiculous. In fact, it would be so ridiculous that they would need to evaluate the situation before deciding what to do," I explained.

Garland paused for a moment. "Reports do say you've become popular among some circles, and the kidnapping attempt has gotten your name out further. What do you think?" asked Garland.

"I think it's worth a try," I said.

"Jenna, obviously, it would only be temporary," I added.

"Why do you say that?" asked Jenna.

"I have a home and a family to get back to," I replied.

"Maybe they'll move here," said Jenna.

"That's not getting ahead of ourselves," I said. "I'll hold the coronation ceremony tomorrow, and we'll leave after your public announcement," said Garland.

"Why don't we just get the ceremony done and do the public announcement?" I asked.

"If we're going along with the plan, we need to give you every symbol of authority we can. Even if it's a spy's report, just remember that you asked for this," said Garland.

That night, while preparing for bed, I was talking to Zora. I had another bad mood set in. She had moved into my room, and we now shared the space. I had offered her a room of her own, but she said that she would rather stay with me.

"I can't believe you're going to become a real princess tomorrow," said Zora.

"It's for a nation that's on the verge of collapse, and a title I don't intend on keeping," I replied.

"Still, even if it's just for a day, how many girls ever become a real princess?" asked Zora.

"All of them do, but I get your point. The truth is that I never actually wanted to be one," I said.

"What do you want then?" asked Zora.

"The same thing everyone else does, I guess. I just want to be happy," I replied.

Early the next morning, under the watchful eye of the few nobles that happened to be at the palace that day, I entered the throne room. Trumpets sounded as I proceeded to walk up to King Garland, who was seated on the throne. I was wearing a yellow and white dress that Jenna had sent up to my room.

When I reached the throne, King Garland declared, "To all who are present here today as witnesses, I do confer upon you the title of Princess of Moltura."

Jenna held out a pillow that had a gem-encrusted tiara on it. Garland picked up the tiara and placed it on my head.

"Rise, Princess Nisha," said Garland.

I stood up and turned around. Everyone in the half-empty throne room began to cheer. On one hand, it kind of felt good—almost like winning a grand prize. On the other hand, I kind of felt like an idiot.

"Hail, Princess Nisha!" shouted Garland. Those in the room echoed the statement back.

As I stepped away from the throne, everyone in the room made a point to come up and greet me.

"You look so pretty!" said Zora when she came up to me.

"Thanks, but I'm sure most of it is the dress and crown," I replied.

"They help, but they don't do all the work," said Jenna. Her hair was a bright blonde today and matched my dress.

"Thanks, Jenna, but do you have something a bit less flashy for me to wear on my envoy mission?" I asked.

"Actually, I had some plate armor made for you a while back when you were still doing your job. I'll have it sent to your room. We're leaving this afternoon, so make sure you get it on after lunch," said Jenna.

"What do you mean? Aren't I the only one going?" I asked.

"Just to approach the army, but the king wants to be close by in case they agree to negotiations," explained Jenna.

That afternoon, I was sitting on a horse wearing the most polished plate armor in the kingdom. *So what exactly was an assassin supposed to do—dress like a mirror?* I asked Jenna.

"The original coating was going to be black, but I changed the order before it was finished," she explained.

The horse I was on wasn't anything like Elvis, but he was black with white socks and looked majestic. I would only ride him as we left the capital for pomp and circumstance. From there, I'd ride in a carriage until it came time to meet with the Central Allied Forces. Leon, Dartan, Cordell, and Zora would also accompany me to meet with them. They were now only a two-day ride from the capital.

I would miss my friends, but I was ready for this war to come to an end. I still had a country to save from the threat of Marx and Berosa. There was no telling what he had been up to since I left Elris. I still had to find out what happened to Lila, Warwick, and the rest of the people I left in Duvort. I smiled to myself as I thought about the irony of the situation. There had been a time when I wanted to destroy this country, and now I was trying to save it.

Two days later, we stopped in the village of Lark. The king and the rest of his staff waited there while my envoy group set off to make contact with the Central Allied Forces.

"What do you mean there's a group of kids riding up to the front line?" asked a sergeant.

"Just that. Take a look for yourself," said the sentry.

The sergeant climbed the watchtower and saw five children. The oldest were two boys in their mid to late teens. The boys were wearing Multiran military uniforms, and the boy in the lead was carrying a white flag.

"Do you think they ran out of adults to fight?" asked the sentry.

"I don't know, but they're too well-dressed to be regular soldiers. Go get the captain," said the sergeant.

The captain stood at the front line, waiting for the five horses and their riders to approach. "They're really sending kids now! That's far enough, Multira! State your business!" shouted the captain as the horses rode up.

"We're envoys of the king. He wishes to negotiate terms of surrender," said a girl wearing plate armor.

"Your king already has our conditions. There are to be no terms," said the captain. "If you want to negotiate, then send for your commander or someone who can," he ordered.

"And what if I don't feel like it?" asked the girl in plate.

"Then consider it a request from the daughter of Count Dylan of Elris for a Royal request from the Princess of Moltura. Whichever gets a proper response," said the girl in plate.

The conditions were too big for him to brush them off. "Give me some time to relay your requests," said the captain.

"Very well, we shall wait for your response," said the girl in plate.

At the camp of the Central Allied Forces, a messenger approached the general's tent. She was currently in a strategy meeting with her officers.

"General, another envoy has come from Moltura," said the messenger.

"Have they decided upon total surrender?" asked the general.

"No, but they have made a request to speak with you directly," said the messenger.

"Send them away," I said, the general replied.

"General, the envoys are strange, and they have requested that you speak with them," said the messenger.

"I don't care who the request comes from. If it isn't unconditional surrender, send them away," instructed the general.

The messenger, at the risk of being yelled at, pushed on. "The request comes from the daughter of Count Dylan and the Princess of Moltura," said the messenger.

The general froze for a moment. "Say that again," ordered the general.

"The request comes from the daughter of Count Dylan and the Princess of Moltura," repeated the messenger.

"You said the envoy was strange. How?" asked the general.

"They were all children," replied the messenger.

"Take me to them!" ordered the general.

Chapter 35

Reunion

I was sitting on my fancy black horse, which I had named Socks, when I saw two riders on burrow dogs coming up to us. I wasn't sure at first, but as they got closer, I recognized the dogs. My heart jumped with joy.

"Leon, hold my horse!" I ordered.

Leon took the reins from me, and I jumped down as the riders came closer. Dart spoke up, "Please be careful around those dogs; they're dangerous."

"Not to me, they're not," I replied as the riders approached.

I called out to my long-lost friends, "Elvis! I missed you so much! Come here, boy!"

Elvis walked over to me, and with one lick, I was covered in dog drool.

I patted his massive snout. "I miss you too, boy," I said. In an instant, a massive bear hug lifted me off my feet.

"I know you're trying to mess with me, but I'll let it slide just this once," said Lila. "I really am glad to see Elvis again, but I'm also really happy to see that you're alive," I replied.

"What happened after you left Dorvas?" Lila asked.

"Ah, it's a long story. There were a lot of strange things that happened, but we need to first end this war. I need to speak with your commander," I said.

"I am the commander," Ashley replied.

"What's going on here?" I asked.

"You're really the commander?" I clarified.

"She's a general," said Lila.

"That's strange, but I suppose that makes things easier. I need you to agree to negotiate the terms of surrender with King Garland."

"Hello, Lark. It's nice to see that you're all right too," I added.

"What's so strange about me being a general?" asked Lila.

"Oh, I just didn't think you had enough patience to be a general," I replied.

"She doesn't, and I'm glad to see you again too," replied Lark.

"Well, I'm so glad I got the approval of both of you. The kingdom will turn. These are our terms. I can't change that, and after everything they've done, I don't want to," said Lila.

"I understand how you feel. They took me and forced me into slavery. I wanted to destroy the entire kingdom too, but there are a lot of good people in this kingdom, and King Garland is trying to protect them. He even killed King Torland, his own father, to do it," I explained.

"Then why did he wait so long to do it?" asked Lila.

"He was third in line to the throne. He had to kill his brother and a bunch of other people just to give him a shot to do it."

"Well, that's pretty true. You were winning the war too fast, so we had to gamble it all on a battle in the throne room, but we came out on top," I explained.

"He had you killing people for him?" Ashley asked.

"Yes, but they were all really bad people. Since he's been king, Garland has issued many reforms, including the abolition of slavery and freedom of commerce. Please, at the very least, just meet with him. We could end this war tonight," I pleaded.

Lila looked at the members of my party, and after a moment, she finally spoke. "I was going to tear down this country brick by brick until I found you. Now that I can see that you're all right, I'll talk to Duke and Daryl and see if he'll meet with the king of Moltura."

"Really? And his brother is your commander?" I asked.

"He is," Lila said.

"Duke and Daryl felt it," I replied.

"I imagined that this whole time. I had no idea," said Lila.

"Are you sure she's a general?" I asked.

"Indeed she is," Lark replied.

"Just stop with it already," said Lila. "Have your friends go back and tell the king we'll agree to a meeting. We'll send a messenger over with the time and location."

"I can't. I've got to stick with them until this is over," I replied.

"You are a member of a noble family of Elris! You belong over here!" said Lila.

"That's true, but I am also the sovereign princess of Moltura, so I have responsibilities over here until this is over," I replied.

"You seriously expect me to believe that?" Ashley asked.

"Ask her if you don't believe me," I said, pointing at Zora.

"It is true," said Zora.

"That's dog shit!" exclaimed Lila.

"So is the thought of you being a general, yet here we are," I replied.

"I suppose that's a fair point, but you still belong over here with me," she said.

"I know I do, so let's get this meeting set up and end this war," I replied.

"All right, I'll get the message to Duke and Daryl, and you'll get a meeting. I can't promise that he'll grant terms," said Lila.

"However things turn out, you're coming back with me," said Lila.

"I'll accept that. But before we leave, Lark, thanks for taking care of Elvis for me. Now give me my dog back! I'll trade you for Socks!" I demanded.

We returned to Lark, and I informed Garland of what had taken place.

"It sounds like they're still pissed off. The resentment for the military runs deep, but I think there are enough level-headed people that reasonable terms can be met," I explained.

"For all our sakes, I hope you're right," said Garland.

"Lila will make Daryl listen. She can be very persuasive when she wants to be."

"How good is your Lumen?" I asked.

"Far better than your Multiran. I've gotten a lot of complaints for making a foreigner out of our princess," replied Garland.

Several hours later, a rider from the Central Allied Forces arrived and told us that the Duke had agreed to discuss terms. The meeting was to take place on a hill south of Lark at sunrise the next morning.

"Will you be going back to Elris once the war is over?" asked Zora as we were getting ready for bed.

"Not right away. There's something I need to do first," I replied.

"What is it?" she asked.

"Either find or kill a dragon or find a dwarven village. I need to find a way to protect my home in Elris from Berosa," I explained.

"That sounds like a long and dangerous journey," she replied.

"Tell me about it. The last time I set out on it, I ended up in a war and was taken as a slave."

"Will I ever see you again?" she asked with a shaky voice.

"Of course you will! I've made too many wonderful friends here to not come back," I replied.

"Good! I hope your journey is short then," said Zora.

"Trust me, I'll get it done as quickly as I can. I actually have a really good friend back home that I want you to meet. Her name is Krisstina, but I call her Kriss. She's the princess of Elris. She's not like a stuck-up princess either; she's really nice," I explained.

"You mean she's not like you?" asked Zora with a grin.

"Haha!" I let out a sarcastic laugh.

We spent the rest of the evening telling stories and jokes. I didn't know how things would go the next morning, but I was glad things had worked out so that I had met Zora.

The following morning, I rode next to King Garland as Jenna, Zora, my escorts, and the king's escorts all headed to the meeting spot south of the village. As we came closer to the hill, there was a large tent set up at the top, surrounded by banners. Just short of the top, we all dismounted. Garland, Zora, Jenna, and I made our way to the tent while the rest of the escort stayed with the mounts.

I had met the Duke several times back in Elris and recognized him as we approached the tent. Lila was standing next to him, and on his other side was Captain LeRoy, only he didn't look like a captain anymore. *Maybe he had gotten several promotions since I last saw him*, I thought to myself.

There were several other people around the Duke, but I didn't recognize any of them. As Garland approached the Duke, he took off his sword and handed it to Jenna. The two leaders bowed to each other.

"Welcome, King Garland," said the Duke.

"Thank you, but I'm content to speak in your language for this meeting," said Garland.

"Very well. Please, come take a seat. Your guests may sit as well."

"I understand that you have turned our lady Nisha into your princess," said Daryl as I came to an empty chair and started to sit down.

"I still hold all my family and values from Elris important to me. There was a time not so long ago that I wished for the destruction of Moltura more than anyone. I came here today of my own free will in hopes that my insight may be of some use to these negotiations," I said as eloquently as I could.

Garland explained as much of the situation as he could. "But we can discuss the particulars of your station later. The first thing I want to know is why I should need to accept anything less than unconditional surrender. I have over 200,000 troops assembled. It would be more than sufficient to take the capital," said Daryl.

"Rather than talking about how you would lose half of your men or more taking the city or any other threats, I'd hope that I could appeal to your better nature. This war was started by men of ill nature for selfish reasons. There are many who have lost much—including life—from both sides because of it. I wish to spare more loss of life and suffering," said Garland.

"Then surrender and be done with it. You know that slavery is illegal to us, and I promise there will be no more bloodshed," said Daryl.

"That's all well and good, but if I surrender, there's still much besides life that could be lost. What would happen to a country with a broken economy? If we were forced to pay vast sums of war reparations or had other harsh conditions placed upon us, history has shown us that under such conditions, the outcome is rarely a good thing. The conditions I would ask for aren't for lands, the wealth of nobles to be spared, or even my own life. It was my father who started the war, so take it if it helps spare more suffering. What I would ask for is that the citizens have a fair chance to keep their livelihoods and have a chance to rebuild," explained Garland.

"That's a noble sentiment. If the nobility of your country had that sentiment in the beginning, this war would have never started," said Daryl.

"That's all too true, but as far as I'm aware, there's no mage or magic strong enough to change what has been done. So I beg you to please let the suffering end with us. I've been taking inventory of the wealth and supplies we have left. We could pay an initial tax of 20%, but any higher than that would cause an economic collapse. People do horrible things when they're starving," explained Garland.

"I get your point, and I'll take it under consideration, but the countries I represent still demand justice for all those taken as slaves from us," said Daryl.

I raised my hand. "May I speak? I feel this is the subject I may offer the most insight," I proclaimed.

Daryl nodded.

"After Dorvas, I was captured and taken as a slave. I had everything short of my life taken from me. I wanted Moltura brought to ruin more than anyone. It was only by fate or chance that I met King Garland, and he began to use my skills. I was skeptical of them at first and believed he had ulterior motives. I still think he has some, but he's proven to be worthy of loyalty and respect time and time again. Those who are loyal to him are not loyal because of fear, but because of admiration. The first thing I did after he became king was go to the palace slaves and inform them of their freedom. Many of those former slaves have already been sent home. The ones from Elris and Alza are waiting for this war to end so that they may go home as well. I know that all those taken as slaves were not as fortunate as me, and some may have even died or been sold to other countries. That said, under King Garland's leadership, the country is changing for the better. I beg you, please give that change a chance to grow."

After I finished speaking, Daryl took a moment before he spoke again. "We need something solid—something that guarantees the submission of Walter and the sincerity of its request for forgiveness," said Daryl.

"Then please take my life as proof of that sincerity," said Garland.

Daryl looked at me. "What does the princess of Moltura think of the king's proposal? It would leave you as the monarch of the kingdom," said Daryl.

"As the princess of Moltura, I say hell no!" I received some odd looks and realized that the expression didn't mean anything. "Let me rephrase that, please. By dark elements, I know I am the last person who should be running a country. King Garland is perfect for the job. As a citizen of Elris, I say make him sign on as a member of the Central Allied Forces. It would guarantee loyalty, cooperation, and tribute," I declared.

"The alliance was only formed as a response to the threat of Moltura. It was never meant to be permanent," said Daryl.

"There will always be more threats. If there is value in it, I'm sure the king of Alza would agree to make it permanent," said LeRoy.

"All right then, list your conditions of surrender. If they are acceptable, I'll agree to them under the conditions that Multira becomes a member of the Central Alliance," said Daryl.

Over the next hour, Garland laid out his conditions of surrender to the Duke. All of them were agreed upon, as they were based on protecting the citizens. Garland had a preliminary document drafted, and both the two leaders signed it.

"We'll have a more official document prepared with signatures from both kings of Elris and Alza, but this should hold for now. I'll have the main force pulled back for now, but I'll leave a contingent at the capitol with you until the official document is signed," said Daryl.

"I think that's more than acceptable," replied Garland.

"Then for now, our business is concluded," said Daryl. The two men were just about to shake hands when I interrupted them.

"There is one more issue to deal with before we're done here," I said. I opened up a bag and pulled out some papers I had prepared.

"What's this?" asked Garland.

"It's an inheritance agreement. I'm signing over my title and rights as princess to someone else, so would you please come sign here?" I asked.

"You can't do that! Only the king can authorize it," said Garland.

"Actually, you never specified that in the inheritance reform you passed. According to current Multiran law, this document is legal," I argued.

"What if I don't want to sign?" asked Garland.

"There are already a number of citizens complaining about the Multiran princess not being native. Not only are you an actual Multiran, you were born a slave. You can inspire people to be more than they ever dared to dream before. Please, I'm begging you to take this from me. Besides, I already have a home with a mother, father, sister, and brother to get back to," I pleaded.

"But if I sign, then you'll leave," he replied.

"I promised you that I'll come back, and I keep my promises," I said.

Zora walked over to the documents I had laid out. I handed her the quill that Garland and Daryl had used earlier.

"I don't deserve this!" said Zora.

"If anyone deserves it, you do," I replied.

With that, Zora signed and became the official Princess of Moltura. I took the tiara off my head and placed it on Zora. After that, I stepped back, and Zora grabbed my sleeves, pulled me to my feet, and wrapped her arms around me.

"You're ruining the moment!" I said as I hugged her back.

"No, I'm not! This moment is fine just the way it is," she argued back.

Epilogue

After saying our goodbyes, Lila, LeRoy, and I rode away from the meeting spot south of the village of Lark.

"Here, I thought you might want these back," said Lila as she handed me my sword and gun belt that still had my revolver secured in it.

"Thanks! You have no idea how many times I wished I had these over the past year," I said.

"Was it more than five?" Lila asked playfully.

"A lot more," I replied with a laugh.

"So what do we do now?" Ashley asked.

"I still need to figure out how to deal with Berosa," I replied.

"But don't you still have responsibilities as a general?" I asked.

"I mostly stayed to find you. Now that you're safe, I'll let Daryl know that I'm resigning. By the way, there is now an alliance of three countries that have agreed to protect each other if attacked. I think Berosa will need to think twice before invading," explained Lila.

"Oh wow, you're right! It wasn't my plan, but somehow it worked out," I replied.

"I swear you are the dumbest smart person I've ever met," said Lila.

I thought about how almost every plan I had fallen through and how, at times, everything had seemed hopeless. Riding alongside friends, it seemed almost silly now.

"Lila, let's go home."

www.ingramcontent.com/pod-product-compliance
Lightning Source LLC
Chambersburg PA
CBHW070727280626
47159CB00023B/2851